THE DEVIL'S PRIEST

By

Kate Ellis

This edition first published in Great Britain in 2005 by
Nirvana Books
Mayfiield Court Victoria Road
Freshfield Liverpool L37 7JL

A catalogue record for this book is available
From the British Library.

10 9 8 7 6 5 4 3 2 1

ISBN 978-09549427-2-4

Printed and bound by
Beacon Printing Keighley

Books by Kate Ellis

The Wesley Peterson Mysteries (Published by Piatkus)

The Merchant's House

The Armada Boy

An Unhallowed Grave

The Funeral Boat

The Bone Garden

A Painted Doom

The Skeleton Room

The Plague Maiden -

A Cursed Inheritance

The Marriage Hearse

The Shining Skull

In memory of my Mum, Mona Ellis.

THE DEVIL'S PRIEST

by Kate Ellis

PROLOGUE

EVE OF ST. MATTHEW - 20TH SEPTEMBER 1539

The tapers by the altar flickered and spluttered as Sister Agnes knelt to pray for forgiveness. Her muttered words rose with the candle smoke in the incense-laden air.

The flames leaned as the chapel door opened and Agnes felt a draught of cool air on her neck. But her thoughts were on her sins so she felt no temptation to look round. She opened her eyes and fixed them firmly on the statue of the Virgin. The Pope had guaranteed forgiveness to pilgrims who prayed at the shrine of St. Mary del Quay. It didn't bother Agnes that King Henry had just robbed the Pope of his authority: she was in need of that forgiveness...in need of a miracle.

As she stared at the gently smiling statue, fervently mouthing the words of the Ave Maria, a dark shape rose behind the fluttering taper flames. Agnes caught her breath and made the sign of the cross. The words came quicker.

"Ave Maris stella. Dei mater alma. Sancta Maria ora pro nobis."

The shape began to loom towards her. She closed her eyes tightly and continued to pray.

"Deus in adiutorum meum intende: Domine ad adiuvandum me festina."

Be pleased, oh God to deliver me: oh Lord make haste to help me. Her heart beat quicker in the silence of the tiny chapel.

When the blow came, Agnes fell senseless to the ground.

Brother Bartholomew - he still thought of himself as "Brother" - walked along the strand, the damp sand penetrating his shoes and the spaces between his toes. No passengers were waiting to be ferried across the grey expanse of the River

Mersey so he would have time to offer an hour's prayer at the church of Our Lady and St. Nicholas.

It was nine o'clock: the hour when he had sung the office of Terce in the fondly remembered days before his ordered world was shaken by the King's commissioners. For one brought up in the cloister since early childhood, the closure of Birkenhead Priory had come as the bitterest of blows. But Bartholomew was still young ...and an optimist by nature.

At the edge of the churchyard stood the chapel of St. Mary del Quay, a small stone building tucked against the boundary of the larger church. Bartholomew felt a sudden impulse to forgo the splendours of Our Lady and St. Nicholas and make his personal devotions in the tiny chapel.

He wasn't sure what he would pray for. Some prayed that the Lord would rid them of the King. Others prayed for the demise of his advisors, as praying for the death of kings was treason, and the punishment of treason was hideous execution. Bartholomew usually contented himself with praying for a change in the King's heart: but, as he was not acquainted with His Majesty King Henry the Eighth, he was unaware that this request was unlikely to be granted.

Bartholomew pushed at the chapel's weather battered door and it opened silently. He stepped from the bright September sunshine into the candlelit gloom and stood near the doorway while his eyes adjusted to the dim light.

Then he approached the statue of the Virgin, so unadorned yet so powerful in its simplicity, and he was about to kneel on the cold stone floor when something in front of the altar caught his eye. A figure lay on the ground, the body too crooked to be a pilgrim prostrate in prayer. The statue of the Blessed Virgin, wondrously escaped from the commissioners' destruction, stared down at him as he approached warily and knelt down.

It was a woman, a young woman, and to Bartholomew's relief she stirred and groaned. She was alive. Blood oozed from a gash on her head and the smooth stone flags beneath her glistened dark red. So much blood for such a small wound.

"Mistress, what happened?"

She looked up at him with grey eyes that kept flickering shut, fighting unconsciousness. Bartholomew touched her face gently, pushing back a strand of fair hair that had escaped from her bloodstained white cap and now intruded onto her lips. She was young, comely. Bartholomew leaned towards her to hear what she was saying, suppressing the thought that the girl was pretty as his training had taught him to do.

"Who are you?" he whispered. "What is your name?"

"Agnes...Agnes Moore."

"What happened here? Who did this to you?"

"He came for me. Satan came for my soul." Her eyes closed as she lost her battle for consciousness.

Bartholomew gathered her up into his arms, strong from rowing against the currents of the river. Moore. He knew the name: all Liverpool knew it. Old Hall, the Moore's house, was nearby. He held the young woman close to him and felt his arms sticky with the blood that was seeping through her russet gown.

As Bartholomew strode out into the daylight with his precious burden, two shapes rose slowly and unseen behind the plain stone altar.

FEAST OF ST. MICHAEL AND ALL ANGELS - 29TH SEPTEMBER 1539

Mistress Marjory Moore adjusted her snowy white cap and prepared to take the bowl of broth upstairs, seething with annoyance. This was servant's work but she wanted to see the girl; to find out the truth.

Agnes had been trouble from the moment she arrived: disappearing for hours on end when there was work to be done. And now this: the girl had lain in bed for over a week being waited on hand and foot. And the disgrace of her condition, the lost baby. And to think the girl used to be a nun.

Mistress Marjory's Christian charity had been sorely strained over the past nine days.

Agnes's disappearances had become a regular thing; Marjory had grown used to them. But when the young monk - no, he was no longer a monk; she must think of him as a ferryman - carried her unconscious, bleeding body into the courtyard for all the servants to see - for the whole town to see for all Marjory knew - her thoughts had become distinctly uncharitable.

Now the girl lay upstairs in her chamber and her silence was causing Marjory further irritation. Marjory Moore was a woman who liked to know what was going on in her own household. The wound to the girl's head had been bad enough: she had either fallen or been hit but claimed to have no recollection of it.

But the blood that had soaked through Agnes's dress... Marjory, having lived upon this earth forty five years, knew the signs. And when the girl had been undressed by Marjory and her maidservant, Griselda, her suspicions had been confirmed. Agnes had miscarried. Marjory had thanked the Virgin that the girl's condition was not too far advanced and she had instructed Griselda to say nothing.

Agnes had not said a word, either about the attack or the other matter. Marjory had asked - could not resist asking - but had been answered by a shake of Agnes's fair head.

Marjory's annoyance bubbled beneath her capable surface. Had she not taken the girl in when the King had closed the nunnery at Godstow? Had Marjory shirked her Christian duty to her dead cousin's only child? Had she not given the girl a roof over her head? And she was repaid with deceit and insolent silence.

Marjory opened the door of Agnes's bedchamber. The girl lay back against the stained linen sheets, staring upwards and Marjory felt another stab of irritation.

"I've brought your broth, Agnes. It would not do to let it grow cold." She put the bowl down firmly on the wooden chest at the foot of the bed.

Agnes looked at Marjory, a strange faraway look. Typical, Marjory thought to herself, not a word of thanks.

After a few moments the girl spoke. "Aunt, I have thought about what happened."

"And?" said Marjory impatiently.

"I saw him rising up behind the altar. Then I remember nothing."

Marjory took a deep breath. This was the most forthcoming Agnes had been since Bartholomew had brought her back unconscious from the chapel.

"Who did you see, Agnes?" Marjory sat down on the edge of the bed.

But the pressure of the question proved too much for the weakened girl. She sank back against the bolster. She would say no more about her experience. Instead she muttered weakly, "I will write to Lady Katheryn. She will advise me."

"And who, pray, is Lady Katheryn?" Marjory felt her impatience rise again as she looked across at the broth which was congealing on the chest.

"Our mother Abbess. She is not far from here...but forty miles away in a place called Cheadle. I will send for her."

Agnes closed her eyes and turned over in bed just as Marjory was about to point out that she alone had the authority to issue invitations to visit the Old Hall: Agnes should be ashamed of her audacity. Then it occurred to Marjory that such a woman as Lady Katheryn would be unlikely to take an interest in the misfortunes of one of her former novices. The Abbess would be leading a new life on a generous pension amongst her gentry kinsfolk and would doubtless ignore a silly girl's ramblings.

With this comforting thought, Marjory left her rebuke unsaid and crept quietly from the room. All this talk of apparitions in the chapel had convinced her even further that the girl's brain was addled. But she would get to the root of this matter and find out the truth.

And she was determined to find the answer to the question that most perplexed her. Who had been the father of Agnes's child?

FEAST OF ST. JEROME - 30TH SEPTEMBER 1539

Salmon were plentiful in the deep green waters of the River Mersey. Peter Fisher owed his livelihood to the glistening creatures, as had his father before him and his father before that.

But sometimes the river gave up other, more grisly, catches from its depths. Peter swallowed hard and made the sign of the cross when he saw what was caught in his net. Like a huge amorphous black jelly fish, the thing was dragged behind the boat as Peter and his son rowed frantically for the strand.

Peter had said nothing: there was no need for words. The poor creature, the bloated thing that was once a man, had to be returned to the shore to be claimed by his kin and given Christian burial. The body, born up by the putrefying gases within, sailed behind the small craft, its voluminous garments spread out in its wake. A monk's habit perhaps, Peter thought. But not the familiar Benedictine habit of the brothers of Birkenhead Priory. A priest's gown maybe? Peter could not quite make it out.

When they reached the strand, Peter and his son dragged their craft up the sand into the shelter of the Tower's high stone battlements, the body slithering behind. Peter approached slowly, signalling to his son to stand back. The corpse stank and Peter's hand went automatically to his face to shield his nostrils.

Peter moved the sodden robes aside to reveal the face, then quickly replaced them, not wishing to look at the horror of the swollen mess and the staring empty eye sockets. He touched the corpse again with his foot and the gown - definitely a priest's gown - fell aside to reveal part of the right arm.

Peter stepped back, staring at the white of the bone protruding from the hacked stump in the place where the corpse's right hand should have been.

CHAPTER 1

Lady Katheryn Bulkeley rose from her prayers. Thomas Cromwell - the Chancellor and the most powerful man in England after the King - had refused her eloquent request to spare her nunnery from the fate of so many others, but he could not stop her doing her duty to her Maker.

A scuffling sound in the rushes by the door made her turn. Jane, the mouse-haired maidservant, stood in the doorway, open mouthed, holding a piece of parchment between two fingers as if she were afraid the thing would burn her.

"Begging your pardon, my lady. I didn't wish to disturb you when you were..."

Lady Katheryn smiled. "What have you there, Jane? Something for me?"

Jane stared at her new mistress cautiously and held the parchment gingerly in front of her. "The chapman called, my lady." She swallowed hard. "He brought this letter for you...from Liverpool he said. From the household of Mistress Moore."

"Did you ask the chapman to stay, Jane? I should like to see his wares. Did you buy anything from him?"

Jane, emboldened by her mistress's friendly manner, relaxed. "Needles, my lady...and some ribbon." She looked down, blushing. "He is still in the village, my lady. I could send for him if you wish."

"I should like that." Katheryn smiled. "Just because I've spent much of my life in a nunnery, it doesn't follow that I've lost all interest in pretty things. Has he any laces?"

"Oh yes, my lady...some fine laces."

"Then please find him and ask him to call again."

Katheryn took the letter graciously and the girl bobbed a curtsey and scurried from the room. Katheryn sighed and smiled to herself: the charm she had used to put nervous novices at their ease seemed to work equally well with maidservants.

She looked at the letter with curiosity. Moore? Where had she heard that name? But if she didn't read it, her curiosity would never be satisfied. She broke the seal.

"Mother Abbess," the letter began - a title to which, according to those in authority, Katheryn was no longer entitled. "I beg you to help me in my time of trouble. I remember with much gratitude your kindness to me at Godstow and I do not know where else I should turn except to you and my Saviour. Having no family, I stay with my father's cousin, Mistress Moore of Liverpool, at the Old Hall there. I have sinned grievously and I fear I am in great danger both of body and soul. I am, Mother Abbess, your humble servant, Sister Agnes Moore."

Katheryn reread it twice. She remembered young Sister Agnes, a pretty, nervous dreamer little suited to the cloister. Katheryn had once suggested to the girl that a husband and string of demanding children would have had a beneficial effect on someone of her over-romantic nature (Katheryn, a realist herself, had never been one for dreaming). But Agnes had been resigned to the religious life: and with her lack of rank and wealth, she had probably had little choice in the matter.

Katheryn looked at herself in the burnished metal of her mirror; a treasure rescued from her well appointed quarters at Godstow and brought to her new home, the family's manor house which - because of her brother's calling - doubled as the village Rectory.

She was still an attractive woman, even at the age of thirty five, she thought to herself murmuring a quick prayer asking the Almighty to forgive her small sin of vanity. She pushed back a wisp of brown hair which was escaping from beneath her white linen cap and smoothed down her gown. A gown that displayed her figure to the best advantage - so much more fetching than her nun's habit.

Katheryn turned her attention once more to Agnes's letter. She read it again and found herself wishing that the girl had been more specific. The devil had devised many traps for the unwary. Grievous sin could mean anything. From what she recalled of Agnes, the girl was far too timid to indulge in serious sin, but who could tell; times and people change. She sighed. Maybe the chapman would throw some light on Agnes's situation when he returned to the Rectory.

Jane's arrival shattered the peace of the chamber. "The chapman's here, my lady. He awaits you in the parlour." Her eyes shone with excitement. "I found him straight away. He was at Mother Gatley's."

"And what else did you find at Mother Gatley's, pray?"

Jane blushed. "Will Gatley bought me some laces, my lady," she said shyly. It was amazing how this mouse of a girl was transformed by the attentions of a well set young man.

"Then I hope you've left some for me. Come along, girl, let's not keep the chapman waiting."

Michael, the chapman, made a little bow as the lady of the manor and her maid entered the parlour, a well lit room strewn with sweet smelling herbs and fresh rushes.

When the business of choosing laces was over, Katheryn bid the chapman put his pack aside and sit down and she sent Jane to fetch some ale.

"You brought me a letter, master chapman? From a lady in Liverpool."

"Aye, my lady. I was there two weeks since. It was Mistress Moore who gave me the letter. All Liverpool knows Mistress Moore. She is widow of the late Mayor of Liverpool and mother to Francis Moore Esquire of Bank Hall. Mistress Moore lives in the Old Hall, the Dower House between the townfield and the strand."

"You didn't see Agnes, the girl who wrote the letter?"

"No, my lady. Just Mistress Marjory." Michael smiled, revealing blackened teeth in a pleasant but pockmarked face. "Mistress Marjory's enough for any man, I'll be bound."

"And she said nothing to you?"

"Only to be sure to deliver the letter when I reached Cheadle." He took a long drink of ale. Trudging the dusty lanes of Cheshire with his heavy burden was thirsty work. "She said nothing more but looked most put out."

Katheryn thanked the chapman graciously and left him to Jane's care. She needed to think.

Sir John Bulkeley, Rector of Cheadle in the county of Cheshire, eyed the new addition to his church with suspicion as he rose from his prayers. The great Bible translated into English was chained firmly to the wooden lectern. It had been planted in the new church of St. Mary like an alien weed, on the orders of Master Thomas Cromwell, at the same time as his men had come to smash the statues and steal what little treasure the village church possessed.

It could not be read by most of his illiterate congregation. But there was always some half-educated yeoman who would stand there at the lectern reading the words to his ignorant neighbours and putting his own interpretation on them. Sir John resented this challenge to his authority. Was he not their parish priest, responsible for the souls of the village? Let the yeoman keep to his own business. Did the priest tell him how to keep his animals or plough his land?

John tried to banish these resentful thoughts from his mind. It was futile to resist the power of the King if you wanted to survive.

The great door opened, letting a shaft of sunlight into the southernmost corner of the church. John turned to see who was disturbing his peace.

"Good day, brother. I had not intended to interrupt your prayers."

"You didn't, Katheryn. I had finished." He paused, noting the expression on his sister's face; the single minded determination. She was planning something. Even as a child, Katheryn had used her formidable talent for organisation to keep her three brothers in line.

"I am summoned to the aid of one of my sisters from Godstow. I intend to go at once."

"But the roads are not safe for travellers. There are rogues and vagabonds roaming the countryside and Oxford is so far..."

"Not Oxford, brother. This girl dwells in Liverpool, but forty miles from here. By my reckoning it will take two days to reach and I will seek a night's lodgings in Warrington."

"But you cannot travel alone." John, a tall man, bent towards his sister with concern. One day Katheryn's determined nature would lead her into peril. He still shuddered as he remembered how she had defied Thomas Cromwell, pleading for her nunnery to be spared from the commissioners. That sort of defiance had led others to the scaffold. He had hoped that now she was home, settled in the fine manor house which doubled as the village's rectory, she would be content with a life of quiet safety. But now he feared his hopes were in vain.

"I will not travel alone," she assured him. "Whatever else I may be, brother, the Lord did not create me a fool. I will take Jane and Thomas the groom. I have given orders for the horses to be made ready."

"But Katheryn..."

She looked around the church, its solid grey stone walls softened in the candlelight and its fine oak roof hardly visible in the smoky darkness. The tall tallow candles in the chantry chapels of wealthy local families, on either side of the altar, burned for the souls of their founders.

Katheryn was in no mood to argue so she changed the subject to one dear to her brother's heart. "I have not forgotten my promise."

"What promise is that, sister?"

"The new chancel. I will pay for its building." She saw John's eyes glow as he contemplated this addition to his beloved church. "That instrument of Satan, Tom Cromwell, gave me a handsome pension when I left Godstow, to buy my co-operation, no doubt. I should like to see it used for the glory of God's house. No argument, John. I am determined."

John, who was not about to argue, smiled. "The Lord will bless you for it, sister." He raised his hand in benediction. "And take my blessings for your journey."

She turned to go and was half way down the church when the Rector spoke again. "I saw our groom entering the White Hart a while back. I doubt he will be sober enough for the journey you intend."

Katheryn turned to look at her brother who was grinning at her. Did he think to prevent her journey so easily? She turned and marched resolutely through the church porch. She then turned right by the church gate and continued towards the door of the whitewashed ale house next to the church.

As she entered the White Hart, Katheryn resisted the temptation to put her hand to her nose to mask the smell of stale ale and foul rushes. The men who sat at the battered trestle tables with their tankards of ale, looked up as she entered and a curious dog, its fur eaten by mange, approached her boldly and sniffed at her skirts.

Unabashed by the silence she had created - the silence of working men unused to seeing the Lady of the Manor enter the ale house they regarded as their sovereign territory - Katheryn spotted her quarry in a darkened corner. Thomas the groom did not see her at first, occupied as he was with his game. He was playing at dice with a stranger. There were many men who made a living roaming the country cheating gullible drinkers. It seemed that one of their number had reached Cheadle.

The weasel-faced stranger threw the dice and grinned maliciously. Thomas took a gulp of ale and pushed two coins at weasel-face. Katheryn stood behind the pair who were too preoccupied to notice her presence. The landlord, a large sweaty man in a stained apron, began to approach deferentially but Katheryn put her hand to her lips, instructing the man to be silent. He obeyed. Her eyes were on the pair playing dice. Weasel-face threw again. Thomas sighed and pushed another coin at him.

Both men looked up, startled, as Katheryn grabbed the dice. The landlord stepped forward, sensing trouble.

Katheryn threw the dice down on the table in front of the gaping men. Thomas blinked at her drunkenly, not believing what he saw. Katheryn addressed weasel-face, who was looking around for a means of escape. "Will you play against me, sir? I favour the numbers three and six." She drew two coins from the purse that hung from her waist and threw them down.

"My lady," the landlord interrupted, worried for a reputation; hers or his inn's, Katheryn could not tell. "It is not fitting."

Katheryn sat down on the bench beside her groom and threw the dice again. Six and three: her suspicions had been confirmed. "I will keep those numbers, sir. If I win again, you will return the money you have cheated from my groom here. Is that agreed?"

Weasel-face knew when he'd been beaten. There was silence in the ale house, broken only by the clucking of the hens who wandered the floor pecking at scraps. Thomas, the worse for drink, lolled on the bench next to his mistress, enjoying the spectacle.

Katheryn threw the dice: three and six. She looked at weasel face triumphantly as he thrust a pile of coins at Thomas who was too far gone to care.

She turned to the landlord who stood open mouthed. "Men like this who prey on honest folk should, by rights, be handed to the constable." Weasel-face looked apprehensive for the first time: he didn't relish the idea of a day in the stocks. Katheryn continued "What do you wait for, Master Brownlow? Have this rogue shown from the village and warned not to return. And have my groom here taken to the pump and given a good soaking to sober him up."

The landlord loomed towards weasel-face, who rose suddenly and made a run for it; getting out while his luck held. Thomas was hauled unceremoniously from his seat by two men sitting nearby and dragged from the ale house. Katheryn graciously bid the landlord good day and swept out into the weak October sunshine.

Thomas would be no use to her for many hours yet and she wanted to be away as soon as possible. There was only one solution; one that she knew would please Jane.

When she reached the Rectory, Jane greeted her eagerly; excited, if a little nervous about her coming journey. When her mistress told her that she should ask Will Gatley to be their escort, Jane tried to hide her enthusiasm, although she was sure that in the quiet dimness of the hall the whole household could hear the quickened beating of her heart.

It took an hour for the pack horses to be loaded with their baggage. Katheryn didn't believe in travelling light. And whatever Liverpool had in store, she intended to be well prepared.

Mistress Marjory Moore had given strict instructions that Agnes should keep to her chamber. Whether this was for the good of Agnes's health or to keep the girl out of trouble, Marjory refused to admit...even to herself.

Agnes was regaining her strength. The daily routine of embroidery and study of the Bible and the lives of the saints was no longer enough for her. But she knew that if Mistress Marjory thought she was recovering, she would be expected to resume her household duties. And Agnes was growing restless: she had to know the truth.

Her legs were still weak as she moved slowly across the rush-strewn floor and almost fell into the window seat. The leaded casement window overlooked the front of the house. From there she could see the rutted line of Mill Street where a cart trundled past on its way to the townfield, followed by a ragged woman and child. She stared out of the window for a further hour, grateful that Mistress Marjory was kept too busy bossing her household to disturb her. Soon the parade of ragged humanity on foot, cart and occasionally on horseback, travelling to the townfield to tend their plots, began to pall. She was not going to see the one she hoped to see; besides, it was growing dark. She watched half an hour more as the twilight gathered but now the road below was empty; few people ventured out after sunset.

Then she saw him. His shape was so familiar; his way of walking, the way he held his cloak around his body. She stood up in the gathering darkness and pressed her face to the window to see better. It was him. She was sure. She struggled with the window catch but by the time she managed to open the casement, the cloaked figure had disappeared quickly in the direction of the townfield.

Tears began to flow down Agnes's cheeks and she sank wearily back onto the window seat. It had been him...she was certain.

CHAPTER 2

The sodden body found by Peter Fisher in the waters of the River Mersey had been taken to the church of Our Lady and St. Nicholas where it lay in a rough wooden coffin before the altar in the chapel of St. John. It was only right, Peter had reasoned, that the church should claim its own.

Father James, the priest, had not looked at the body too closely. It had been in the water for several days and the face had been eaten away by the fishes. When it had been stripped, washed and coffined, all the dead man needed was his prayers.

When Father Clement, the priest in charge of the chantry chapel of St. John, had disappeared a few days before, Father James feared that he had met with an accident; or worse, been robbed and murdered by the villains who roamed the land. Gone were the days when a man's calling was respected and the murder of a priest would confer everlasting damnation. This was a Godless and lawless age. Now it seemed that Father James's worst fears for Father Clement had been justified: the rogues had even hacked off the corpse's hand, no doubt for reasons of their own which Father James did not dare to contemplate.

Father James knelt before the coffin and muttered a prayer. He prayed for Father Clement's soul and for the souls of his killers. But he added a further prayer begging forgiveness for himself: he had not liked Clement. Even now, when he lay dead before him, Father James could not bring himself to think well of his fellow priest.

Father Clement in life had been a handsome, well built fellow of about twenty eight summers, with an easy charm and - Father James suspected - an eye for the ladies of the parish. James recalled the time when he had caught Clement alone with one of the Mayor's daughters, his hand upon her breast as he purported to settle some complex theological point which she claimed had puzzled her?

Clement had served as chantry priest for three months, having come with a letter of recommendation from Abbot

Birkett of Norton. But James had had misgivings from the start. Clement had been lax in saying the required masses for the souls of the founders of his chantry and James had noted his absences with increasing irritation. The Augustinian canons of Norton Abbey had always had a good reputation in the district for their work in the local churches: so why had Father James's church ended up with one who did not justify the high standing of his order?

But now the man was dead. He lay, battered, in his linen shroud; his black priest's gown, heavy with river water, having been stripped from his body. Father James muttered another prayer of repentance for thinking ill of the dead.

He did not hear Valentine approaching. The chanting of latin verbs by the boys of the small grammar school held in the chantry chapel of St. Catherine on the other side of the church had masked his footsteps on the stone flags.

"Good day to you, Father."

James turned his head and rose from his prayers, glad to see his old friend.

"I heard of your loss, Father James."

"I was praying for his soul, brother. How goes it with you?"

Valentine smiled. He was a wiry man of middling height and middling years. His hair, once jet black, was now streaked with grey. With his olive complexion and warm brown eyes, the former infirmarian of the Priory at Birkenhead over the river had been taken more than once for a foreigner, his dark looks being a legacy from his long dead Spanish mother.

"There are many in Liverpool in need of my services, Father. Business is good." With the forty shillings given to each monk as they left the shelter of the Priory, Brother Valentine had set himself up as an apothecary in the town of Liverpool. His skill with medicines and reassuring manner had ensured the venture's success.

Valentine looked at the coffin. "Do you know how he died?"

"Set upon by thieves, or at least that's what I surmise. His hand has been hacked off. The world is a sorry place."

"May I see?"

Father James was surprised at Valentine's request. "His face is mutilated, eaten by river creatures. He was in the river a few days. It is not a pleasing sight, brother."

"I have seen worse, no doubt." Valentine lifted the coffin lid and put his hand to his face as the smell hit his nostrils. He pushed aside the shroud. "He is indeed battered but it was done after death, probably on the rocks beneath the water. The marks have not bruised." He studied the man's bloated chest and gingerly turned the body over. "He was stabbed with a long sharp dagger by the looks of it. And his hand; I should say that was hacked off with a dagger too...not a clean cut. Did he wear rings on that hand?"

Father James's brow furrowed as he tried to remember. He thought of the hand that had lain on the gentle swell of the Mayor's daughter's breast. Was there a ring? He thought not. "I couldn't say. But they have left the ring on his other hand. See." He indicated the corpse's swollen left hand. On it, stuck fast on the bloated white middle finger, was a ring, plain gold with a matt black stone: not a common design. "It is the one he always wore. I recognise it well. Surely they would have taken it."

"There are reasons other than theft for removing a dead man's hand," said Valentine softly. The two men looked at each other.

Father James could stand the stench no longer. He flicked the shroud back into place so it covered the mess that was once a face and replaced the lid of the coffin. "I cannot believe... I have heard no rumours of such things in the town."

"Nor I, Father James. But we must remember that Satan is everywhere."

Katheryn's journey had been uneventful apart from Will Gatley's mount losing a shoe; this misfortune being swiftly remedied by a large sweating blacksmith in the village of Lymm. The inn at Warrington was comfortable and respectable and the landlord had welcomed Katheryn according to her rank, with a tankard of his best ale and a tasty meat pie.

Refreshed after a night's rest and grateful that the ragged vagrants they had passed on the dusty highway had done nothing more threatening than beg alms, the three riders crossed the great heath and approached the Townsend Bridge with relief. Liverpool was in sight and the weather had held fair.

Will Gatley rode in front of the party leading the packhorses. Katheryn, on her fine white mare was in the centre of the party and Jane brought up the rear. Katheryn had noticed Jane and Will exchanging glances and the girl seemed to have acquired a new radiance, elevating her mousiness to a delicate prettiness. The power of love, thought the former Abbess, was a wonderful thing...not that she knew much about it from personal experience. She would not be surprised if her brother, Sir John, had another wedding to perform at the church of St. Mary before the year was out.

Katheryn gathered her cloak about her. The wind was starting to bite. The autumn had been unseasonably warm but now the first chill of winter was making itself felt.

A yeoman near the Townsend Bridge bid them a cheery good day as they passed. They could see the town in the distance: the tower of Our Lady and St. Nicholas; the bulk of the castle; and the huddle of houses radiating out from the ship-strewn, glistening river.

The sight of three decomposing corpses hanging from gibbets by the roadside caused Jane to avert her eyes. Katheryn, used to such sights on her journey from Godstow, rode on. The gibbets were full across the land since King Henry had declared that the Pope was no longer head of the church and had claimed to fill the position himself. His agents looked for treason in every quarter and it was a time to keep thoughts to yourself.

Even in such far flung towns as Liverpool there were spies only too eager to report dissent to the authorities.

They continued down Dale Street into the bustling hub of the town. At the cross-roads, by the tall stone High Cross, a pasty faced man stood in the pillory, a smouldering fish stinking beneath his nose; a tradesman who had sold bad fish and was now paying for his greed. He was taunted by a group of jeering youths and a trio of barking dogs joined in the administration of town justice.

Groups of roughly dressed men strolled down the streets or hung about the tavern doors. Some, by their appearance and their voices, were foreign; some spoke with accents Katheryn knew to be Irish; sailors from the tall masted merchant ships they had seen anchored in the river.

Katheryn halted her horse at the High Cross. Looking left she could see the grey mass of the castle with its round towers, perched on its red rock base. She bid good day to a chubby merchant's wife in a neat grey wool gown, and asked her the way to the Old Hall. There was no hesitation; Mistress Moore's house was known to the whole town.

Their horses clattered down the hard packed dirt of Juggler Street until they reached another cross-roads. To their left was Chapel Street and the parish church, with the tiny chapel of St. Mary del Quay nestling in its shadow. Ahead was the road out to the townfield, Mill Street, furrowed from the passage of carts used by the townsfolk as they cultivated their plots. It was here they found a handsome stone house with neatly dressed servants hurrying about its courtyard and outbuildings.

Katheryn made a quick appraisal. The signs of a well run household were everywhere. A manservant, will scrubbed and alert, came forward to take their horses' reins and ask them their business. It soon became clear that they were not expected.

When Mistress Marjory Moore swept out into the courtyard to greet Katheryn, the servants backed away respectfully and went about their duties with self conscious diligence. Katheryn studied her hostess. Marjory was in her mid forties and still clung precariously to her beauty; although the lines on her face had increased and the flesh had begun to sag, she possessed a fine bone structure and tall slim figure. She would remain a handsome woman, long into old age.

She led Katheryn into the hall and gave orders that Jane and Will were to be looked after. The servants jumped to their tasks like well trained soldiers. There was no slackness allowed in Mistress Marjory's household. The thought came to Katheryn that Sister Agnes must have fitted awkwardly into this efficient establishment.

"I am grateful to you for coming, Lady Katheryn. Though I must say I did not expect you to answer the request of a silly girl so promptly, if at all." Katheryn detected a touch of bitterness in Marjory's speech, but the mistress of the house did not forget her manners. "I trust you had an uneventful journey?"

Katheryn smiled warmly. It would need all her charm to coax confidences from this woman. "Indeed. The weather held fair and the roads have not yet become quagmires."

Marjory clapped her hands and a maidservant, not more than thirteen years of age, scurried forward with two goblets of the finest wine Katheryn had tasted since her days as Abbess of Godstow. She appreciated good claret and complimented Marjory on her choice.

"We are not at the heart of the wine trade here in Liverpool, my lady, but there is always a merchant ship with wares to sell. My steward knows many of the ships' masters... and he drives a good bargain."

"You are fortunate, Mistress." There was a pause while she sipped the warming ruby liquid, so welcome after the dusty journey. She thought it time that she mention the reason for her visit. "And how is Sister Agnes? Her letter sounded most urgent. I hope I have arrived at a fitting time."

"Indeed you have," Marjory said unconvincingly. "Somebody needs to talk some sense into the girl." She invited Katheryn to sit on a well carved chair by the roaring fire and drew another chair near for herself.

"Since Agnes arrived here she has brought nothing but trouble." Katheryn inclined her head, hoping Marjory would elaborate. "She seemed willing enough when she first came and she went about her tasks without complaint." Marjory's lips tightened. Agnes, Katheryn thought, would have been expected to work hard about the house for her keep; such is the fate of poor relations. "Then she began to absent herself from her duties without any explanation. She started daydreaming. I had to tell her more than once about her sewing ...that her stitching was large and clumsy. The girl's mind was on other things."

"What things, Mistress? Do you know?"

"Do you think I did not question the girl? She is sly. She said nothing."

"At Godstow I always found Sister Agnes...how shall I put it best?...a little inattentive; a dreamer, perhaps. But I should scarce have thought her sly. I knew of no malice in the child."

"Then, my lady, what of the girl's condition?"

"Condition?"

"She was with child. She miscarried."

Katheryn took another sip of wine. "She spoke of sin in her letter." Clearly the girl's romantic nature had got the better of her. "That might be an indication of a lack of control, Mistress, but not necessarily of wickedness. Who was the father of her child?"

"I have no idea. I never knew of a young man. Whoever it was, they met in secret."

This did not strike Katheryn as being necessarily sinister. Mistress Marjory would hardly have welcomed the swain of a poor relation into the house or condone any relationship that might distract Agnes from her duties. If Katheryn had been in Agnes's place, she might have done the same. "Many young lovers meet in secret, Mistress. Has he not called to enquire about Agnes? Or enquired of any of the servants?"

"No. There has been no one. Only the monk who found her unconscious in the chapel. He has called several times to ask after her health. Though he has not asked to see her; she has kept to her chamber."

"What monk is this?"

"I should call him a monk no longer. His Priory at Birkenhead over the river was closed by the King's commissioners some three years back. His name is Bartholomew. He sails the ferry across the river. The monks at Birkenhead have always kept the ferry. People need to cross the river, priory or no priory."

"This Bartholomew, has he visited the house before? Did he have any contact with Agnes before he found her?"

"I know what you think, my lady...that they were lovers. But I think not. The young man shows concern but his behaviour is most proper. He was a monk and, by his demeanour, one who still holds to his vows."

Marjory had obviously taken a liking to this young ferryman and was refusing to cast him in the role of Agnes's errant lover. Katheryn would keep an open mind. She had known many monks and nuns who were as susceptible to the temptations of the flesh as any other man or woman...and his attentions might indicate an uneasy conscience.

"Tell me how she was found? What happened to her?"

"Indeed, my lady, you deserve to hear the full tale as you have taken so much trouble to answer Agnes's request." Marjory took a deep breath, settling down to tell a long story. "Agnes came, as you know, from Godstow. When your house was dissolved she wrote to me, as her only relative, to beg a roof over her head. She is my husband's late cousin's child. He died soon after Agnes's birth. Her mother's name was Blanche but I hardly knew her. She was a delicate woman in body and mind, given to ill humours and imaginings." Marjory looked disapproving. "Her daughter, it seems, has inherited much from her mother. Blanche's father was a merchant of Oxford but apart from that I know nothing of him. Blanche died when Agnes was but ten years old."

Katheryn interrupted. "Then she came into our care at the Abbey. I recall her mother's family had some connection with our house and that it was assumed that she would join our order. It often happens thus. She was a quiet girl...much given to dreaming, if I'm not mistaken." There was gentle humour in Katheryn's voice but Marjory missed this and took the last remark as criticism.

"You are right, my lady. The girl is lazy. Give her a task to perform or an errand to run and she would disappear for hours on end. I have had words with her more than once, I can tell you."

Katheryn suddenly felt sorry for Agnes. Life as a nun may not have been ideal for her, but at least it was better than the semi-slavery expected of a poor relation in return for food and a roof. She interrupted Marjory's bitter complaints, feeling an urge to defend the girl. "I felt poor Agnes was unsuited to the life of our order, but she made the best of it and would have taken her vows in the next year. Sister Magdalen, our Mistress of Novices, had much praise for Sister Agnes. She said the girl had a loving heart and an aptitude for scholarship."

Marjory snorted. "But they don't pay for her keep. Am I to keep her in good food and idleness for her loving heart. The girl must work, my lady. It is her only contribution to the household. Book reading and Latin do not pay the butcher and baker." Mistress Marjory sat back, arms folded, and looked at Katheryn who sat toying with her goblet, eyes downcast.

Agnes's situation was indeed a sorry one. Any money she had inherited from her merchant grandfather would have been given to the Abbey as her dowry and was now in the coffers of the King. Without the pension given to the older nuns, Agnes was truly penniless and thrown upon Marjory's mercy. Katheryn had even heard tales of girls in Agnes's situation turning whore to keep themselves alive. Had Agnes tried this way out? Katheryn did not think the idea would have occurred to her, but in desperate times one never knew.

"What happened when Agnes arrived?" Katheryn tried to return Marjory to her narrative.

"She wrote to tell me she was coming and claimed to have nowhere else to go. Her mother had spoken of her father's relatives in Liverpool, it appears, so the girl travelled all the way from Oxford with a group of travellers. Well, you know how careful you have to be nowadays. She fell in with some merchants travelling to Chester...and some monks were in their party. At Chester she found more companions at an inn and made her way to Liverpool by boat." Katheryn raised her eyebrows. She hadn't given Agnes credit for such an enterprising spirit. To travel from one side of the land to another on the perilous roads, showed initiative for a young girl whose head was filled with dreams.

"Did she speak of anyone she met on the road?"

"She spoke of her companions but not one name that I remember."

"And when she arrived?"

"She rested a day after her journey. Then she was shown her duties in the household."

"And how long before she began to absent herself?"

"Almost right away. I was most displeased but when I tackled her about it she would say nothing."

"And you have no idea where she went or who she was with?"

"If I knew, my lady, I would tell you. I did suspect she was hiding somewhere...daydreaming or reading." She made the last activity sound like a deadly sin. "But in view of her condition, we must assume that she found other ways of amusing herself."

"Do you know if she stayed about the house or if she went out? Did anyone see her return, for instance?"

She is not a prisoner here, my lady. She is free to come and go as she pleases. So if she chooses to abandon her duty and disobey my requests..."

"Quite." Katheryn noted that Marjory was bristling with righteous indignation. "So what happened on the day she was found unconscious?"

"It was in the morning. I had asked her to run an errand for me...to Brother Valentine, the apothecary." She corrected herself. "Or I should say Master Valentine? One grows used to..." Katheryn nodded and willed her to continue. "But instead the girl is found half dead in the chapel of St. Mary del Quay. I have mentioned the young ferryman who found her, Brother Bartholomew, he went into the chapel to pray. It was the hour of Terce and he still observes the discipline of his order when his duties permit."

Katheryn nodded. She knew the difficulty of observing one's vows when one is thrown out into the secular world. One by one the offices would be left unsaid: she was as guilty of this as any.

"He found Agnes lying before the altar. He saw nobody else about."

"And Agnes miscarried?"

"To her shame."

"How far advanced was her condition?"

"Master Valentine said about ten weeks. She has been with me but three months. To think how she has repaid my trust."

"Could she have fainted with pain? Hit her head?"

"That is what I thought - what Brother Bartholomew thought. Master Valentine says different."

Katheryn sat forward, suddenly interested. "What do you mean?"

"He says the injuries to her head show that she was struck...not that she fell. But I cannot believe... Who would wish to attack her?"

Katheryn said nothing but had her own thoughts. She drained her goblet and Marjory, the good hostess, refilled it. The claret was smooth and warming. Katheryn knew she shouldn't have accepted more if she wanted to keep a clear head, but the journey had given her a thirst.

"Do you want to see Agnes now, my lady. After all, that is why you came, is it not?" Marjory asked sharply.

Katheryn nodded and stood up, feeling a little light headed.

Valentine hurried back to his shop, avoiding the stinking stream that ran down the middle of the narrow street. His apprentice, Ralph, couldn't be left on his own for too long, even though the boy was learning fast.

It was nearly dark and the sharp autumnal wind from the river held a bitter salty chill. Valentine pulled his cloak about him for warmth. There were many figures scuttling down Juggler Street, heads down against the breeze, making for the warmth of their firesides before the curfew sounded. Small groups of sailors swaggered into the taverns, anticipating an evening's drinking and, if their luck held, a night in the arms of a whore.

Shopkeepers, putting up their wooden shutters for the night, bade Valentine goodnight as he strode past. Candles were beginning to flicker in windows, creating a moonlike glow behind the oiled parchment which provided small protection against the weather in the poorer dwellings.

As Valentine walked down Dale Street, looking forward to a bowl of hot broth before the fire, a figure, cloaked and bent, emerged from an alleyway and crossed his path in the twilight. The man - he was certain it was a man - stopped and turned towards him. Valentine could not see the face as it was hidden by a hood pulled down so that it concealed the wearer's identity. But he recognised the style of cloak, though this one was stained and torn. The Augustinian canons of Norton had worn such a garment against the cold when their abbey had been in existence...the abbey where the late Father Clement had taken his vows.

"Alms...alms, sir, I beg you."

So this shabby creature was a beggar. There were many of them about. If this man was caught by the constables he would be sent from the town or imprisoned for the night in the ground floor of the Guildhall with the other common criminals. Valentine drew a coin from his purse and held it up for the man to see. The beggar, seeing Valentine staring at him, pulled his hood down further to hide his face.

"If I were you, my friend, I should keep hidden. If the constables..." He stepped forward, offering the coin. "Buy yourself a bed for the night and a hot meal and take this with God's blessing. Do you come from Norton, my friend?"

There was no answer. Valentine placed the coin in the outstretched left hand, avoiding the temptation to hold his nose against the stench of unwashed clothes and urine. The beggar's heavy fleece-lined black cloak fell open as he muttered his thanks then he quickly gathered the folds together before he turned and hurried away. It was dark and the cloak had only fallen open for a second, but Valentine had noted in that brief moment that the beggar's right hand was missing.

CHAPTER 3

Agnes had been asleep when Mistress Marjory had taken Katheryn up to her chamber the previous evening. Marjory had been all for waking her, but Katheryn begged her to let the child sleep: she had been through an ordeal and rest would speed her recovery. Marjory agreed reluctantly, but not before she had cursed the girl for the wantonness that had brought her to her present state.

Katheryn, exhausted by her journey, had been glad to retire to her chamber early after the splendid supper provided by Marjory Moore for her honoured guest. The best cloths had draped the table, the best silverware brought out for the occasion. The cook had sweated over juicy joints of meat since Katheryn's arrival had been announced in the kitchens. It wasn't every day that the former Abbess of a great religious house, the sister of Sir Richard Bulkeley of Beaumaris, came visiting the dower house of the Moores of Liverpool. Wealthy burgesses though the Moores were, they still did not aspire to the status of gentry.

Jane went eagerly to her mistress to help her prepare for bed. Katheryn yawned and relaxed as her maidservant brushed her hair. She was glad to be in the privacy of her bedchamber. Mistress Marjory was not the most comfortable of companions.

"Are they treating you well, Jane? How are your quarters?"

"Well enough, my lady."

"Have you spoken with Will? Is he comfortable?"

Jane blushed. "Oh yes, my lady. He is to sleep above the stables with the grooms. He says he has naught to complain of."

"And you?"

"I share with Griselda and Margaret, the maidservants."

"Have they said much of the household?"

Jane looked down shyly.

"Come along, girl, what have they said? Whatever you tell me shall be our secret. What do they say?"

Jane shuffled her feet. She knew her mistress would not give up until she had learned the truth. "They talk of Mistress Moore, my lady. They say she's...she's a harridan. That she likes everything her own way...and that she is over strict and works them hard...and that she is mean. I'm sorry, my lady, but that's what they say."

Katheryn smiled. "I think I've discovered all that for myself, Jane. Do they speak of Agnes?"

"Only that they are sorry for her...and they think she had a secret lover." The last words were said with relish. Jane enjoyed gossip and could always be relied upon to keep Katheryn informed about the more intimate aspects of life back home in the village of Cheadle.

"Tell me all you know, Jane. Who is this secret lover?"

"They know nothing of him, only that she would disappear for hours to meet him. She would say nothing concerning him even when Griselda questioned her."

"Is Agnes unhappy here?"

"Griselda thinks so."

"And desperate to get away?"

Jane shrugged.

"Maybe Agnes was so desperate that she...that she sought to obtain money by means that would imperil her immortal soul."

Jane looked at Katheryn blankly, not grasping her meaning. "I talk of the sins of Saint Mary Magdalen...before her repentance, of course. Could Agnes have become a whore, do you think?" Jane looked shocked but Katheryn continued. "There are many sailors in this place. And the men of the town: many who would be willing to pay for a pretty girl's favours. Have Griselda and Margaret considered this possibility?"

"I'm sure they haven't, my lady. And I don't think we should speak of such things. The girl was a nun."

"And I have known many nuns who could not count chastity amongst their virtues. Did not the King give immorality as one of the reasons for closing the religious houses of this land?"

"But my lady, you must know..."

"I know only that I tried to run my own Abbey as a house of prayer and devotion. I cannot speak for others. Why even at Godstow it was not unknown for young monks studying at Oxford to navigate the Thames and call upon the young nuns of my Abbey." Jane gasped, shocked. "The flesh is always with us, Jane." Katheryn turned and looked at her reflection in the mirror. "When you have lived longer you will understand such things."

"But the young monks and the nuns of your Abbey...did they?"

"Katheryn turned to the blushing girl. "I could only advise against sin, my child. It would have taken a better one than I to stop it altogether."

The two women said nothing for a while, their silence amicable, as Jane continued to brush her lady's hair. Then Jane remembered what it was that was bothering her.

"There was one thing Griselda said, my lady."

"What was that?"

"When Margaret told Agnes of her young man and said that he'd not been attentive to her of late, Agnes told her she knew someone who could make a love potion...someone skilled in the black arts. She remembered it because she was surprised that Agnes should know of such things, having been a nun."

Katheryn smiled, sceptical. "There is always some crone ready to provide a giddy girl with a love potion."

"Margaret says there is a woman in Liverpool who deals in such things...Mother Sherratt. But when Agnes talked she said "he". Do you think it could be important, my lady?"

Katheryn stared at the mirror and spoke slowly; she was tired. "I don't know, Jane. It might be. Sister Agnes has many matters to explain."

Katheryn awoke and threw back the bed curtains to find Jane pouring hot water from the kitchens into a bowl. Katheryn was in the habit of washing each morning; most were not. Jane was shaping up well. The girl was anticipating her mistress's needs without instruction: that was good. Katheryn would miss her when she married and had a family of her own to look after, and from what she had observed between Jane and Will Gatley, that day would not be too far away.

"Jane turned to see Katheryn watching her and bobbed a curtsey. "Your water's ready, my lady."

"Thank you, Jane. I trust you slept well?"

"Quite well, my lady. But those girls I share with are such gigglers and gossips. They talked well into the night."

"What did they gossip about?" Katheryn was keen to glean any bits of juicy information connected with Agnes before she actually faced the girl.

"Griselda thinks Agnes is enamoured of a sailor and that he has returned to some foreign land and that is why he has not called."

"A reasonable explanation. What evidence has she?"

Jane shrugged. Gossip needs no evidence. "It seems that Mistress Agnes looked out to sea a great deal. That is all, as far as I know. Griselda is courting an sailor herself so..."

"As your new companions are such tale tellers, we are bound to come by the truth eventually." Katheryn grinned. "Or their version of it. Do tell me, Jane, if you discover anything of interest."

"I shall, my lady." Their eyes met conspiratorially.

Katheryn washed and dressed in her third best gown of dark green, with russet embroidered kirtle and fashionably wide sleeves. She had to keep up appearances in front of Mistress Moore, a snob if ever Katheryn saw one. She prayed and broke her fast with some smooth ale and fine white bread that Jane had been thoughtful enough to bring to her chamber.

After examining her appearance in her mirror, Katheryn descended the oak staircase. The Old Hall was a comfortable house, kept clean with fresh rushes and herbs. The hangings on the wall were of rich tapestry and the wood was polished by a small army of well-trained servants. Mistress Marjory was captain of a tight ship.

Marjory Moore greeted her guest in the parlour. After the usual polite enquiries, Katheryn came straight to the point. "Is Agnes well enough to receive me, Mistress Moore?"

"The girl still keeps to her bed but..."

"Then I will go to her, if you have no objection."

Mistress Marjory's lips tightened. She issued the invitations in her own household, controlled the comings and goings. But she reminded herself that Katheryn was there to help and that she might even persuade Agnes to become a useful member of the household once more - or even take the disgraced girl with her when she returned to Cheshire. "Of course, my lady. If you do not mind the girl being in a state of undress and neglect, brought on by her own idleness."

"Agnes is ill, mistress. I quite understand if she does not dress to receive me." With this Katheryn bowed her head to the mistress of the house and swept back up the staircase. She remembered the way to Agnes's chamber, a small room at the south end of the front of the house; almost an antechamber to the empty larger room one had to pass through to reach it. The poor relation had been put well out of the way so that she would know her place. Katheryn felt the presence of cold charity. She knocked on the door and gently pushed it open.

Agnes was huddled in bed, dressed in a plain white shift which sapped the colour from her already pale face. It took her a few seconds to recognise Katheryn - dressed as she was in a fashionable gown rather then the black habit and white wimple of the Benedictine Order - but then her eyes lit with surprise and delight. Agnes almost leaped from her bed and, to Katheryn's dismay, knelt at her feet and kissed her hand.

"Mother Abbess, I have sinned grievously. I beg you to pray for my soul." Agnes's eyes filled with tears. She continued, sobbing. "I did not think you would come. I have been so wicked. But I cannot repent of my sin. I still long for it. Oh, Mother, what can I do?"

Katheryn bent to help the shaking girl to her feet, then put her arm around her and held her close. She could feel the warm dampness of Agnes's tears penetrating the thick cloth of her bodice. "Do not distress yourself, my daughter. There is no sin that God cannot forgive. Tell me about it. That will help."

Agnes took a deep breath, composing herself. Katheryn noticed that he shift was grubby and stained with crusted brown blood about the middle. Mistress Marjory had washed her hands of her relation, denying her even fresh linen. The room was bare, the bed but a board in the corner with a straw filled mattress, and the rushes were old. There was no polish and sweet herbs here.

Agnes sat on the bed, her hands between her knees, rocking to and fro. There was no fire in the room: the child was cold. Katheryn rummaged in the wooden chest at the foot of the bed and drew out a shabby cloak. She put it around Agnes's shoulders.

After a minute, Agnes looked up at Katheryn and spoke softly. "I have committed the sin of fornication, Mother, and God has punished me."

"I know you lost your child." Katheryn sat down by Agnes and put her hand on the girl's shoulder. "Who was the father, Agnes? Does he know you were with child?"

"I cannot tell you. I promised I would tell no one."

"Surely he should know. Is he here in Liverpool now?"

Agnes sat tight lipped.

"Is he a sailor? Is he from some foreign place?"

Agnes smiled, a secret smile. Katheryn gathered that this guess was way off the mark.

"Does he wish to marry you?"

Agnes looked down at her ringless hands. "He cannot."

"He is married already?"

Agnes hesitated. "In a sense. I can say no more. I cannot go against my word."

"You asked for my help. I can do nothing for you if you do not tell me."

"I should never have written to you. I should never have put you to the trouble of coming here. I'm so sorry. I am beyond all help. You cannot understand."

"I cannot understand if you will not tell me." Katheryn sighed. The conversation was going nowhere. She tried again. "What happened in the chapel, Agnes?"

"It was a judgement on me."

"What was?"

"I saw..."

"What did you see?"

"He was behind the altar. I saw him."

"Who did you see?" Katheryn was losing patience.

"I sensed such evil." Agnes was shaking her head.

"Who was it, Agnes? Who did you see?"

Agnes looked up, her eyes filled with terror. "The devil. I saw the devil."

Katheryn took her leave of Agnes after persuading her to return to bed and rest while she could.

Katheryn desired to see this remarkable chapel for herself: the place where, it was reputed, miracles had occurred and where even Satan himself had made an appearance.

With Jane beside her and Will bringing up the rear, she walked down Chapel Street, her cloak wrapped about her firmly against the chill wind from the river. The handsome church of Our Lady and Saint Nicholas stood like a beacon, greeting the seafarers who put into the port. At the corner of its churchyard next to the sand at the edge of the river, stood a humbler, older building: the ancient chapel of St. Mary del Quay. But before she went in, Katheryn led Jane and Will down to the shore and they stood on the damp red-gold sand taking in their surroundings.

The strand was littered with small boats; even those who didn't make their living by fishing used their free time to catch fish for their tables. Small single-sailed craft sped across the expanse of the Mersey like white winged insects while larger ships bobbed on the river; merchantmen anchored on the wide waters. Further along the strand men were unloading cargoes of linen and leather from ships standing at the end of wooden jetties. The people of this small, busy port made the best use they could of the sea's bounty.

Near the chapel stood Lord Derby's fine fortified house, the Tower; another landmark for sailors, its red stone walls solid against wild coastal storms. Further in the distance stood the castle, squatting malevolently on its red rocky outcrop. Across the river, amidst the green of open fields, Katheryn could make out a small group of stone buildings dominated by what looked like a church tower: was this, she wondered, what remained of the Priory at Birkenhead?

She turned back towards the chapel. "What think you of Liverpool, Jane?" she asked amicably.

"Chilly, my lady."

"I agree. It is ever thus on the coast." Katheryn noticed that Jane was shuffling her feet to and fro on the sand as if testing the ground. "You have never seen a sea shore, Jane?"

Jane shook her head. "All this water...and the boats..."

"It is the Mersey: the same river we have in Cheadle." Jane looked at her disbelievingly.

"The Mersey is but a narrow river, my lady. This is not..."

"All rivers flow to the sea, Jane. And this is where our river joins it. Look out there at the headland. It is the sea."

Jane gaped at one of nature's miracles until her mistress broke the spell. "Before we go to the chapel I will ask for the ferryman who found Agnes. He may be about if he is not on the water."

Katheryn, to Jane's unease, approached some fishermen who pointed down the beach at a tall young man standing by a simple jetty further down past the Tower. At the end of the jetty a modest open craft bobbed on the waves, its single sail furled.

Jane and Will watched as Katheryn strode across the sand, lifting her skirts carefully, and greeted the young man.

"You are Bartholomew, the ferryman?"

"Indeed, madam. Do you wish to cross the river? We have a good breeze today and the tides are with us. The passage should be swift." The young man was strong in body with dark curly hair and an open smile. Katheryn liked him on sight.

She explained her presence and Bartholomew's expression changed to one of concern. "It is good that Sister Agnes has a friend in the town, my lady. I feel that Mistress Moore regards her as a nuisance. I have called several times to ask after Agnes but Mistress Moore wouldn't let me see her. I have suggested that Brother Valentine visits her again. He examined her after she was found in the chapel. He was the infirmarian of our priory at Birkenhead and is skilled in the care of the sick."

"And what did Mistress Moore say to your suggestion?"

"That Agnes was recovering and there was no point spending good money on a physician." This sounded typical of Mistress Marjory Moore.

"I think that your Brother Valentine should see the girl. I will pay for any medicines. Mistress Moore need have no worry for her purse."

"Thank you, my lady. It would put my mind at rest. I have prayed constantly for Sister Agnes's recovery."

"Yes. She is pretty, is she not?" said Katheryn with a mischievous grin. Bartholomew blushed in reply. "I should be grateful, brother, if you would show me the chapel where you found her. I have heard much of it."

"Indeed, my lady, it is a most holy place. To think it has been desecrated by..."

"So you know it was no accident?"

"Brother Valentine told me that Sister Agnes had been hit. Though I can hardly believe it in a holy place."

"When so many are homeless and dispossessed, it is small wonder the desperate turn to wickedness."

Bartholomew nodded. "The King has much to answer for."

"Take care, brother. There are many who would report such talk as treason." Katheryn's concern was genuine. She had no wish to see this likeable young man hanging from a gibbet.

"I guard my tongue well, my lady. I have to when I take the ferry across the river. I do not always know who my passengers are or where their sympathies lie."

They had reached the chapel door. Bartholomew lifted the latch and they stepped into the incense scented gloom.

Katheryn and Bartholomew knelt to pray: Jane and Will, a few paces behind, did likewise. After a while Katheryn got up and wandered round the small chapel. The prayers of generations of importuning pilgrims had permeated the stones and the chapel's simplicity enhanced its holiness. A statue of Our Lady, delicately carved from ancient and battered oak, stood to one side of the plain stone altar, surrounded by dancing candle flames. Katheryn approached the altar in the flickering light of the tallow tapers.   What had Agnes said? That the devil had risen from the altar? There was a space behind the slab large enough for a man to squeeze into. She examined the ground. The space was well swept in common with the rest of the chapel floor. There were bunches of fresh michaelmass daisies placed before the statue and the altar. This place was lovingly cared for. There was no sign of anything out of the ordinary. No sign of Agnes's devil.

The silence was broken by the nearby jangle of church bells. Bartholomew stood up. "It is time for mass, my lady...at the church of Our Lady and St. Nicholas. I hear mass whenever my duties permit."

"Then we shall accompany you, brother."

Shutting the chapel door behind them, the group strode across the churchyard accompanied by the sound of bells and the cry of seagulls overhead. The church of Our Lady and St. Nicholas was a well sized, airy building, lit by a kaleidoscope of stained glass. Katheryn counted three chantry chapels as well as the high altar. The church had been well endowed by the donations of the wealthy.

Out of one of the chapels in the south aisle, walked a line of boys with their pale-faced schoolmaster. Townspeople filed in through the great west door, summoned by the bells to mass.

When the service was over Katheryn, refreshed by an hour's prayer, blinked as she emerged from the church into the watery sunlight.

"I must attend to my ferry, my lady." Bartholomew looked over to the jetty. "It seems I have passengers waiting."

"Would you direct me to the house of Brother Valentine? I should like to speak with him."

Bartholomew nodded. "You will find him in Dale Street, just past the Guildhall. Anyone will direct you. And may God's blessing go with you."

Katheryn touched Bartholomew's shoulder. "I will do my best for Agnes, brother, be assured of that."

With a weak smile, Bartholomew turned and walked down the crowded strand towards his craft and the waiting passengers. Katheryn, Jane and Will made their way back past the church towards the High Cross and Dale Street.

The beggar with one hand took up his position by the White Cross at the end of Juggler Street. It was a good spot; there were many passing to and from the townfield to tend their plots. He had to take care to be inconspicuous if he wasn't to be ejected from the town or shut up in the jail. Every so often the Mayor and Aldermen engaged on a campaign against vagrancy, but in between times an individual beggar could live comparatively undisturbed, providing there were not too many of his number making nuisances of themselves to the good burgesses of the town.

The wind was cold. He drew his stained cloak about him; a warm cloak: so good of Father John to give it to him. There had been some good - much good - among the monks of Norton Abbey, now themselves dispossessed and scattered across the countryside.

He sat shivering at the foot of the White Cross. Most passers by ignored him; the more charitable minority tossed him a small coin. A small group of foreign sailors jeered at him in some incomprehensible tongue as they passed: it was too early yet for drink to increase their generosity. Hunger gnawed at the beggar's stomach. But at least he would soon have enough money to buy a bowl of stew at the Mayor's House - not the dwelling of the town's chief citizen but an inn near the Guildhall famed for its cheap and filling victuals. And maybe there would be enough left for a loaf of stale bread from the baker's. And tomorrow was market day. There were many who would take pity on a poor man on market day....and many who would, after too much ale, be ready to give a beggar a sound beating. On the streets you had to take care.

A figure approached. A man, tall and well built, wearing a good brown woollen cloak, new by the looks of it: its wearer had money. The beggar held out his left hand.

"Alms, sir, I beg you. Of your charity give alms to a poor man who has lost all he had. God will bless you, sir. Alms, I pray you."

But as the man drew nearer, the beggar saw his face and fell silent. His heart pounding, his hunger forgotten, he gathered his cloak about him and ran down Chapel Street towards the church, all the time keeping his hand firmly on the dagger that hung from his belt. He only stopped to catch his breath when he reached the safety of the strand.

It was impossible...he must have been mistaken. Surely a dead man could not walk the streets of Liverpool?

CHAPTER 4

Valentine's shop smelled of herbs. Katheryn paused for a moment by the door, breathing in the delicious aroma. Inside, a red haired boy of about thirteen was sweeping an already clean stone flagged floor. Katheryn bade him good day and he looked up, smiling welcome, at the gracious lady with the kind face who was asking for his master.

Ralph, the apprentice, hurried into the back of the shop with the news that Lady Katheryn Bulkeley of Cheadle wished to speak with Master Valentine.

Valentine emerged from his fragrant domain, wiping his hands on a clean white apron. "Forgive me, my lady, I was mixing some medicines. Agnes Moore mentioned you. You were her Abbess at Oxford were you not?"

"I had that honour, sir...until recent events overtook us."

Katheryn and Valentine's eyes met in understanding.

"How is Agnes? I have not been called by Mistress Moore so I assume she is recovering."

"In body, perhaps, but not in spirit. She is still in great distress."

Valentine nodded. "I knew it. I was concerned for her state of mind. She spoke of strange things."

"The devil?"

He nodded. "Do you stay with Mistress Moore, my lady?"

"For now. I feel that my rank causes Mistress Moore to offer me the hospitality of her house but I think I shall soon outstay my welcome. She has no patience with Agnes or her fancies."

Valentine smiled. This woman was perceptive and had read Marjory Moore correctly. "Then we must do our best to help Agnes, my lady. Does she still keep to her room?"

"Yes. And looks quite uncared for."

"I wonder that Mistress Moore does not have the girl working about the house again. Poor relations are cheaper than servants."

"Doubtless she would if she could. I should be grateful if you would come with me and see Agnes. I should like your opinion." She studied Valentine and liked what she saw. A kindly man, quite handsome, with a refreshing air of good sense. It was good to share the worry of Agnes's care with another.

"I have some medicines to make up urgently and I have a funeral to attend, but I will call the Old Hall as soon as I can."

"I shall tell Mistress Marjory of your visit." She grinned. "I trust it will not make me too unpopular."

Valentine took Katheryn's hand, the ring she wore as Abbess still in place, and kissed it. "Sister Agnes is indeed fortunate to have a friend such as you, my lady."

Their eyes met once more in understanding. Katheryn dismissed the quickened beating of her heart as due to the brisk walk round the windswept streets of Liverpool. She joined Jane and Will who were waiting for her in the street, deep in conversation, their hands touching. There must be something in the air, she teased herself. Master Valentine was a good man - and attractive. Nothing more.

There was an appointment Valentine had to keep: he had promised Father James. There would not be many mourners at Father Clement's funeral. He had not served the church long enough to be a well known figure in the parish and those that had known him had regarded him with indifference rather than love. Valentine, with his tentative interest in the man's death, would be there to make up the numbers.

The wind bit hard as they stood by the fresh dug grave in the churchyard. Father James recited the prayers for the dead quickly. Like everyone else he did not relish standing in the windswept graveyard any longer than he had to. The pale schoolmaster, Master Culver, was there, having sent his pupils home as a mark of respect for the dead priest, much to their delight. A couple of soldiers from the garrison at the castle slouched in the background, their presence incongruous and unexplained.

The church's other chantry priest, Father Nicholas, had not much liked his colleague and found it hard to muster any grief. He fidgeted at the graveside, anxious to be out of the cold and into the bed of his new and unofficial wife: they had married before the King had passed the new Act of Six Articles, forbidding the marriage of priests by law. But he would not abandon his Mary: Liverpool was not London and much here went unnoticed provided the King's security wasn't threatened.

The small assembly broke up as soon as the sexton began shovelling earth into the grave. Father James turned to Valentine. "You will take a cup of wine with me, brother to keep out the cold?"

Valentine accepted the invitation, sensing that James wanted company. He followed James to the small thatched stone house next to the church, walking in silence as they considered the briefness of earthly existence.

They were so deep in thought that they did not notice the cloaked figure of the beggar with one hand watching in the shadow of the church wall.

Mistress Moore's lips tightened as Katheryn told her of the apothecary's impending visit. "I shall, of course meet any expenses," she stated with ingratiating charm. "It is to put my mind at ease, Mistress. I feel a responsibility for my sister, you understand."

Will returned to his duties in the stables as Katheryn and Jane helped Agnes to wash and put on a clean shift. There was nothing so demoralising as filth, Katheryn thought. With Griselda's help Jane even found fresh linen for the bed. Agnes, at least, now looked presentable. But the girl was lethargic and lolled against her bolster as if she no longer had the spirit to help herself.

When Valentine arrived he found Katheryn reading to Agnes from the lives of the saints. Katheryn had hoped it might prove inspiring - or at least relieve the tedium of Agnes's existence - but the girl hardly seemed to be listening. She said nothing as Valentine examined her.

"She is well enough in body," he said confidentially to Katheryn outside the chamber door. "But, as you say, she has sunk into melancholy. I will give her valerian to calm her and help her rest. But I think we should try and discover the true cause of her condition."

"Find the child's father?"

"That would help. I will leave it to you, my lady. You are best placed to gain her confidence."

Katheryn sighed. "Do you think I have not tried?"

"If we can find the young man and tell him what has happened, perhaps bring him to her."

"I feel it may not be that straightforward. I fear that this was not merely a case of young love but something more."

"More what?"

"I don't know. Could she have been violated?"

Valentine looked at her sharply. "There was never any suggestion. I found no signs of violence but after that time... I admit I had not considered the possibility. But she spoke of a lover. And she claimed that she had sinned."

Katheryn shrugged. "It was but a thought. I will try to question her further when she is more receptive. She was never a secretive girl at Godstow. I am sure I can discover the truth but it will take time and patience." She smiled. "I will endeavour to keep Mistress Marjory from interfering."

"A wise course of action, my lady." He handed her the medicine. "I will return when you call for me."

"I am most grateful, Master Valentine." He raised her hand to his lips again. She lowered her eyes modestly, feeling a tiny thrill of forbidden excitement.

She watched him go down the staircase then returned to Agnes's bedside. She found the girl staring into space. She was certainly worse today; more preoccupied.

"Agnes," Katheryn began. "Master Valentine says that you are well again in body. Will you not tell me what distresses you?"

Agnes looked at her and shook her head.

"I promise I shall say nothing to Mistress Marjory. It shall be our secret." Agnes's eyes filled with tears. Katheryn was getting through at last. "You wrote and asked for my help. I cannot give it if you do not tell me what troubles you."

Tears began to flow down Agnes's pale cheeks. "I am beyond help, Mother."

"Nobody is beyond help, even the worst of sinners." She put a comforting arm around Agnes's shoulders. "Tell me. Please. I will try to help."

"He would be angry. I promised."

"Who would be angry? Please, Agnes..."

"I cannot say..."

"Is it the man you lay with? Your lover?"

Agnes nodded.

"Why would he be angry?"

"I should not tell."

"That you lay together?"

She nodded again.

"Is he married already?"

She shook her head.

"A priest? One who has taken a vow of chastity?"

Agnes looked up, her eyes wide with alarm. Katheryn's question had hit its mark. "Can you tell me his name?"

"I cannot. He would be angry."

Katheryn sighed and smoothed her skirts. "You do know, Agnes, that many priests have married. And as St. Paul says, it is better to marry than to burn. Our Lord understands that in changing circumstances our vows of chastity..."

"Oh Mother, it is not so simple."

"He no longer wants you?" she said gently. "He used you to satisfy his lust with no intention of marriage?" She knew the question was blunt but she felt she was getting near the truth.

"He said he loved me but he walks past the house. I see him sometimes when I look from the window. He has abandoned me."

Agnes began to weep. Katheryn held her, stroking her hair. "Tell me his name, Agnes. I will speak with him."

"I promised I would never tell," she sobbed. "Please. I am tired. I want to rest."

"Take Master Valentine's medicine, my child. It will calm you."

"Leave it there, Mother. I will take it later."

Katheryn felt that until she knew the man's identity there was nothing more that she could do. She left the room quietly. Agnes should get some sleep.

As soon as the door shut, Agnes rose from her bed and went to the chest where her clothes were kept.

It was almost dark when the bald headed priest knocked at Father James's door. Father James, expecting no one, opened his door with caution. One never knew.

The bald priest, clad in a shabby black gown, introduced himself as Father Theobald, late of Norton Abbey. James, satisfied that the man's inclinations were spiritual rather than villainous, opened the door wide and admitted him to his sparse lodgings.

He poured his guest some ale. Father Theobald looked in need of refreshment. His cloak was travel stained and he seemed tired.

"I have travelled from Chester, Father," Theobald began. "I was...I was held at His Majesty's pleasure in the castle there, along with two of my brothers and our Father Abbot."

James nodded. He knew that Norton Abbey had not surrendered to the King's commissioners peacefully and that some of the brothers were still paying for their disobedience. "You are fortunate to have your liberty, Father Theobald. There are many who have paid for dissent with their lives."

Theobald smiled. He was a chubby man: his imprisonment in Chester had clearly not been too harsh. "The High Sheriff, Sir Piers Dutton, had no taste for bloodshed and he was most skilled at ignoring the King's orders when it suited his purposes. He took a liking to our Father Abbot and we were treated well. Now the events at Norton are all but forgotten, we have been released. One of my brothers is intending to seek passage to Ireland. That is why I am here. I thought to join him."

"Many ships go to Ireland, Father. When would he have arrived here?"

"We were released two weeks since. I do not know if he intended to come straight to Liverpool or if he had other business to attend to before he left. He did not say. But I wanted to ask you, Father James, if you had met him or had word of him. His name is Father Edmund. He is a dark haired, well built, handsome fellow and of good nature."

"I will certainly keep watch for him and tell him of your destination if I meet him. It may be that he is in Ireland already. Will you take a meal with me, Father Theobald? There is an inn on Juggler Street that is clean and respectable. You look in need of refreshment."

"I thank you, Father, but I sail on the next tide. An Irish captain gladly allowed me passage on his ship in return for my prayers and the celebration of mass for his crew." Theobald stood to leave.

It was then James remembered that the sad events of that day would be of interest to his visitor. "I have some unhappy news concerning one of your brothers," he said solemnly. "Father Clement of Norton was a chantry priest in my church. He was buried today...murdered by footpads, I fear. A sad loss." He spoke with a conventional piety he did not feel.

Father Theobald looked genuinely upset. "I am sorry to hear it, Father James. We live in violent times." He made the sign of the cross. "I shall pray for Father Clement's soul. He was a good man: a true man of God."

When Father Theobald had taken his leave, James knelt and prayed afresh for the soul of Father Clement. From what Theobald had said, Clement had changed since his days at Norton or maybe James had misjudged the man.

Then he wondered whether he ought to have mentioned the other matter to Father Theobald. He would certainly have been in sympathy with their cause: his imprisonment would have assured that. But the man had been in a hurry. And it was better to keep such things secret. Who knew where the King's spies watched.

Agnes was still weak. Her legs shook a little, but she knew she had to find the strength from somewhere. She had seen him. He must be nearby.

It was pitch dark and the household had retired to bed. The only sounds were the gentle lap of waves outside, the distant drunken carousing of sailors in the town and the shriek of an owl as it flew through the velvet sky. She knew that she would have to take care going out after curfew but she had to see him. She had to tell him of her suffering.

She dressed in her plain grey gown. Her only other gown, the russet one, had been taken from her for the blood to be washed off and hadn't yet been returned. The grey would have to do. The shabby hooded cloak she drew about her had served her well in her days as a novice and on her journey from Godstow. Now it was torn and frayed, but it was all she had.

There was a window near the kitchen that opened easily. If she was careful and didn't quite shut it, she could get back in that way too when the time came.

The stairs creaked as she crept down. She stopped, listening for the sounds of disturbed sleepers. But all was silence. The window by the kitchen opened as easily as she remembered and Agnes, feeling a little stronger with the excitement of her mission, climbed out carefully.

She flitted through the streets, sinking into the shadows to avoid the groups of drunken men outside the ale houses and the sharp-faced rogues who slid through the stinking thoroughfares. Beggars and vagrants, risking arrest or an unofficial drunken beating, begged alms from the night time revellers before shrinking back into the doorways and alleys to huddle in sleep. Hard faced whores, their hair dyed red and their faces painted, flirted in the narrow streets with potential customers. A leering man, stinking and staggering with drink, grabbed Agnes's waist as she passed him but it was easy to shake him off. She muttered a quick prayer for safety...although she had lost the will to pray, being so deeply sunk in wickedness.

Running past the High Cross, she saw her final goal. The castle rose forbiddingly before her. The place looked cold; merciless; a thing of repression. But she had no choice in the matter.

Her lover had mentioned Captain Wharton many times. He had done the captain many services of a nature she did not care to think about.

She stood staring at the great stone walls while she considered what to do next. A postern gate: he had spoken of a postern gate.

"Who goes there? Show yourself," a deep rough voice barked, shattering the darkness.

Agnes, heart pounding, stepped forward.

The beggar with one hand who had followed her from the Old Hall, sank back into the shadows of Castle Street and watched silently.

CHAPTER 5

Agnes stepped forward and the soldier stared at her appraisingly. She looked down, uncomfortable, sensing the lust in his eyes.

"What do you want?"

She didn't answer.

"I've not seen you before." He approached her slowly and reached out his hand. He held her chin while he studied her face. She could smell the ale on his breath. "You're not one of the usual girls. New to the town are you? Come here for a bit of trade amongst the garrison?" His hand slid down to her breast. Agnes flinched and stepped back. "Oh, we have a coy one here." The soldier leered, putting his arm round her waist and drawing her to him.

Agnes tried to pull away but he held her fast. "I am no lady of the night," she said with as much spirit as she could muster. "I seek Captain Wharton. Would you tell him I wish to speak with him on a private matter?"

"And what do I get in return, eh?" He drew her closer. She could feel him hard against her as he pushed her against the castle wall.

He pressed against her as he began to lift her skirts. She tried to push him off but he has a big man with ale-fuelled determination.

"When I tell Captain Wharton, he will be most displeased at the treatment I have suffered."

But the man's lust had deafened him. As Agnes felt his hand on her thigh, she managed to utter a scream. The sound made the man stop and he looked at her with fury. This wasn't what he had expected.

He struck Agnes across the face with a stinging slap. "Shut up, whore. Just lift your skirt and let me have my way. I'll pay you well." He threw three coins to the ground. "You can get them after."

He lunged at Agnes again. She threw herself to one side but he caught her arm and drew her to him again. He was enjoying the challenge. He pushed her against the wall again. Agnes closed her eyes. She hadn't sufficient strength to continue the fight.

A kick to the backside made the man release Agnes as he swung round.

"So you have a whore when you're meant to be guarding us, eh?"

The speaker was considerably smaller than the guard but he spoke with authority. The soldier slouched to attention as Agnes, uncertain what to do, hung back, eyes downcast.

"Go to the guardroom, man, and send Tilletson out. I'll attend to you later you bastard son of a bitch."

The guard hesitated.

"Go," the newcomer barked before turning to Agnes. "And you'd better make yourself scarce, my dear. The men can have whores all they like but not while they're on duty. Off you go, girl."

Agnes raised her eyes to his. He was young, small, dark and wiry. His face was even featured, even womanish, and by the richness of his dress Agnes judged he was a gentleman. She experienced new hope.

"I beg your pardon, sir, but I wish to speak with Captain Wharton."

"Do you now? And what is it you wish to speak of?"

"It is a private matter. I will tell only the Captain."

"Owes you money does he?"

"I am no whore, sir. I am Agnes Moore, cousin of Mistress Moore of Old Hall."

He looked her up and down. The girl was young and pretty with swelling breasts but, by her dress, she was lying. This was no kinswoman of the wealthy Moores...more likely a serving girl. "Sure you are." He smiled sardonically. "And you've met Captain Wharton? You know him?"

She hesitated. "No...er...I have never met the Captain."

"You have not? Then what is it you would tell me?"

Agnes sighed with relief. "Oh, Captain, I have risked much to see you. It is about a mutual acquaintance of ours...a certain priest."

She looked into his eyes. They still held a look of mild amusement. "I know who you mean. What about him?"

"I have seen him passing my window but he does not contact me. If you know his whereabouts, sir...or if you would give a message..."

He sighed. So this is what it was about. A lovesick girl rejected by her illicit lover. He suppressed a smile, sensing there was sport to be had. "Your name is Agnes, you say?" She nodded. "He spoke of you only yesterday. He said that if I saw you, I was to bring you to him."

Agnes's face lit with joy. "Oh, sir, I thank you. You could not have brought me better tidings." She looked round. "But are you able to leave your garrison, sir?"

"I am in charge, Agnes. There is nobody to challenge me." He took her hand and led her towards the overshadowing bulk of the castle gatehouse where a new guard now lurked self-consciously, watching them. They passed without challenge, the guard standing to attention.

They met no one else as Agnes's guide led her through grey castle passageways lit by flaming torches, and out of a small wooden wicket gate into the moonlight again. He helped her down a set of steep steps, warning her to take care.

"Where are we, sir? Where are we going?"

"Do not fear, Agnes. It is but a tunnel cut in the rock. Have a care where you step."

The tunnel through the red sandstone castle base was dank and chilly and the fetid air made Agnes shudder. She was glad when she saw the shimmer of moonlight at the far end as they approached the strand. The Captain explained that the tunnel was there in case of siege. She was glad of his confident presence in that place which reminded her of tales of purgatory and the nether cold reaches of hell. It was with relief that she walked out onto the shore. The tide was advancing and a flotilla of little boats bobbed nearby.

"He waits in the boathouse. It is not far. I will take you there." He took her arm, linking it in his as they walked along the sand beneath the castle rock. She could smell his clothing, leather and sweet herbs. The firmness of his grasp on her arm gave her no comfort but she made no effort to withdraw it. She must go with him: she had no choice.

The night air was cold and she shivered. She wanted to get this over with; to be rid of her companion. He looked into her face appraisingly, a slight smile on his lips, then he leaned towards her and whispered in her ear. She could feel the heat of his breath on the side of her face. "Do not be afraid. Just think of the pleasure that awaits you."

There was something about the officer's words and the way he said them, thick with innuendo, that made Agnes feel uneasy.

Captain Wharton had just won at a game of dice with one of his sergeants when the guard came into the chamber rubbing his backside.

The captain stood up, menacing. He did not tolerate neglect of duty. "Manners, you stinking son of a whore, why aren't you at your post? I could have you whipped."

"But Captain, Sir Edward told me to return to the guardroom and ..."

"Sir Edward!" Wharton roared angrily. "Does that little snake think he can give orders here just because his father is constable of the castle. Does he seek to undermine my authority?" He flung the dice he held across the room in fury. "I shall speak to My Lord Molyneux and tell him how his younger son abuses his position. Did he give any reason for this...order?"

The guard, seeing he was on a winning streak, was not going to tell of his encounter with Agnes. While Sir Edward was getting the blame, he would make the most of it. "No, sir, no reason. But there was a woman. Sir Edward was with a woman."

Wharton's bulging eyes rolled to heaven. "Typical. He gives orders to my guards to impress some doxy with his importance. Is anyone guarding the gate or shall we be overrun with Spaniards and Frenchmen at any minute?"

"Tilletson replaced me, sir."

"Very well. Back to your post. Tell Tilletson to go to the postern gate. I expect a visitor who might come that way."

Manners bowed slightly to the Captain and got out while the going was good. A pity about the doxy, but there were plenty more like her in the taverns and molly houses. Pleasure could always be had if you knew where to look.

Sir Edward strode towards the boathouse, watching Agnes as a snake watches a rabbit. The river air was cold and he wondered if he dare put his arm around her shoulder to keep her warm...make her more amenable.

Agnes walked in silence, hardly noticing her surroundings and the moonlight on the rippling water. Her heart beat fast. He would be there waiting for her. She would see him; talk to him; tell him all she had suffered for him. She pulled her cloak closer about her. There was something in the way Captain Wharton looked at her that made her feel uncomfortable. Perhaps it was the way he walked as closely to her as possible and stared at her body, her breasts, rather than looking at her face.

Agnes tripped on a rock protruding from the sand and clung to her companion's hand to steady herself. He caught her in his arms and held her much longer than she considered necessary, his hand sliding down across her breast.

"There is the boathouse over there. The brothers of Birkenhead Priory used it," he said conversationally, though she sensed his mind was on lower things.

She could make out the shape of a small wooden building against the sky. That part of the strand was deserted but further down towards the Tower, in the distance, Agnes saw points of light from flaming torches as fishermen landed their catch and sailors returned to their ships after a night in the tavern. It was a faraway world, oblivious to Agnes Moore.

"He is hiding in the boathouse," said her companion, clutching her arm more tightly. "Come."

Holding his hand, she followed. The boathouse was in darkness with no sign of life. Edward pushed the door and it opened slowly. Agnes could see nothing in the darkness but she could smell the damp and the salty tang of seaweed.

"Where is he?"

Edward went in first then drew Agnes inside, shutting the door firmly behind them.

"I lied. He isn't here."

Agnes took a deep breath in panic. "Where is he? Take me to him. Please. You promised."

"I made no promise that I would take you straight there. I have been your guide and now I claim my fee."

She tried to push him away as he held her to him and kissed her, his hands fumbling inside her cloak. Before she knew it she was lying on the hard damp boards of the boathouse floor and he was on top of her, lifting her skirts. Agnes, unprepared and numb with fear, lay still. If this was the price to be paid, then so be it. Her soul was damned already. She had no will to fight as he went into her, and after what seemed like an eternity he sighed with satisfaction. It was over. Agnes lay still and breathless as he rolled off her.

"Now take me to him," she whispered.

His laugh was gently mocking. "I don't know who you're talking about?"

"What do you mean?" Her voice rose in panic. "Where is he? Tell me."

"Whoever you seek, my dear Agnes, I do not know him...or where he is."

"But you said... Did you just bring me here for...?"

"I can't think of a better reason on a moonlit night." He put his arm across her. "We can relive our pleasure if you like."

She pushed his arm away. "He said he knew you. He spoke of you."

"He spoke of Edward Molyneux, did he?" He laughed. "All men speak of me. Some good...some bad."

"But you are Captain Wharton."

"I never said I was. You assumed it." He fondled her breast. "You should never assume, my dear Agnes."

She turned away from him, her last hope gone. His hand moved to her hair but she brushed it away. He was repugnant to her: the very sight of him reminded her of her foolishness, her gullibility. She put her head in her hands. "I did not want... I should never have done..."

"You only did what any doxy does when she is alone with a man aroused by her sweet looks. I've taken a great liking to you, Agnes. Come, I will take you back to the castle. Another walk in the night air might refresh our appetites and you will find my quarters most comfortable...better than the bare boards of a boathouse."

He put his hand round her breast and would have kissed her neck but she pushed him away with a violence that surprised her and stumbled blindly out of the blackness of the dank boathouse. She did not know if he was following and she did not care. She felt sick with disgust at herself: how she had let herself be used.

She ran across the sand, making for the glistening edge of the River Mersey, then she waded out into the waves and flung herself on the cleansing water.

Agnes Moore needed to wash: she needed to be clean again.

CHAPTER 6

Katheryn awoke and heard the sounds of activity outside her window. She realised she had slept late and she saw that there was a bowl of hot water standing on the oak chest: Jane had been in and had not liked to wake her.

She threw back the covers and rose from her bed. Then she crossed to the window and looked out on Mill Street below. A stream of people passed in the grey morning river mist, driving carts, carrying sacks or leading animals. It was market day: Mistress Marjory had mentioned it the previous evening. And there was always entertainment to be had on market day. She would take Agnes: the market would take the girl's mind off her problems.

After a hasty visit to the guardrobe, she summoned Jane to help her wash and dress.

Jane was excited. "The whole household is going to market today, my lady. May I go too?"

"Of course. And you and Will must allow me to come with you. We will take young Agnes: it may cheer her a little and distract her mind from her troubles. Have you seen her this morning?"

"No, my lady. But she usually keeps to her chamber."

"Then go there and tell her of our plans. And tell her I shall tolerate no refusal. We will raise the child's spirits whether she wants it or no." She paused, looking at Jane. "What say you we take her home to Cheadle with us when she is stronger? She has had naught but bad fortune here. If she could forget her errors and begin anew..."

Jane nodded and agreed it was an excellent idea. It seemed as though Agnes's fortunes were about to improve. She hurried to Agnes's chamber, hoping she would find her receptive to Katheryn's plans for the day and not sunk in melancholy: Jane was not adept at dealing with such humours.

She knocked gently on Agnes's chamber door but there was no answer. Agnes must be sleeping. It was unlikely she would be up and about. Jane lifted the latch very carefully and when she opened the door, her eyes were drawn to the small truckle bed in the corner. The sheets were tossed aside as if someone had risen in a hurry. The room was empty.

Hurrying across the landing, Jane nearly collided with Mistress Marjory who shot her a killing look. Jane bobbed her deepest curtsey, fit for the King himself, in reparation. "Begging your pardon, ma'am, but do you know where Agnes is? She is not in her chamber."

Marjory looked more irritated than worried. "I have not seen her. You must ask the servants." Marjory swept past, nose in the air, putting Jane firmly in her place.

But none of the servants had seen Agnes. Reluctantly, Jane reported back to her mistress . Agnes was missing.

The house and outhouses had been searched. Agnes was nowhere to be found. Mistress Marjory cursed the girl: she had been nothing but trouble from the moment she arrived. And she had expected her former Abbess to talk some sense into her but, if anything, Agnes had become more stubborn since Lady Katheryn's arrival. So much for the effects of a youth spent in a nunnery.

And Lady Katheryn herself was not what she had expected. She had thought to find an Abbess cold, regal and formidable; instead she was attractive, smiling and good natured...and possessed of a worldliness that belied her spiritual authority. The woman even dressed in the latest fashions. Maybe it was true that religious houses were dens of secular iniquity after all.

Now the servants were being kept from their duties while they searched for Agnes - under orders from Lady Katheryn of course. It was too much: who was to attend to the running of the house? Besides, the pest of a girl would doubtless return when it suited her.

Marjory stood, arms akimbo, in the courtyard seething inwardly at the loss of control over her domain. It was three hours now since Agnes's absence had been discovered and most of the servants were about the town making enquiries. The weekly market would make their task more difficult: Liverpool would be teeming with strangers converging on the town from the surrounding countryside. Marjory resisted the strong temptation to aim a kick at a passing hen who strolled, clucking complacently, across the cobbles. It was the last time she would show charity to a poor relation if all she got in return was trouble and worry.

At last! One of her idle servants was returning to his post. John, the gardener, rushed into the courtyard, breathless and stood before his mistress panting, hardly able to get the words out.

"Mistress....I have news." He paused for breath again. He was a big man, past his first youth, and unused to running about the streets. "I asked at the Mermaid if anyone had news of Mistress Agnes. One of the, er...ladies there..."

"You mean the whores?"

The gardener flushed. "Indeed ma'am."

"Yes..yes, man. Get on with it."

"She said she saw a girl in a cloak like Mistress Agnes's...you know, the black one she had as a nun. She saw her hurrying by late last night, going toward the castle, she reckoned. The, er...young lady was with a, er...friend on their way back to the Mermaid." He cast his eyes downwards and shuffled his great feet on the well swept cobbles, unsure what to do next."

"Thank you, John. Return to your duties now and I will inform Lady Katheryn of what you have said."

John lumbered away, glad to return to his vegetables, while Marjory went in search of Griselda. She would send her maid to find Lady Katheryn. There was no hurry. Let that silly creature, Agnes, stew for a while.

The Mermaid bubbled with chatter and activity...lively even for market day. Mine Host sailed from table to table carrying brimming tankards of ale while his buxom wife and chubby daughters hurried to and fro with dishes of steaming meat pies and thick spicy stew. The Mermaid was well known for its victuals...and for other delights.

It was market day. The place was packed with farmers and their families, come to sell their produce, and tradesmen and women, hungry and thirsty after a morning on the bustling stalls. The inn was clean and the food and ale appetising, the best in Juggler Street...the best in Liverpool. Master Turner, the landlord, considered he had much to be proud of: and as for the other side of the business, he was providing a service for the good citizens of the Borough...as did many others. And in difficult times, every little bit helps.

The sight of Father James, the parish priest, conversing with another man at a corner table below the leaded window, was not unusual. The Mermaid catered for everyone, from Mayor to the humblest freeman. Even King Henry himself would be welcome in the Mermaid...by some at any rate.

Father James looked round, checking there was nobody listening, then leaned forward to hear what his companion had to say. The two men spoke softly, not wishing to be overheard.

But Captain Wharton, his cloak covering his leather jerkin and his hood pulled down over his face, sat very still at a table behind the men, careful not to alert them to his presence, and strained to hear over the hubbub of conversation. He knew who the priest's companion was: Francis Wells, the former cellarer of Birkenhead Priory, who was now landlord of an inn near the site of his deserted monastery.

Wharton listened, hardly drawing breath, but he could only make out the odd word or phrase. "In the north....support for our cause....the Virgin's table." He could hear nothing that made any sense.

Wharton drained his tankard. The inn was packed with people who chattered like magpies. There was nothing more to be discovered. The one who sent him would have to wait for his information.

He stood up and left, passing Katheryn on his way out. Katheryn, who was thirsty but too preoccupied to be hungry, sent Will to fetch ale and sat in Wharton's vacant seat, Jane settling down beside her.

"Shouldn't we ask, my lady...for the girl? What was her name?"

"Melisanda." Jane raised her eyebrows. "I doubt that's her real name, Jane. When one is in that occupation one is expected to take a few liberties with the truth. I will enquire of Mine Host, if I can find him."

But, having spotted a lady of quality in his establishment, Master Turner found her. He approached the table, wringing his hands obsequiously.

"Madam, if I may be of service..."

Katheryn smiled sweetly. "You may, landlord. I would speak with a Mistress Melisanda. I have been told I may find her here."

Master Turner looked wary. "What is your business with her, madam?" He feared some domestic entanglement. Was this lady a wronged wife seeking the one with whom her errant husband sought outside entertainment? He did not think so. There was no anger in her eyes.

"I would speak with her concerning a missing kinswoman of Mistress Moore's"

Turner relaxed a little. He didn't want trouble but he could see no harm in giving this lady her will. "I will fetch her for you, madam." He backed away, almost bowing. Katheryn inclined her head graciously.

It was then she noticed the two men at the next table. The priest she recognised even though he had his back to her. He had said Mass at Our Lady and St. Nicholas and Bartholomew had named him as Father James.

The other men she had not seen before: he was grizzle-haired and rotund - a man who liked his food by the look of him. She watched the incongruous pair out of the corner of her eye and noted how they spoke in whispers, huddled together as though in conspiracy. She was careful not to let them see her watching them: conspiracy meant danger. But she couldn't help being curious about their dealings.

Turner appeared again, followed by a girl who couldn't have been more than seventeen years old. Her face was round and pretty and her hair the colour of ripe corn. The low cut of her bodice, revealing a good proportion of her ample breasts, gave a hint of how she made her living. The landlord scurried away leaving Melisanda standing, hands on hips, staring with cautious insolence.

"Master Turner said you would talk with me. If it's about that girl that's missing, I told that gardener of the Moores all I know."

"Would you be kind enough to tell your story to me?" Katheryn smiled charmingly. "Agnes, the girl we seek, was once in my care and I am most concerned about her safety."

The young whore nodded in understanding. "And so you should be, ma'am."

Katheryn sat forward. It was clear that Melisanda knew more than she had revealed to John the gardener. "What do you mean? Please sit down and take a drink with us." She nodded to Will who stopped staring at Melisanda's breasts, gave up his stool and went to fetch more ale. Melisanda sat down and began to relax.

"Be assured that I fear only for Agnes's welfare. She is missing...gone without a word to anyone. If you know anything...anything at all that may help to find her..."

"She was talking with a soldier."

"A soldier?"

"I was speaking with a...friend in a doorway of a fishmongers in Castle Street. We were, er...talking business."

Katheryn noticed Jane staring, open mouthed, and gave her a gentle nudge under the table. Jane had never encountered such things before - Cheadle was a quiet place - but Katheryn didn't want to lose Melisanda's co-operation if she were to take offence. "Please go on," Katheryn encouraged, sweetly.

"I was bringing him back here when I saw a girl passing, going towards the castle. She did not look like... I did not know her for one of my calling," she said with studied delicacy. "I watched her over my shoulder, wondering what she was up to. Those such as me do not like our trade stolen by newcomers. We have to live."

"Of course. What happened then? What did she do?"

"She walked on towards the castle. As if she know where she was going; she didn't stop nor hesitate." Katheryn nodded, willing her to continue. "I did not think she was looking for business so I brought my gentleman back here. A girl has a living to earn," she concluded defensively.

"So you didn't see where she went?"

"Oh yes. My, er...friend...we had a disagreement about the price. He's a juggler and he said he couldn't afford to pay what I asked until market day on the morrow: he is paid well for his skills on market day. We stopped and I showed him how much I was worth."

"Oh yes?"

"Some men need to be...you know...aroused to desire. Once I have them in that condition, I can name my price."

Katheryn raised her eyebrows. The girl was remarkably businesslike about such matters: a born expert on the laws of supply and demand.

"I saw the girl in the distance. It was a full moon and the light was good. She was at the castle gate, talking with one of the guards."

"Was she indeed? Did you see anything more? Did she enter the castle? Return the way she had come?"

"I do not know for by then my friend was in a hurry, if you understand my meaning."

Jane covered her mouth with her hand and blushed, avoiding the eyes of Will who had just returned with the ale and was hovering behind Katheryn.

"But all I know," Melisanda continued, "is that the one who followed her did not turn and come back the way we were going."

Katheryn sat forward. "The one who followed her? Who? Who was following her?"

"He wore a long cloak and his face and form were hidden."

"But it was a man?"

"Well, I think it was a man but I do not know for sure. I caught but a glimpse."

"But you are sure he followed her?"

"Oh yes. He stopped every so often to watch her from the shadows. I thought him a father or husband. I did not think much about it." She shrugged. "Such things happen."

"And you can say no more about him?"

"It was dark." She picked up her tankard and drank thirstily as though unaccustomed talk had parched her throat. "And I had other matters to think of. But he followed her all right."

Melisanda rose and, giving Will a sensuous wink that made his cheeks redden, left the table, her tankard drained. She disappeared into the crowd of market-day drinkers, her ample hips swaying provocatively, a saucy smile on her face showed that she knew that the eyes of the men she passed on her travels were watching her appreciatively. Melisanda, at least while the bloom of her youth lasted, would never be short of customers.

"So what do we do now, my lady?" Jane asked anxiously, watching Will's eyes follow Melisanda across the crowded inn.

"I return to the Old Hall and make enquiries about the castle, Jane. That was clearly Agnes's destination last night and I would know more of the garrison and those in authority over them before I make my next move. I cannot arrive at the gates and demand entry to Liverpool castle, much as I should like to. But you and Will must not miss market day. Walk with me to the Old Hall then take your leisure for a while."

They stepped out into Juggler Street and the bustle of the market. Katheryn saw that Father James had still been deep in discussion as they left. She wondered what he had to talk about for so long and so secretively. But that was not her concern: Agnes was. Katheryn lifted her skirts and fine woollen cloak and stepped over the filthy debris of the market stalls and through the milling, odorous throng. She kept her hand tightly on her purse, knowing only too well that where there were crowds there were pickpockets and cutpurses.

Next to a stall, piled high with stinking fish, a small group of gawking citizens gathered to watch a juggler. Katheryn stopped to watch as he flung his brightly painted clubs into the air with casual grace. The things flew faster and faster above the man's tousled head. He was tall with a mop of curly yellow blond hair and a permanent grin. He smiled with his mouth but his ice blue eyes were coolly watching his audience's reaction.

With a final flourish the juggler jettisoned all the clubs into the air at once and caught them one by one, ending with a deep bow to his applauding public. Katheryn looked round at Jane and Will who were clapping ecstatically. They were impressed...as was she. The man possessed a remarkable talent and, judging from the coins tossed into his waiting cap, he made a good living from his skills.

Then Katheryn recalled that Melisanda's male companion had been a juggler? But there would be more than one entertaining the crowds on market day and, besides. Melisanda's customer would have been too preoccupied to be observant.

When the performance was over, Katheryn resumed her slow journey through the crowd, followed by her servants. She resisted the temptation to stop at a stall piled high with richly coloured cloth and ribbons: she had more important matters to attend to that day than the adornments of the body and she regretted wasting those few precious minutes watching the juggler. If Agnes was to be found safe and well, time could be of great importance.

Bartholomew steered his craft gently to the Birkenhead jetty and it moored with a soft thud, wood against wood. He was glad of the stiff breeze which had set his boat racing across the Mersey. Rowing the vessel - laden with people, goods and animals on a market day - would have been a difficult task in becalmed water...even for one as well muscled at Bartholomew.

He helped his chattering passengers to unload their market day acquisitions: a brace of clucking hens; bales of cloth; plump cheeses; even a remarkably well behaved goat. Bartholomew smiled cheerfully as he worked and touched the purse that hung from his belt. Market days paid well.

There was nobody waiting on the Birkenhead side. Soon the beacon would be lit on the Liverpool strand, a signal that more people waited to return home over the water. But until then, with the tides satisfactory for the next couple of hours, Bartholomew could stretch his legs. He pulled his cloak around him against the chill of the wind and strode off in the direction of Tranmere Pool.

He could just see the Priory at the top of the rocky cliffs. It was now falling into ruins as local people took advantage of the ready supply of good stone to repair and build their homes and barns. Nature was encroaching on the great buildings and soon the red stones would blend with the woodland beyond. To this place of peace Bartholomew had come, expecting to lead a life of contemplation; to die and be buried with the other brothers in the shadow of the great Priory church. But times had changed.

Tranmere Pool, that tree lined inlet just south of the Priory grounds, was a place where the river's dead came to shore. Bartholomew had dragged many unfortunates from the water there and taken the soaked corpse to lie in the Priory church and receive Christian burial. He was no stranger to death by drowning.

When he saw the billowing bundle of clothes near the shore and the golden hair spread out in the water, shining like salmon in the weak autumn sunlight, he knew. He quickly made the sign of the cross and uttered a prayer for the dead.

Then he waded out to the body and disentangled the clothing from the clinging seaweed.

He looked at the face, serene and lovely in death...released from all the troubles of this world. He knew her. Poor girl. Poor lovely girl. Poor Agnes.

CHAPTER 7

Bartholomew's heart beat fast as he navigated the ferry over the choppy waters of the Mersey, the wet sleeves of his gown clinging to his flesh. He had picked Agnes out of the shallow water gently, almost reverently, and carried her up to the Priory church, her garments dripping and adorned with seaweed. Tears had pricked his eyes as he had laid his burden - a surprisingly light burden - on the spot where the great stone altar had been. He recalled the last occasion he had carried her thus; but then she had been alive, there had been hope. Now Agnes was dead and he would pray for her soul and for the forgiveness of her sins. According to Brother Valentine, she had talked much of her sins: but she was so young and her face so innocent in death. Surely God would have mercy on poor Sister Agnes.

A sudden squall rocked the boat and the wind caught against the sail almost turning the vessel over. Bartholomew wasn't concentrating. He tried to bring his mind back to the task in hand. He had to cross the river safely; to see Brother Valentine and share the knowledge of Agnes's death. He needed to talk to someone who would understand.

He reached the Liverpool side, still dazed, and tied the boat against the jetty automatically: he had performed that action so many times that it did not need thought or concentration. There were a handful of passengers starting to arrive at the jetty carrying their market day purchases but, Bartholomew told himself, they would have to wait. He ran past them with no explanation and he didn't hear their muttered grumbles as they saw their ferryman deserting his post

Bartholomew pressed through the chaos of the market around the High Cross, cursing the crowds that slowed his progress and made him take tiny steps when his urge was to run as fast as he could.

Valentine was in the back of the shop crushing herbs calmly with a pestle. He looked up and smiled when he saw his visitor: it was good to see one's brothers. But he sensed that something was wrong.

Bartholomew put his head in his hands, too distressed to speak. Will had been sent by Katheryn earlier that day to inform Valentine of Agnes's disappearance. He made a guess. "Is it Agnes? Has she been found?"

Bartholomew nodded. Then the tears came. Valentine put a comforting hand on the young man's shoulder.

"It's my fault," Bartholomew muttered between sobs.

"How so, brother? Surely you have not harmed her?"

"I had such thoughts about her...desires. I have never thought that way about a woman before and when I first held her in my arms..."

Valentine could see the way Bartholomew's thoughts were turning. "So you were attracted to her. It happens, brother."

"Now she is dead and it is a judgement on me. What must I do?"

"How did she die?"

"Drowned. I found her in Tranmere Pool. I took her to our church." His sobs resumed. Valentine watched him speculatively.

"You had nothing to do with her death?"

Bartholomew looked up horrified. "How can you say that? I...I loved her."

Valentine spoke gently. "There is no shame in love, brother. Your conduct towards her was ever honourable. You have nothing to blame yourself for."

"But my vows..."

"There is nothing sinful about love, brother, and your love for Agnes, brief though it was, was sincere, was it not?"

Bartholomew nodded, reassured.

"She was drowned, you say?"

"It appears so, brother."

Valentine thought for a moment. "I will send the boy Ralph to fetch Lady Katheryn. She will want to know the news, bad though it is."

He said a few words to the boy who had been sweeping the shop floor assiduously while they talked, and the lad disappeared into the crowded street, glad to be relieved of his tedious task. Valentine gave Bartholomew a calming infusion of herbs while they waited for Katheryn to arrive.

Bartholomew felt steadier and took several deep breaths, ready to face the ordeal ahead. Valentine was right; his behaviour towards Agnes had never been too forward. But a niggling, sinful thought in the back of his mind suggested to him that maybe, in view of the briefness of life, he should have been bolder.

When Katheryn arrived with Ralph, Valentine told her the news as gently as he could, and the three sat for a while in silent prayer for Agnes's troubled soul.

"We must bring her home," said Katheryn quietly. Bartholomew nodded.

Katheryn drew Valentine to one side and spoke softly, not wishing Bartholomew to hear. "Do you know how she died?"

"Drowning. Bartholomew found her in Tranmere Pool. If a body goes into the river on the far side, it commonly ends up there."

She nodded. "An accident then?"

"I shall examine the body. If there are signs of anything else, I shall see it. I wish this affair had ended happily. You come all the way here to care for the girl and..."

"If she has come to harm through the wickedness of others, Master Valentine, I wish to discover it."

"Of course, my lady. But what makes you think...?"

"Agnes was seen last night going towards the castle. She slipped out of Mistress Moore's house and was alone. But I believe she may have been followed."

Valentine sighed. "I see." He turned to Bartholomew. "Are you ready to return to Birkenhead, brother. We should go soon before the tide turns."

The three walked through the bustling streets to the strand in solemn silence.

The passengers on the ferry found their ferryman morose and silent. He collected their money without a smile. The ferry secured, Bartholomew led his two companions up to steep pathway to the deserted Priory.

It was almost three years since the Priory had been abandoned. The lead from the roofs had gone first, stripped off by the commissioners, allowing the elements to do their destructive work in the refectory and the dormitories. The chapter house with its scriptorium above stood virtually intact but the sandstone walls of the remaining buildings were being eaten slowly away by nature and theft.

The once beautiful priory church with its fine windows and elaborately tiled floor was now a shell. They approached the west end of the great church and entered through the great west door, now hanging off its iron hinges like the door of an derelict barn. Ahead lay the stone slab that marked the site of the altar, and lying on it the bundle of black sodden rags that had once been Agnes Moore.

Katheryn paused in the doorway. Her beautiful abbey at Godstow would soon be like this; weeds growing through the floor of the choir; the great carved roof open to the sky. She felt a pang of bitter regret for the passing of their way of life. The three made their way eastward in quiet procession, as they had done many times before to sing the offices of the day. Agnes lay there, serene, as the three crossed themselves and knelt to pray for her soul.

It was Valentine who stood first and, brisk and businesslike, undid Agnes's cloak, the better to view the body. Katheryn, still kneeling, watched him as he examined the face and neck. He turned to her.

"I will not be able to say for certain until I have had a chance to examine her further but my first observations tell me that Agnes's death may not have been accidental.

Bartholomew looked up sharply. "What do you mean, brother. Surely nobody would..."

Valentine turned to the body and gently pushed back the damp strands of fair hair from the face. "Do you see these marks?" He put his hand gently over the dead girl's face. "Like the marks left by fingers...by a hand? They were made when she was alive. Somebody held her head under the water as she struggled. She faced him and he put his hand to her face and pushed her backwards. See?"

Katheryn, now bent over the body, nodded in agreement. "Who would do such a thing to the poor child?"

"You must remember, my lady, that she was attacked before. Somebody wanted Agnes Moore dead. I hate to speak of such wickedness, but I fear it is true."

"What could one such as Agnes have done to arouse so much hatred? She was young and innocent. She had no real knowledge of the world. Who would hate her so much?"

"Maybe not hate, my lady," Bartholomew said quietly. "Maybe love...jealousy."

"Why do you say that, brother?" asked Katheryn sharply.

Bartholomew looked flustered. "I did not mean... It was just a thought."

"Or perhaps she knew something. Perhaps she'd seen something she shouldn't have seen. Perhaps someone was afraid that she would betray them," suggested Valentine.

"I think that more likely," said Katheryn thoughtfully. "Poor Agnes was not one to inspire hate enough to lead to murder. Of love I cannot say," she smiled wistfully. "Having no knowledge of such matters myself."

"We must take her back to Liverpool," said Valentine, laying a comforting hand on Katheryn's arm. "Take her to the church for requiem mass and burial."

Katheryn nodded and looked down. She did not want the two men to see the tears that had begun to fill her eyes as she thought of young Agnes growing to womanhood at Godstow...and now lying lifeless before her.

They stood for a minute in silence, heads bowed in the presence of death. Then Bartholomew lifted Agnes in his arms and started back towards his boat. The other two followed, a strange little funeral procession, and boarded the ferry without a word.

Marjory Moore took the news calmly. "I dare say I could have predicted it, my lady. The girl brought nothing but trouble." She sat there looking at Katheryn, her face impassive. "Of course I'm sorry that the poor child's dead, God rest her soul. But I can't help feeling that she probably brought about her own misfortune. If a girl behaves thus, she must accept the consequences."

Katheryn wrestled hard with her temper. "But Agnes was killed, Mistress: probably murdered."

"Agnes was a fool. Didn't you teach her anything about the world at that nunnery of yours? The girl becomes enamoured of the first undesirable man she meets and this is what happens." She looked challengingly at Katheryn.

"Nunneries, I confess, are not the best places to learn of the world but then we never thought to be part of it." If Marjory was trying to lay the blame for Agnes's death at her door, Katheryn was not going to let her get away with it. "If she had been shown more understanding when she entered the outside world..."

"Do you suggest, my lady, that the girl was not well cared for?" Marjory leaned forward angrily. "Did I not take her under my roof and care for her? At my own expense, I may add...and for no thanks."

"I blame no one, Mistress. Please, let us be calm and remember that Agnes needs our prayers."

"The girl has brought nothing but trouble to my family. My son, Master Francis of Bank Hall, says it is the last time I should let anybody take advantage of my generous nature."

Katheryn, who had seen many examples of Marjory Moore's generous nature, thought it best to take her leave before she was tempted to confront her hostess with a few home truths.

"I shall not prevail on your hospitality any longer, Mistress. I shall seek lodging elsewhere. I thank you for your hospitality. I shall not forget it."

Marjory nodded smugly. To have the sister of Sir Richard Bulkeley of Beaumaris praise her hospitality was a small advancement in the Moore family's social standing, so precious to Marjory's heart. "You are welcome to stay on at Old Hall, my lady. It would be an honour," she said with as much sincerity as she could muster, hoping Katheryn would refuse. The woman was too observant by half...and she had strange notions about how to treat those of lower social rank.

"That is most kind but I have intruded enough. When Agnes has been buried, I shall depart. I have taken the liberty of bringing her body to lie in the church of Our Lady and St. Nicholas for the time being. If you wish to make arrangements for her burial..."

Marjory was relieved. She wanted no part in the disposal of Agnes's body: she did not even want to be reminded of the fact that the girl had existed. "No, I insist, my lady, you must do as you think fit. You knew her better than I and she would have wished you to make the arrangements. She thought highly of you."

So Marjory was washing her hands of the whole thing. It did not surprise Katheryn, who smiled sweetly and agreed that she would put all the necessary arrangements in hand and would even pay for the funeral from her own pocket...a welcome suggestion for Marjory who was already thinking how she could cut down on the costs that would be bound to accrue from a funeral, however humble

Katheryn took her leave of Marjory and made her way with Jane to the church where she had agreed to meet Valentine.

The market stalls were being dismantled and the debris thrown into the middle of the streets. On their way to the church they passed many people wending their way home; some drunk, some sober; most subdued after a long day at market. Of the juggler and the other entertainers there was no sign. They would be in the ale houses spending their earnings.

Agnes lay in a coffin of plain wooden boards, hastily knocked together by a nearby carpenter who owed Valentine money for medicines and was only too glad to pay in kind. Mother Bilton, who assisted the townsfolk of Liverpool at the start and the end of their lives, being midwife as well as tending to the dead, had washed Agnes and dressed her in a clean linen shift ready for burial.

Valentine kept vigil, kneeling in prayer by the coffin in the chapel of St. Nicholas. Katheryn found him thus and knelt beside him. Jane did likewise.

Their spiritual duty done, they stood up, their eyes drawn to the face of the girl in the coffin, a pretty face; sweet and innocent. Such a waste.

"Father James will bury her on Monday," Valentine said practically. "And he will say a mass for her tomorrow."

"I will pay for a mass to be said for her once a week," said Katheryn, staring at the lifeless beautiful face. "It is the least that I can do."

"Your generosity does you credit, my lady."

"It is not generosity. I could have done more for her when she was alive; perhaps prevented this."

"You must not feel guilt for something you could do nothing about. She is at peace now and our prayers will shorten her time in purgatory."

Katheryn was surprised to find herself leaning for comfort against Valentine's shoulder, his arm about her supportively. He smelled of herbs and clean linen. She stayed there longer than she knew was proper, drawing warmth and strength from his closeness.

Valentine spoke first. "While Mother Bilton was about her work, I had the opportunity to examine the body more closely."

"Did you discover anything?" She stood back slightly as Valentine's arm slipped away from her shoulder.

"Apart from the bruising I observed on her face, there was bruising to her thighs. I cannot be sure you understand..."

"You think she was violated before death?"

"It is possible."

"Poor Agnes." Katheryn tore her eyes away from the dead girl's face.

"We must find the man responsible for her death, Katheryn." He spoke with quiet determination.

Katheryn looked at him and nodded. It was the first time he had used her Christian name. "I shall not leave Liverpool until our task is done."

"Will Mistress Moore allow you to stay at Old Hall now that Agnes is gone?"

"I had words with that lady an hour since. I feel I have outstayed my welcome so I should be grateful if you could recommend a respectable inn where we can stay until this matter is resolved."

" The previous tenant of my shop had a large family and many relations and the accommodation is too large for my needs. There are two spare chambers, clean and swept. If I may offer you and your servants the hospitality of my humble house..."

Katheryn smiled. What Valentine suggested may not have been wise, but she felt a recklessness that she had never experienced before. Outwardly calm, she thanked Valentine for his kind offer and said that she was delighted to accept. It was not that she was unused to the ways of the opposite sex: she had three brothers and it had been her duty, as Abbess of a great religious house, to entertain the landowners and noblemen of Oxford. But none of the self opinionated grandees at Godstow had ever been particularly welcome companions.

"I will send Will for our horses and baggage. Thank you," she said simply.

Father James hurried from the church where he had spoken with Valentine about the arrangements for the girl's burial. It was the same girl, he was sure of it; the one who had been in St. Mary del Quay that day. Now she was dead and Father James was afraid.

There were few people about, only the last stragglers returning from market; a group of sailors just arrived in port wandering aimlessly looking for drink or women; and a handful of drunken men returning from the inns of the town to their long suffering wives. As James entered the chapel of St. Mary del Quay, shutting the door quietly behind him, he was sure he had not been observed.

Francis Wells, once cellarer of Birkenhead Priory, was waiting for him in the chapel, standing next to the altar in the flickering candlelight. With him was another man. James shot Wells an enquiring look and Wells smiled as the stranger opened his cloak. There pinned on the inside was the familiar badge: the badge of the five wounds of Christ. The stranger was one of their fellowship. James relaxed as the man was introduced.

Then Father James returned to the chapel door and wedged it firmly shut. What was about to happen was for the eyes of the initiated only.

CHAPTER 8

Katheryn's new chamber was smaller and humbler than the one she had been given at the Old Hall, but the room was spotless with clean linen and fresh rushes provided by Matilda, Valentine's cheerful cook and maid of all work. Jane was to sleep on a small truckle bed in the corner and Will was to share with young Ralph. Matilda, a large and talkative woman, seemed pleased to welcome the new visitors. The house was quiet, she complained, with just Master Valentine and young Ralph. She was glad of female company.

Matilda was an excellent cook: the fish pie she presented to them for supper proved that. After they had eaten (Ralph, Jane, Will, and the cook herself sitting at table with them - a social situation that would have filled Mistress Moore with horror) Katheryn complimented her on her skill. Matilda, blushed, taking a liking to their new guest at once, fine lady or no fine lady.

When the meal had finished and the others got up to go about their business, Valentine poured Katheryn some ale and they drew their stools closer to the fire. The nights were growing chilly.

They sat in amicable silence for a while, gazing into the flames. The events of the day had tired them both. Valentine spoke first. "Agnes was seen going to the castle you say?"

"Last night after curfew. A young lady of the night from the Mermaid was about her work and saw her, thinking her another of her calling. She thought that Agnes was being followed but she could see nothing of her pursuer because he was well hidden by a cloak. She also said that Agnes spoke to one of the castle guards. But she could tell me no more: she had her living to earn, poor child."

"Then we must make enquiries at the castle. I visit there often. You would not believe soldiers to be such babies with their aches and pains. On Monday, I am to change a dressing for one of the men of the garrison who injured his hand in sword practice. You could come with me if you wish."

Katheryn nodded. It was wise to start their enquiries where Agnes was last seen and the sooner the better while memories were still fresh.

Her eyes felt heavy with the ale and the heat of the fire. She wished Valentine goodnight and retired to bed where she slept soundly until morning.

Sunday passed slowly. Valentine and Katheryn, accompanied by Jane and Will, heard the mass that Father James said for Agnes's soul and returned to the house subdued.

Mistress Marjory had been at the church and had bowed her head politely to Katheryn as she passed. Agnes still lay in the side chapel awaiting burial but, as far as Katheryn could see, Marjory had made no effort to go there and pay her respects. Katheryn watched Marjory leave the church, head held high, receiving the greetings of the less prosperous burgesses of Liverpool who were dressed in their Sunday best for the whole town to see. The households of Lord Molyneux at the castle and Lord Derby at the Tower, celebrated mass in their private chapels. But at the church of Our Lady and St. Nicholas it was the Moores who ruled supreme.

Griselda had followed her mistress from the church and had given Jane a wide grin as she passed. She missed the girl from Cheshire with her innocent country ways. She missed telling her of the delights of Liverpool, the taverns and the sailors, and seeing Jane's eyes widen in disbelief.

When Griselda got back to the Old Hall, Marjory sent her to fetch some fresh herbs from the garden to throw on the fire. Griselda felt a prick of resentment: it was the Sabbath. But she knew that at Old Hall there was one law for Mistress Marjory and another for the servants and even the Almighty himself could not change that. But if she had to go out, Griselda thought, she would go a little further than the herb garden. The weather was fine and if she walked along the shore she might just see the dark haired, blue eyed young sailor from Ireland who was currently taking her fancy.

So she hurried across the garden and out of the wooden gate that separated it from the townfield beyond. She wouldn't be too long; just long enough to see if her sailor was there. She trudged across the sparse grass that grew on the sand ridge between the fields and the shore and she saw the bulk of the old disused mill on her right. She hadn't entered the mill since it was abandoned for a new one nearer the centre of the town a couple of years before. There was something about the deserted building that made her uneasy. Besides, Mistress Moore had given strict orders that no servant was allowed in there.

The brickwork on the mill was starting to crumble and its windows stared like hollow eyes in a decaying face. There had been a time a few weeks back when her sweetheart had wanted them to go inside the mill...to be alone. But Griselda had refused. She had heard tales of the place.

Maybe she would go back. It was starting to get dark and there was no sign of her sailor. He was most likely at an inn somewhere with his shipmates, she thought bitterly, and he was due to sail on the first high tide tomorrow. But he would not be away for long: he would soon be back bringing more Irish flax for the merchants of Manchester. Griselda was ever the optimist.

She turned reluctantly and started to walk back towards the Old Hall, glancing at the mill, brooding against the darkening sky.

Then she saw the face at one of the upper windows: a blur of hair and flesh, watching her, staring at her. She could almost feel the eyes on her back as she quickened her pace. Her heart beat faster. She reached the gate and fumbled with the fastening, her panic making her hands clumsy and useless. He could not reach her...surely he could not reach her.

The gate opened and she almost fell into the garden. The herbs quite forgotten, Griselda stumbled down the path and pushed at the kitchen door.

Monday morning was grey. Katheryn awoke early and the aroma of fresh baked bread from the baker's shop next door made her realise she was hungry.

After breaking their fast, Katheryn and Valentine put up the hoods of their cloaks against the fine drizzle that was dampening the streets and slowly turning them into alleyways of stinking mud. The streets were busy as people ignored the weather and went about their business. Servants and goodwives with baskets haggled noisily with shopkeepers; an unfortunate man who had been caught fighting drunk by the constable the night before, stood in the pillory, his lank hair hanging wet around his face as a group of ragged children threw at him any rubbish they could find on the ground. The man cursed his tormentors with as much strength as he could muster then vomited dramatically on the ground in front of the pillory, narrowly missing a skinny dog who was about to urinate against his leg.

Valentine hurried past the pillory and the steps of the guild hall, ignoring the commotion. Such sights were commonplace. But Katheryn stopped, noting the pallor that had come to the prisoner's face. "Should we not help the man, Valentine. He might choke."

Valentine smiled. "That man is in the pillory at least twice a week. He is well used to it. Save your pity for those who deserve it."

She walked on. Valentine was probably right. He knew this town and its people better than she did. They hurried up Castle Street, avoiding the newly made barrels stacked up outside a cooper's noisy workshop and the shiny pieces of offal and fish thrown out from shops for the dogs who scavenged in the streets. When they reached the castle the guard let them through with a friendly greeting. Valentine was a welcome visitor.

First he attended to the injured soldier's hand and changed his dressings. Katheryn hovered in the background, handing

Valentine what he needed and trying hard not to look at the unbandaged wound. Whatever other talents she possessed, she would not make a good physician's assistant: she knew her limitations and hoped they would not be too obvious to Valentine.

As Valentine knew the castle and its people better than she did, Katheryn left the next move to him. The soldier dealt with, he led her down the bare stone corridors to the quarters of the Captain of the garrison explaining that, as he knew Captain Wharton, this would be as good a place as any to begin their investigation.

Captain Wharton was sitting alone examining some papers which he hastily rolled up when they entered the room. He greeted Valentine respectfully and bowed to Katheryn who was introduced as Lady Katheryn Bulkeley, sister of Sir Richard, Constable of the King's castle at Beaumaris. Wharton, a career soldier, was impressed by authority and rank and treated Katheryn with due deference, inviting her to sit and clumsily pouring her a cup of wine: Wharton was no courtier and his rough manners did not allow him to hide his curiosity about the reason for her visit. He scratched his greasy and thinning black hair and stared at Katheryn uneasily.

She decided to speak plainly. "A young lady who was once in my charge, became the victim of unfortunate circumstances and found herself here in Liverpool in the care of Mistress Moore of Old Hall. The poor girl became ill and on Friday night she went missing. I have made enquiries and it seems that she was seen talking with a soldier of this garrison at the castle gate. We are anxious to discover what became of her and I thought to enlist your help."

She smiled her sweetest smile at Wharton, who looked down embarrassed. She had thought it best not to mention Agnes's death. If he thought murder was involved, Wharton might be more likely to guard his tongue.

"Friday night, you say?" Wharton stroked his chin. "I recall that Manners was posted at the main gate that night. I heard nothing of a young lady from Old Hall: I should have remembered. Surely such a lady would have been instructed to report to me unless..."

"Unless what, Captain?"

"Unless she went straight to one of my officers. Did she have a sweetheart in the castle? That is the most likely explanation." Wharton sat back, satisfied with his deductions.

"I know of no sweetheart amongst the soldiers here, but I am prepared to consider any possibility of course. If I may speak with the guard who was on duty that night..."

Wharton nodded. It could do no harm. And if there had been a lapse in discipline - if any member of the garrison was entertaining his woman when he should have been about his business - Wharton wanted to know about it. He sent for Manners.

When the guard arrived, Katheryn looked him up and down. He was a big man who smelled of sweat and stale beer. It was difficult to calculate his age, but it must have taken many years to cultivate the characteristic stoutness of an ardent ale drinker. Manners stood, humble, in front of his betters. He was a soldier with a soldier's taste for ale and women. His needs were simple. He mistrusted the Captain and the strangers who watched him speculatively.

When Katheryn spoke, Manners doffed his cap and bowed his head. He recognised natural authority when he saw it. "Master Manners," she said in a pleasant but determined voice. "You were guarding the castle gates on Friday night, were you not?"

He nodded. If it was about that whore, he was saying nothing.

"A young lady who was in my care has gone missing. She was seen approaching the castle and speaking with one of the soldiers here. Did she, by any chance, speak with you? Or did you see her with anybody else? She was about my height and she wore a black cloak. She was a pretty girl of eighteen years with fair hair." Katheryn looked him straight in the eyes and he looked away.

"Er...no, my lady. I saw nobody. T'was a quiet night."

Katheryn inclined her head graciously. "Very well, Master Manners. Thank you. You may go."

Manners shambled out, leaving the odour of his sweat behind him. Wharton, relieved, waited for his visitors to make the next move. He was glad when the lady got up and thanked him for his help.

When they were safely out of the castle, Katheryn turned to Valentine who was walking beside her, deep in thought. "He was lying."

"Who was?"

"Manners...and Wharton too probably. It's their word against Melisanda's and she has no reason to lie, nothing to lose or gain."

"As far as we know."

"I spoke with her, Valentine. I'm sure her word can be trusted. If somebody from the garrison is involved in Agnes's death of course they would hide the truth. And I did not think Master Manners was a very practised liar. Did you see how he would not look me in the face?"

Valentine nodded. He was inclined to be more tentative in his conclusions. "If we take on the garrison," he reminded her, "We take on more than Manners...more than Captain Wharton."

Katheryn looked at him, a smile playing on her lips. "Why, Master Valentine, I do believe you're afraid."

"Not afraid," he replied. "Just cautious."

Wharton called Manners back as soon as his visitors were gone.

"What the devil happened that night, Manners. Tell me now, damn you or I'll see to it that..."

"That whore Sir Edward had...the one that asked for you. It could have been her. It was like her..."

"You're sure?" Wharton's voice was anxious.

Manners shrugged. He wanted to forget the whole incident. "She might have been, sir. I did not see clearly. She was just a whore."

Wharton sighed. "Very well. There is no need to say anything more about it. The girl they spoke of was not here. Is that clear?"

Manners fought the compulsion to grin with relief. "Yes, sir. Very clear, sir."

"And perhaps you would tell anyone else who was around that night not to mention the matter. Let's keep this between ourselves, eh." Wharton winked confidentially, an understanding between two soldiers with a common enemy.

"Yes, sir. You can trust me, sir."

Wharton doubted the truth of Manners' last statement but he trusted in one thing. There would be no more talk of Sir Edward's whore in the castle. The matter was dealt with. Closed.

The drizzle had stopped. Katheryn picked her way carefully through the rubbish strewn streets, narrowly avoiding the stinking corpse of a dead dog that lay in her path. Valentine walked behind her as the street by the shambles was too crowded to walk two abreast and too noisy for conversation.

Out of the corner of his eye Valentine spotted a cloaked figure: that beggar again; the one with the missing hand. The man would have to take care if he was not to be arrested. But then, from what Valentine had observed, the beggar seemed to have the ability to disappear into the shadows at will...a vital skill for one in his situation.

When they returned to Dale Street they found that Ralph had dealt with the routine requests as best he could, sending people home with common medicines and ointments. But there were still a few who wished to consult the apothecary for themselves about some new ailment or symptom that had appeared. While Valentine dealt with his patients, Katheryn went upstairs to her chamber to say the morning office before joining Jane who was mending linen in the back parlour. Will, Jane explained, was feeding the horses, now stabled in the yard at the back of the shop and Jane had been busying herself helping Matilda and Ralph. Katheryn smiled. Their new living arrangements seemed to be working well.

The parlour door opened and in walked Griselda, who smiled widely when she saw Jane but whose smile faded as she spotted Katheryn. She bobbed a curtsey.

"Begging your pardon, my lady. I thought to speak with Jane. It was nothing important. I'm sorry, my lady."

Katheryn stood up. "No, you must stay Griselda. I was about to see if Master Valentine needed help. Sit down. I'm sure Jane will be eager to hear your news."

Katheryn thought that half an hour's escape from Mistress Marjory's domination would do Griselda the world of good. And who knows what gossip Jane might pick up as a result. She left them alone together.

Griselda spoke first. "Mistress Marjory has one of her headaches. She sent me for some of her usual physic. How are things with you?"

"Very well. The household here is, er...easier than Mistress Moore's."

"And Will? Is he still attentive?"

Jane blushed. "Indeed he is. And my lady is kind enough to leave us together."

"You are so lucky, Jane. If I want to see my young man I have to sneak out like a thief."

"Your sailor? How is he?"

"In Ireland again. He sailed this morning on the first tide. But he will be back by and by." Griselda leaned forward. Her face suddenly looked troubled. "I went to see if he was on the strand last night."

"And was he?"

"No. But I saw something; something that frightened me."

"What do you mean?"

"There's a mill at the back of the Old Hall. It belongs to the Moores but they have built a new one near Castle Street: it is more central there for the townsfolk to take their grain and the Moores were ever ones to make a greater profit." Jane nodded; she was beginning to understand all about the preoccupations of the Moore family. Griselda continued. "The old mill's deserted now...falling to ruin. It is not a place to be after dark."

Jane was beginning to find the tale interesting. "Go on...what happened?"

"I looked up at the mill as I passed and in one of the windows I saw a face. It was horrible...like something from the grave."

Jane hurriedly crossed herself, enjoying being frightened in the safety of Master Valentine's back parlour. "What did it look like?"

"Like a corpse. White with staring eyes." Griselda's eyes sparkled. Jane suspected some use of poetic embellishment.

Jane leaned forward further, open mouthed. "Who was it, Griselda? Who was it?"

Griselda opened her eyes dramatically. "I reckon it was Old Nick himself. I reckon it was the devil."

CHAPTER 9

The great bell tolled across the river Mersey, tolling for Agnes. The little party of mourners filed into the church of Our Lady and St. Nicholas for the requiem mass. Father James officiated with solemn dignity but instead of dismissing the congregation with a blessing, he stood by the side of Agnes's coffin and looked at the mourners, scanning their faces.

"My friends," he began. "We are here to pray for the soul of our sister here. One that was a sister...a nun of the Abbey of Godstow. How then does she come to be lying violated and dead here before us?"

Katheryn shifted uneasily and hoped that Father James would show some restraint, some discretion. But the passionate tone of his voice made her suspect that she hoped in vain.

"You will all know of the events that have overtaken this land. How our King has rejected Christ's words that the descendants of St. Peter should rule over the church and usurped that authority for himself."

Katheryn looked down, praying that no King's agent was present to report the priest's words back to the authorities. Such talk was dangerous...such talk was treason. And treason resulted in a hideous death. Valentine caught her eye: his thoughts clearly matched her own. They willed Father James to stop but the priest carried on.

"And hunger for power and worldly wealth has made our sovereign lord King Henry look with avaricious eyes upon the property of our Holy Mother Church...on the places where God's faithful servants have spent their lives in prayer and devotion. This is why our dear martyred sister lies dead before us today. The King seized the wealth of her hallowed house and had no thought for the poor creatures thrown out to fend for themselves in a wicked world."

Katheryn and Valentine exchanged glances again. Although there was some truth in what Father James said, there were many like themselves, furnished with good pensions and a new way of life, who could not count themselves amongst the

King's unfortunate victims. But whether or not the priest's words were accurate, they were better left unsaid.

"Sister Agnes was a martyr...a symbol of the suffering caused by the wickedness of those who rule over us. The devil stalks this land." Father James was becoming more carried away with his words. His eyes glowed with conviction. "And that devil's name is Henry..."

"Enough, Father." Katheryn could stand it no longer. If this speech carried on to its natural conclusion they would all be in danger. Father James looked at her surprised, the spell of his eloquence broken. "Let us all pray for poor Agnes's soul and pray that the one responsible for her untimely death will be brought to justice."

Father James, realising that he had perhaps gone too far, looked at Katheryn with understanding. He made the sign of the cross and began the prayers for the dead. The crisis was over. Katheryn felt Valentine's hand on hers. "Well said," he whispered.

Father James confined himself to the standard litany from then on, much to Katheryn's relief. She had no wish to see the priest suffer the death of a traitor; to be half hanged then cut down and disembowelled, his entrails burned before his eyes.

When they reached the graveside she looked around. A few of the Moore's servants, including Griselda, were present, shifting uneasily from foot to foot and wrapping their cloaks around them against the cold breeze that blew from the river. The only other mourners were Bartholomew, Jane, Will, herself and Valentine. There was nobody she had not seen before: nobody, she hoped, who would repeat Father James's indiscreet words to the authorities.

Soon it was over. Agnes was in the ground. Katheryn stood watching as the gravedigger covered her coffin with sandy earth. Valentine took her hand and she was glad of his comforting presence. As she contemplated the pathetic grave, she resolved to discover the truth, whatever dangers that discovery might bring. She would stay in Liverpool until she discovered who had killed Agnes.

When they returned to the shop, Valentine poured ale for Katheryn and himself and harboured the uncharitable wish that the townsfolk of Liverpool would suddenly be struck down with a mild and unthreatening malady which would distract him from the sad events of that afternoon. But nobody came.

Katheryn broke the silence. "Father James is a danger to himself. He must learn discretion...as we all have had to."

Valentine nodded. "I had not thought him so foolish. He has never spoken thus to me...never."

"We must hope that he was merely carried away with the sadness of the occasion and that he will learn to conceal his thoughts in future."

"There was nobody there, surely, who would report his words."

"You can never be sure, Valentine. Any of those servants of Mistress Moore might tell tales. There are many about who would gain advancement by betraying their fellow citizens."

Katheryn was right. An act of betrayal could lead to preferment, to a new and better position: and ultimately to wealth and power. He had seen it happen. So had Katheryn.

It was then that Valentine's wish for a distraction was granted. A servant from Crosse Hall came, breathless, into the shop to ask Master Valentine to come right away as the young master had a swelling of the finger. Valentine packed up his ointments and left. Jane came in and, seeing her mistress alone and staring into the fire, turned and was about to leave her to her thoughts. But Katheryn called her back.

"You have not told me what news Griselda had to bring. Come and sit down. Let us try and forget our sadness for a while. Entertain me with the latest gossip."

Jane needed no encouragement. She sat down, eyes aglow. "Griselda said the strangest thing, my lady."

"What? What did she say?

Jane looked down, half grinning. "She said she saw someone in the mill behind the Old Hall."

Katheryn looked disappointed. She had expected something more exciting. "Who was it? Who did she see?"

"She reckoned she'd seen Satan himself, not that I believe her," Jane stated solemnly. She had not taken Griselda's half-baked revelations seriously. It was just the sort of story Griselda would make up to make herself seem important.

Katheryn noted that Griselda was the second person to claim to have seen Satan in the flesh. Agnes had told a similar tale when she had been attacked in the chapel of St. Mary del Quay. Although Katheryn was in no doubt that the devil was constantly about his work, she did not think he was in the habit of making himself quite so visible.

"And did Griselda seem frightened by what she saw?"

Jane thought for a moment. "Yes. She said she would never go past the old mill alone again, not even to meet her sweetheart on the strand. She would ask him to meet her by the gate, even if it risked being discovered by Mistress Moore."

Whatever Griselda saw, Katheryn thought, must have been more fearful than Mistress Marjory's tongue. She sat back and looked at Jane. "Are you feeling courageous, Jane?"

"Me, my lady?"

"And Will, of course. I think we should take a look at this disused mill to see if there is any sense to be made out of Griselda's story."

Jane looked wary. She had never been of an adventurous nature. But if Will was going with them, the enterprise might not be without its compensations.

Marjory Moore's head felt a little better. Master Valentine's potions always worked swiftly. She lay on her bed, eyes shut against the light, wondering what her household was up to. Those servants couldn't be trusted: if she did not watch them every minute of the day who knows what they might get up to and what duties would be left neglected. Without her ever watchful presence the idle, ungrateful creatures would slacken off their efforts and the house and lands would sink to decay and ruin.

She opened her eyes. The pain was virtually gone. Tentatively, she pushed herself into a sitting position and looked around. The rushes on the floor needed changing. That girl, Griselda, was becoming a slattern, too busy dreaming of that Irish sailor. Marjory resolved to confront her about her ever lengthening absences next time the girl deigned to show her face.

Marjory rose from her bed, went to the window and looked out over the herb garden to ensure that none of the servants were idling their time away out of doors. Beyond the garden she could see the old mill. Her son, Francis, had said that if it was not to be used again as a mill, perhaps he could find another use for it...or have it pulled down. His own mother should not be expected to view an unsightly ruin from her chamber window; a scar on the otherwise uninterrupted view across the townfield to the river estuary. But she had kept silent. Francis would forget about the old mill; he was a very busy man.

A movement caught her eye. Someone was at the entrance to the mill. Three people intruding where they had no right to be. She looked more intently, realising that one of the figures was familiar. Surely it could not be that woman: surely it would not be appropriate for one of her rank to trespass in derelict buildings.

Marjory went to her chamber door and shouted. But no servant came. She stepped into her shoes and bustled down the stairs and out of the back door into the herb garden, startled servants curtseying as she swept past.

"Lady Katheryn," she called as she opened the wooden gate that led onto the open land. "May I enquire what you are doing?" She made a imperceptible curtsey for appearances sake and tried to hide her anger.

Katheryn smiled sweetly, sensing trouble. "I have heard reports of an intruder in the old mill, Mistress Moore. I thought to investigate but did not wish to disturb you. I apologise if..."

"You do realise, my lady, that you are on Moore land?"

"If I trespass, Mistress, it is with the best of intentions. I have vowed to discover the truth of Agnes's death. I am sure as her kinswoman, you would add your prayer to mine that I may be successful in bringing her killer to justice."

"It was but an accident, madam. I have put the matter from my mind and do not wish to be reminded of it. It would oblige me if you would leave my land at once."

Katheryn smiled sweetly once more. "All I request, Mistress, is that my servants and I take a look inside the mill. Surely that would do no harm and satisfy us that nothing untoward has taken place on your land. Think of the danger of lurking thieves and footpads on your own doorstep: think of the threat to your property."

Katheryn could see Marjory weighing the arguments against her personal prejudices.

"Perhaps a quick search, just to satisfy us that no villains lurk there unseen."

Katheryn nodded to Will who cautiously pushed open the battered wooden door, half falling off its hinges. Marjory watched them intently.

The interior of the mill was unthreatening in the daylight that streamed in through the unglazed windows. The floor was covered in dusty chaff and straw: machinery rotted on the ground, piled up by the ramshackle ladder that led to the upper storeys. There was nothing here on the ground floor to give rise to suspicion. Katheryn looked at the ladder. There was no way she could investigate the upper floors herself.

"If I wore breeches, Will, I should go up myself but..."

Will, not wishing to appear a coward before Jane and his mistress, put a testing foot on the ladder. The first rung, at least, was firm and safe. Surprisingly, so were the rest. He went up slowly, testing each one.

"Can you see anything, Will? Are you all right?" Katheryn called up after a minute's silence.

"Yes, my lady," came the muffled reply. "I can see nothing amiss."

Marjory, who had been shifting from foot to foot impatiently, could contain herself no longer. "It is quite plain that there is no one here. I suggest we leave this place." She shouted up to Will. "Come down at once, man. There is little purpose in tarrying here longer than we need to. It grows cold. Come down."

Katheryn did not like to countermand Mistress Moore on her own property. She just hoped that Will had conducted a thorough search, though she feared he would not have had time. He came down the ladder as carefully as he had climbed it.

Will reached the ground, grinning at Jane. "I reckon the ladder's been mended, my lady. See those new nails and that lighter wood near the top."

Katheryn nodded. "It has been in somebody's interest to keep the place in good repair." She looked questioningly at Marjory.

"It was only shut up two years back, my lady. The work might have been done just prior to that. It means nothing." Marjory went to the door and waited. It was obvious that she meant to escort them from the premises.

But Katheryn did not intend to be hurried. "Did you find anything, Will?" she whispered.

"Only this, my lady." He held out his hand. In it was a lump of solid wax, moulded into a strange shape, almost as if someone had been modelling a human form with it and had stopped before the legs were fashioned. "What do you think it is, my lady?"

"I could not say, Will. Did you find nothing else of interest?"

"There is much debris up there, but I found signs that candles had been burned...and some bones. I did not search the top floor. I merely looked and I could see nothing amiss but it was dark."

"You found bones, you say?"

"Animal bones...meat, my lady."

"I see." She turned to Marjory who was standing by the door, anxious to be gone. "You're sure nobody's been here, Mistress? You've seen and heard nothing?"

"Nothing, my lady. I told you." Her irritation was becoming obvious. "If you have seen all you wish to see, I should be obliged if you would leave this place now."

Katheryn knew when she was beaten. She bade Marjory farewell with studied politeness and left with as much dignity as the setting allowed.

When they were back at Valentine's shop Katheryn turned to Will. "Have you kept that piece of wax you found?"

"I have it safe, my lady." He laid it on the table in front of them and they stared at the strange object. Katheryn knew she could be wrong - she would seek Valentine's opinion on the matter - but she had heard of such objects before...and knew their meaning.

When Katheryn had spoken with Marjory Moore outside the mill, they had been watched by a man, well wrapped in a thick brown cloak, who stood in the shelter of the hedge that marked the townfield boundary.

The watcher knew one thing for certain; he couldn't return to the mill until they had gone. So he fell in behind a cart that was trundling along the lane, and walked slowly back towards the town, his cloak and hood concealing his face and body. The mill had been a useful place for concealment...and other things. There were not many hiding places in a small town like Liverpool where one could remain undisturbed for so long.

But if his refuge was discovered it meant that the girl, Griselda, must have seen him; must have said something. Servant girls were notorious gossips. He would have to take care. He reached Juggler Street, busy with people, and pulled his hood down further.

When the commotion started, his first instinct was to hide. He ran to the junction of the Shambles and stood in a doorway watching the citizens running to and fro like ants while the dogs barked with excitement and the shopkeepers hammered at their shutters. Goods fell out of shopfronts and were trampled and kicked into the stinking stream that ran down the centre of the street.

Somewhere in the distance could be heard the rhythmical beat of a drum. People ran out of their houses, more purposeful now, to put up their shutters. Then they hung about talking to their neighbours, their hands firmly on their purses, waiting to see the spectacle. Groups of sailors slouched in the tavern doorways, more curious than anxious: they had nothing to lose. There was cautious excitement as the drum beat drew nearer. Other instruments were audible now and voices raised in disharmonious song.

The first to appear round the corner by the High Cross was the upright man, leading the ragged procession in a shabby, frayed silk, scarlet gown. An escort of yapping dogs ran about his feet like attendant heralds as he swung his heavy staff, his wand of office, in time to the beat of the drum. The beggars had come to town.

The crowd of shoppers stared, half repelled, half fascinated, at the outlandish parade. The abraham men, mad and marching in their rusty chains, made forays into the crowd: the goodwives backed away nervously before throwing them a coin. Cutpurses darted amongst the spectators like rats as their victims were distracted by the beggars. The marchers formed themselves into a ragged line, some deaf mute, many limbless and on crutches, some able bodied and willing to entertain in exchange for their alms by playing instruments, singing or juggling. There were also the able bodied who, having no skills worth paying to watch, feigned sickness by limping and rolling their eyes alarmingly. It was these who watched the crowds slyly, assessing how much they could trick out of the inhabitants of each new town or village they reached.

Beggars from all around had joined the line: the local unfortunates resenting the newcomers and wanting a share in any public generosity that was going.

The man in the brown cloak stood at the corner of the Shambles scanning the faces of the beggars as they passed. Near the back of the procession marched the one he was looking for. So he was here: he had not been mistaken. The beggar held the stump of his right hand up for all to see. It was certainly him.

The watcher's heartbeat increased with fear and he pulled the hood of his cloak down further so that it hid his face. He pushed his way through the crowd and made his way to the castle. When he reached the gatehouse he was greeted with a routine challenge. The guard, who looked little more than a fresh-faced boy, was unknown to him: probably a newcomer to the garrison.

"Tell Captain Wharton that Master Mires wishes to speak with him on an urgent matter." The folds of his brown cloak muffled his voice. The young soldier looked him up and down suspiciously and beckoned to Manners who was standing on the far side of the gate. He sauntered over and his young colleague whispered something in his ear.

"It's all right, Jones." Manners nodded to the visitor in recognition. "Our Captain is well acquainted with Master Mires. Go through, Master. You'll find the Captain in the usual place."

"The new guard looked perplexed as the cloaked figure strode past into the castle. "Who is he? Is he connected with the garrison?"

Manners laughed unpleasantly. "There are some questions you'll soon know not to ask, my lad. You've a lot to learn. Stick with me and we'll make a soldier of you yet."

Wharton took another sip of wine. His visitor always made him nervous. There had been times over the past year when his bowels had loosened at the very sight of the man. But he needed him and his need was becoming all the more desperate as each day passed. If he could not have the woman, could not possess Rosina, her brute of a husband certainly would not.

Mires put out his hand, showing the translucent white object. "See how carefully I have fashioned it...and the hair I obtained. It can not fail."

"I only pray you're right."

"That depends on who receives your prayers. God or..."

Wharton looked away. This was madness. It had begun in Chester with small matters, the removal of inconveniences. Then there had been his promotion; when Mires had got rid of that bully March. It had worked then only too well. March had been found at the bottom of the castle rock, his neck broken.

Wharton looked at the object. He hardly dared to touch it. It had seemed like a game back then, the answer to his problems but now... There were tales that the devil had brought Mires back from the dead. Wharton was a hardened soldier; he had seen many things in the course of his life. But Mires frightened him.

Take it," Mires hissed. Wharton did as he was told and took the cold waxy thing in his hand. "You know what to do, do you not?"

Wharton knew. He nodded and pushed three gold coins towards his visitor. Soon Rosina would be in his bed, would be his. It was worth it for that prospect.

"Have you any news on the other matter?"

Wharton shook his head. "Not yet. You must be patient. These things cannot be hurried."

Mires, who had kept his hood up throughout the transaction, took the coins from the table and left the room silently. Wharton sat down and poured himself another drink to steady his nerves.

It was late afternoon when Mires slipped from the castle. The streets were quiet now after the excitement of the beggars' procession. He knew they would be spending their alms in the ale houses that night before taking unoffered accommodation in barns and outhouses, then moving off to another town or village the next day. Some of the beggars were lounging on the steps of the high cross accosting passers by, the constables not daring to confront them for fear of their numbers.

But the one Mires feared was not amongst them. With any luck he would be gone with the rest of the group at dawn to test the bounty of some other town. Mires ignored their whining requests as they stretched out their hands for a coin, and made his way purposefully past the white cross to the Old Hall.

CHAPTER 10

Master Jacob Multhorpe of Manchester was a man who liked his food. The Mermaid suited him well when he came to Liverpool to buy flax to make his cloth. The victuals were excellent and, of course, there were the other attractions...though he took care not to mention these to Mistress Multhorpe when he talked of the place.

The pie had been delicious; well up to Master Turner's usual standard. With good food in his belly and a good deal agreed with Captain Flynn, Jacob felt pleased with himself. He sat back and loosened his belt. Trade was prospering and it was good to get away from Manchester...away from Mistress Multhorpe's nagging tongue.

The journey had been smooth as the weather had held fair. And he enjoyed haggling with the Irish captain with his quick wits and good humour. The price of flax was good and the customs dues small, better than those of Chester. Liverpool, as many Manchester merchants were discovering, was a good haven for the man of business.

He rubbed his stomach. He had eaten that pie too quickly and would, no doubt, suffer for his lack of delicacy for the rest of the afternoon. There was one he knew in Liverpool who could make his discomfort disappear; one who could achieve miraculous results with an infusion of herbs. He threw some coins on the table, nodded to the landlord, and went out into the street. He had been to Master Valentine's shop before, always with a successful outcome.

The apothecary was there in the shop and gave him a friendly greeting. "It is good to see you again, Master Multhorpe. I hope your business prospers well." Valentine liked the bluff merchant and enjoyed passing the time of day with him when he visited the port.

"The cloth trade prospers, Master Valentine, as I am sure does the trade in medicines."

"People are always ill, my friend. It is a fact of life. But I hope I find you in good health."

"Apart from my old trouble: Master Turner's excellent pies."

Valentine took a jar down from his shelves. "I have the remedy, although you realise that the solution lies in your own hands. If you would only eat slower, the indigestion..."

"I know...mea culpa. I will take more care next time. How are things in Liverpool. It was late September when I was last here. How is Father James? I thought to see him at the Mermaid."

"Father James is well enough." Valentine thought it best not to mention the priest's indiscreet words at Agnes's funeral. "Though one of the chantry priests of his church, Father Clement, was found in the river. He had been murdered, God rest his soul. Footpads."

"Nowhere is safe, Master Valentine. I always travel with others; it is the only way. There are many out there too idle to work but not too idle to wield a cudgel against somebody's head."

Valentine kept his thoughts to himself. "There are indeed many desperate souls, Master Multhorpe."

Multhorpe paused for a moment, deep in thought. "The dead man, Father Clement, I met him. He was on his way here a few months back. We travelled together on a boat from Chester. He said he was taking up a post in Liverpool, but he said little else. We did not talk much. He preferred the conversation of a pretty girl and I can't say I blame him. When did he die?"

"He was found a couple of weeks ago floating in the river. He had been dead a few days, poor man."

Multhorpe's brow furrowed beneath his thinning hair. He sat for a while, thinking. Suddenly he looked at Valentine and spoke. "I saw him...Michaelmas eve it was. When was he found, did you say?"

"Feast of St. Jerome. The thirtieth; two days after."

"Then I must have seen him just before his death." He leaned forward confidentially. "I did not greet him as we were not on those terms. But I have a good memory for faces. And I particularly noticed because of the company he was keeping."

"What do you mean?"

"I would not have expected a priest to be walking with such a man. But I suppose all souls need saving, do they not, Master Valentine?"

Valentine nodded, wishing Multhorpe would get to the point. "Who was he with?"

Multhorpe drank deeply of the infusion Valentine had made for him and sighed, rubbing his swollen stomach. "They made a strange pair. When you see a priest deep in talk with a yellow haired juggler you can't help but notice."

"If you saw this juggler with Father Clement shortly before his death, doubtless the constables would wish to speak with him," said Valentine practically.

This had not occurred to Jacob Multhorpe. He nodded his head sagely. "That is true, Master Valentine." He leaned forward with the self righteous enthusiasm of the good citizen anxious to be seen doing his civic duty. "I will alert the constables if I should see the fellow again."

"I have a better suggestion, Master Multhorpe," said Valentine calmly. "Send word to me if you see this juggler and I will do whatever is necessary. I am well acquainted with the constables and magistrates of this town."

Multhorpe nodded. Master Valentine was a man to be trusted.

When Valentine reported his conversation with Multhorpe to Katheryn she listened carefully. The yellow haired juggler again. Though what connection he could have with the deaths of Father Clement and Agnes, she could not imagine.

"I have been thinking about Agnes's death," she said, glad to have the opportunity to share her thoughts.

"And have you reached any conclusions?"

"None. There is her lover of course, but all we know of him is that he is bound by a vow of chastity. Until we know his identity..."

"If he was her lover, the father of her child, would he need to ravish her?" said Valentine, matter of factly.

"That is true enough. But still we must find him. You must know the people of Liverpool well."

"Indeed. There are several priests and former monks, myself and Bartholomew the ferryman amongst them, but I think them all honest men."

"What of the priests who might have known Agnes? The priests of Our Lady and St. Nicholas?"

"I cannot see our Father James in the role of libertine," he smiled. "There is Father Nicholas, newly married and much abed with his wife so I hear. There is Master Culver, the master of the school there: he was a monk I believe; but I have heard nothing but good of the man. And Father Clement...but he is dead."

Katheryn shook her head sadly. Father Clement: another hapless victim. There were many tales of travellers and other innocents being killed for a few coins or a decent gown. And evil doers would make no exception for a priest.

"Where did Father Clement live?" she asked.

"He had a small cottage next to Father James's."

"Is it occupied now?"

"Why do you ask?"

"I should like to see it."

Valentine looked at her, puzzled. "But why? It is a simple case. The man was murdered by footpads and thrown into the river, as many have been before him, alas. There is no mystery about it."

"I should still like to see his lodgings."

Valentine was beginning to realise that once Katheryn had something on her mind there was little purpose in argument. With luck it would not take long to satisfy her curiosity. "Very well. I can leave young Ralph to look after the shop."

As he walked with her through the streets it occurred to him that he enjoyed being in her company. But he suppressed this thought and tried to turn his mind to other things.

Father Clement's cottage was a tiny whitewashed dwelling, leaning up against Father James's house like a child against its mother. Katheryn lifted the latch and stepped inside. There was one room with a bed in the far alcove next to a small fireplace. A battered table stood in the middle, and on it stood half a loaf of mouldy bread and a jug of stale ale with bits of blue mould floating on the surface of the liquid. Two stools stood by the table and a high backed chair was drawn up to the ashes of the fire. The only other furniture was a plain wooden cupboard standing against the left hand wall. The walls were lime washed and the earth floor swept clean but the place had a bare feel. Father Clement had done little to make the cottage his own.

Katheryn opened the cupboard. There were a few books inside of a devotional nature and behind them was a folded square of parchment with a broken seal: a letter. She opened it, read it and passed it to Valentine, who was hovering uneasily behind her. He read the letter reluctantly: he was not comfortable searching other people's quarters...even those of the dead.

There was no salutation. The letter came straight to the point. "I am in need of your services. I shall expect you at the castle at sunset. I remain, sir, your friend, Thadeus Wharton."

"So Captain Wharton was in spiritual need. Surely there is nothing unusual in that. Father Clement often said mass for the garrison. The Molyneux family have their own chaplain but the garrison relies on the services of priests from the town."

"So we have discovered nothing of great interest. Does Father James visit the castle?"

"I believe he does sometimes: more so since Father Clement's death."

"How well do you know Father James?"

"Well enough. He often said mass for us at Birkenhead. There were none of our number who were ordained, you understand. We were all lay brothers, even our prior. Father James has always seemed to me an honest man; good at heart."

"And his speech at Agnes's funeral?"

"We all have our opinions and it takes an honest man to voice them so openly."

"And Father Nicholas, the other chantry priest. What of him?"

"He was a brother at Whalley Abbey; a Cistercian."

"And his character?"

"I know nothing against the man. In fact I have had few dealings with him." He smiled. "He and his wife appear to enjoy good health."

"When did he marry?"

"Two months ago. Her father is a tanner with premises on Moore Street."

"Does Father Nicholas live nearby?

"Very near. In Chapel Street."

Katheryn continued to search the cupboard, looking for any more clues to Father Clement's life in Liverpool. But there was nothing more of interest: a pair of pewter drinking vessels, a pewter plate, a knife, some blank parchment, a couple of sharpened quills and a half empty pot of ink. Father Clement had led an austere life: the sum of his possessions had not increased since his days as a brother at Norton Abbey."

Katheryn looked over at the bed. It was tidily made and looked as if it had not been slept in. The discipline of monastic life must have given Clement the habit of neatness, thought Katheryn.

She took one last look in the cupboard, running her hand against the back of the shelves. There was something wrong here. The place was too bare.

A board at the back of the cupboard was loose. She rattled it, pushing it to and fro. Eventually it slid back, revealing a small hiding hole. Katheryn bent down to see it better. The hole was empty apart from a single small copper coin.

Whatever treasure or secret thing Clement had kept there was gone. They had walked into the cottage freely; maybe others had too and had stolen what money the priest possessed. There was no way of knowing now.

"Come," said Valentine. "I feel uncomfortable intruding on a dead man's privacy."

"You are right as always, Valentine. And there is nothing more to be found. But we know now that Father Clement had connections with Captain Wharton."

"He said mass at the castle. Must you make so much of every innocent thing?" He touched her hand gently and she did not move it away.

"There is something amiss in this town, Valentine, and right now it seems that Captain Wharton is at the centre of it." She moved away towards the door. "And as we are nearby I think we should pay a call on Father Nicholas and his wife."

Katheryn needed an excuse to visit Father Nicholas. She thought it appropriate to buy a few more masses for Agnes's soul. Her conscience still troubled her concerning Agnes. Why hadn't she looked after the girl better when she asked for her help?

Father Nicholas's cottage was no bigger than Father Clement's. It was situated further down Chapel Street at the end of a row of fishermen's' dwellings. Broken fishing nets waiting to be mended lay in front of the cottages like the discarded webs of some giant spider.

The door was answered by a plump dark-haired young woman with a pleasant face. Not everybody, particularly those of a religious vocation, could accept the wife of a priest - and the King's new law forbidding the marriage of priests had made her position illegal. She greeted Katheryn and Valentine civilly but warily, as though she feared their disapproval.

"My husband is at his work," she said, self consciously. "But if you wish to come in..."

They stepped across the threshold. Father Nicholas's wife had endeavoured to make their humble cottage as homely as possible. The rushes were fresh and the wooden furniture, though sparse, was as polished as Mistress Moore's. The smell of fresh baked bread filled the small room and the bed next to fireplace was neatly made up with clean linen.

Father Nicholas was sitting at the table, bent over a piece of parchment. His quill pen scratched as he formed the letters. He looked up at his visitors.

"You must forgive me. I write a letter for one of the townsfolk. His landlord is threatening to increase the rent for his plot on the townfield to an extortionate sum."

"I hope your words move the landlord to justice, Father," Katheryn said with sincerity. "I would buy some masses for the soul of a girl who was buried this morning. Her name was Agnes Moore."

She watched the priest carefully, waiting for signs of guilt. She saw none. He merely nodded as she handed over the coins. "I will indeed pray for her, madam. A tragic business. There is much wickedness in the world."

"There is indeed, sir."

She saw Nicholas glance across at his wife, who smiled back at him affectionately.

"Did you know Agnes Moore, Father?"

Father Nicholas looked up. Something had disquieted him. "No...er...no. I never knew her."

Katheryn politely took her leave. It would be fruitless to question the man further in his wife's presence.

When their visitors had gone, Father Nicholas turned to his wife. "Do they suspect anything, do you think?"

"No, my love." She put her arms about his neck. "They know nothing. All will be well." She began to kiss the back of his neck. He discarded his pen and pushed the parchment aside.

She gently led him to the bed in the corner and began to undress.

CHAPTER 11

The evening meal had been good. Matilda had excelled herself with a fresh salmon, caught in the Mersey that very morning.

"I think it is time I took advantage of my eldest brother's position," Katheryn said, taking a sip of wine. Valentine looked at her warily, wondering what she was planning. "His office as Constable of Beaumaris should ensure that I am not turned out of Liverpool Castle like an inquisitive serving wench."

"Take care, Katheryn. We are seeking a killer, remember. You should not do anything that might endanger..."

"There is little risk to myself. And I do it for Agnes. I let her down so I feel it is my duty to..."

"You have done all anybody could reasonably expect. Leave it to the constables to bring the culprits to justice."

Katheryn snorted with derision. "The constables! They are too busy chasing beggars and cutpurses and dealing with those who have taken too much ale. If a murder is committed and there is no culprit at hand, you know as well as I that the matter is quietly forgotten. What have they been doing to apprehend Agnes's killer? Or Father Clement's? Nothing. It is my duty to do what I can, Valentine. And I will hear no arguments."

Valentine looked at her. Not the first time he noticed that she was an attractive woman; slim, with good complexion and even features, her chestnut hair peeping from the front of her fine linen coif. He could not face the thought of her walking into danger.

But she seemed confident that her family connections would protect her from serious harm...and she could well be right. It would be harder to explain the disappearance of a respected member of the Bulkeley family than that of one of lower social class. Valentine did not agree with this state of affairs - we are all equal in the eyes of God - but this was how the world worked and Katheryn might as well take advantage of it.

"What do you propose to do?" he asked.

"Everything we have heard so far about Agnes's death - and Father Clement's murder - leads us to the castle. Do you not agree?"

Valentine nodded reluctantly. "I know the castle as well as any. Wharton is a tough man - but fair, I should imagine. And his men are a mixture of good, bad and wicked like any other group of soldiers; no better, no worse."

"And the Constable, Lord Molyneux? What kind of a man is he?"

"Absent most of the time in London or at his estate in Sefton. His sons use the castle as their base in the town, however. The elder, Thomas, seems well enough; but the younger, Edward, is said to like his pleasures. I know of no facts, you understand. I only repeat what I hear."

"Gossip, my friend, is the best source of information. I found out years ago when I was a young novice that it pays to know what is going on in the world. Tell me more of Edward."

"He is young. He likes his wine and the ladies of the town. Honestly, Katheryn, I hardly know anything of the man..."

"But what have you heard?"

Valentine looked sheepish. He was loath to slander a man without evidence. "I have no reason to believe the tales."

Katheryn was becoming impatient. "What tales. Tell me, Valentine. Whatever you say will go no further, I assure you."

"I have heard that he entertains ladies at the castle, in his chamber. There has been talk of..." Valentine blushed, clearly embarrassed. "There has been talk of more than one lady at a time."

Katheryn resisted the impulse to smile at Valentine's embarrassment. "There is no need to say more, Valentine. I understand. Such things go on, I believe. I have even heard rumours of monasteries where..."

"Surely not."

"When the commissioners came to Godstow, I overheard much. Though I am sure they exaggerated the amount of licentiousness that occurred in some religious houses. After all, they had to have some excuse to throw us out of our establishments, did they not?"

"Nothing of that sort went on at Birkenhead, I assure you."

"I am sure nobody would suggest that it did, Valentine. But the temptations of the flesh are always with us." She stood up. "I will go to the castle tomorrow and ask to speak to Lord Molyneux; or in his absence, one of his sons."

"I am coming with you, Katheryn. You cannot go alone."

"I do not intend to. Jane and Will will accompany me. You must stay here as the sick of Liverpool may have need of you and I shall report all when I return."

"Katheryn, take care."

"I shall, Valentine. And pray that I discover something of relevance."

The castle loomed before them. Katheryn strolled boldly to the gatehouse and gave her name. The guard, bowing, hurried off to see if Sir Thomas would receive her.

It wasn't long before Will and Jane were offered refreshment in the kitchens and she herself was escorted across the bustling castle courtyard to the great hall. An impressive chamber, its great stone walls were hung with shields and tapestries and its stone flagged floor was strewn with rushes that could boast of being fairly fresh. A huge fireplace almost filled one end of the room; the royal and the Molyneux coats of arms carved above. This hall was for the Molyneux family and their guests, not for the common soldiers.

Katheryn was not kept waiting long. A dark haired man in his mid twenties strode into the room and bowed with perfect politeness.

"Lady Katheryn, this is an honour. If I had known you were in Liverpool, I should have invited you to dine at the castle. You must think us lacking in manners."

"Not at all, Sir Thomas."

"How is Sir Richard, your brother? Beaumaris is a fine castle is it not? Much larger than our humble defences here on the Mersey."

"It is indeed, Sir Thomas, and my brother is well, I thank you. I am sorry your father is not here. I should have liked to pay my compliments to Lord Molyneux."

"He will be sorry not to have greeted you himself, my lady. But I trust I shall do in his stead." He poured her a goblet of very fine claret. Katheryn noticed that his manners were impeccable. "Is this your first visit to Liverpool, my lady?"

"It is. But I have been here a while."

"It is a pity then that you have left it so long before visiting our castle."

Katheryn smiled. Sir Thomas had not been told of her earlier visit with Valentine. Why, she wondered had Captain Wharton kept it quiet? Sir Thomas bade her sit. His expression was serious. Here was a young man who didn't take life lightly, she thought...unlike his younger brother.

She explained her business and watched Sir Thomas's expression when Agnes's name was mentioned. He made the usual noises of sympathy but it was obvious the name Agnes Moore meant nothing to him. She felt a pang of disappointment. Her journey was wasted. It would, perhaps, have been better to concentrate on Captain Wharton.

"I should be honoured if you would join me for supper one evening if you plan to stay in Liverpool. I am away on my father's business for a few days but I return on Sunday." He looked slightly embarrassed. "We sorely lack good society here at the castle. Liverpool is hardly London."

"You know London well, Sir Thomas?"

"I have had the honour of being at court with my father, my lady."

"You are acquainted with Master Thomas Cromwell, by any chance?"

Sir Thomas gaped with awe. "All men know Master Cromwell. But to be in his service is to be at the heart of government and I have not yet..."

"Of course." Sir Thomas Molyneux, Katheryn suspected, was an ambitious young man.

"Are you yourself acquainted with Master Cromwell, my lady?"

"Master Cromwell and I have exchanged many words," she said, smiling. She was giving nothing more away. Let Sir Thomas remain impressed: it would be to her advantage. She changed the subject. "You have a brother, I believe. I wonder if he would be able to help me in this matter."

"That I doubt, my lady." His lips tightened with disapproval. "My brother would not concern himself with ladies of virtue. His taste is for the other kind...if you will forgive my bluntness."

Katheryn nodded. She had omitted any details of Agnes's recent indiscretions, mentioning only that she had been a novice in her charge and had gone missing.

The door of the great hall opened and a young man stood on the threshold. He bore a resemblance to Sir Thomas and shared his colouring, but he was smaller in stature and his features were more delicate. He was more richly dressed than Thomas, with a fine gown of slashed velvet. This, she guessed, was Sir Edward. Seeing that his elder brother was engaged, Edward swiftly withdrew, closing the door behind him. Katheryn stood up.

"I thank you for your hospitality, Sir Thomas, and I look forward to our next meeting."

Sir Thomas bowed deeply and escorted her across the courtyard. She had hoped to go out alone, maybe to find Sir Edward, but she should have anticipated that Sir Thomas would not abandon etiquette. He was a man destined for the King's court.

The guards, who had been slouching against the gatehouse, pulled themselves up to attention as Sir Thomas kissed Katheryn's hand. She bade him farewell with dignity and beckoned to Jane and Will to accompany her.

"Did you find out anything, my lady?" asked Jane when they were out of earshot.

"Nothing at all, Jane. But I did get a look at Sir Edward Molyneux: and I do have an invitation to dine at the castle so all is not lost."

In the small whitewashed cottage in Chapel Street, Father Nicholas picked up the leather pouch and looked at it. His wife, standing behind him, kissed his neck sensuously, taking his mind off what he had to do.

He turned and took her in his arms. How had he ever thought he could lead a life of chastity? He had first discovered the pleasures of the flesh as a novice, when one of the older monks of his house had taken him to a tavern. What he had tasted in a chamber above the inn with a young redhead, he had been unable to abandon.

Then, a few months back, he had met Mary, the tanner's daughter when she came to him for help in drafting a letter. From that time on the prospect of marriage had begun to have its attractions. And now he was glad he had repented of his licentiousness and taken St. Paul's advice that it was better to marry than to burn. Mary, with her soft skin, eager lips and talent for thrifty housekeeping, suited him well.

He kissed her, letting his hand travel slowly down to her breast. "I must go, Mary. I must go to the Captain. He will be waiting."

Mary moved away reluctantly. Must you go?"

"I must, my love. I do it for us."

"But is it not dangerous?"

"Everything has its dangers nowadays. We must just pray that I shall not be apprehended."

Mary turned away and said nothing more. She would be on her knees in front of the statue of the Virgin that stood in a niche in the corner of the room, praying until her husband's return. He slipped out into the street, shutting the door quietly behind him and hurried down Chapel Street towards the Strand.

His footsteps slowed as he reached the sand and he covered his nose against the stench of rotten fish as he passed the foot of the Tower. The Captain had said he would meet him at the end of Bank Street. The afternoon strand was quiet apart from a few groups of fishermen who were too preoccupied with their business to notice a lone priest in a threadbare gown.

The Captain was not there. Nicholas looked round. Maybe he'd misunderstood; perhaps he waited in the wrong place. Then a young man in sailor's dress half walked, half ran down the jetty and Nicholas stepped forward expectantly. The man greeted him, looking about him as he spoke.

"Father Nicholas?" His English was not good and his accent was almost impenetrable. "Captain Sanchez...he no come...you come Friday...yes?"

Father Nicholas fingered the object inside the pocket of his gown. "Yes. You tell the Captain I will be here."

When the sailor had given a toothless grin, and departed, Father Nicholas almost ran home across the sand, anxious to get back to Mary...and their bed.

CHAPTER 12

When the band of beggars had passed through the town, the beggar with one hand had been tempted to leave with them; to enjoy some fellowship and share in their pickings. But he knew he had to stay in Liverpool now that he had seen the man in the brown cloak. He had to find out if it was really Mires...or if he had been mistaken.

The girl he had followed to the castle that night had been found dead and he felt that he must stay to find out the truth before more innocents suffered harm. But had the girl been innocent? She had been the creature's whore He had watched them together through the window...had seen her lie beneath him, her legs apart and her skirts up, giving herself willingly. Now she was dead: and perhaps she had got what she deserved.

The beggar huddled against the bales of hay stacked in the Mayor, Master Crosse's barn. He had been fortunate to discover this haven. There were many in his situation who would dearly love to bed down in dry straw.

Suddenly, with a great crash, the huge barn doors opened. The beggar moved quickly and sunk himself down deep behind a pile of hay. The straw stuck into his flesh as he kept perfectly still, his heart beating fast, hardly daring to breath.

There were men - a number of them by the sound of it - calling to each other, shouting remarks. He could hear their banter; the ribald remarks about the women they had met with at the tavern and about Master Crosse's daughters. Their master could not have been within earshot or they would have been lucky to have escaped with a whipping. From their talk, he gathered that they were taking a proportion of the hay to place in the tithebarn...but that Walton church would not be the recipient of Master Crosse's bounty. The Molyneux had bought the tithes of Walton church some time ago.

It was the dog that gave him away. A great grey brute of a thing, scampering over the hay as the men worked to fork it out of the barn and onto the waiting carts. The dog approached the beggar, wagging its tail and enjoying its private game. Each time it came up to him with its wet inquisitive nose, he tried to push it away. But this seemed to encourage it further. Then, tired of rejection, the dog started to bark loudly.

The beggar tried to bury himself further in the hay, burrowing like a mole to avoid detection. But he wasn't quick enough. One of the workers, a big man with lank blond hair that hung about his face, accentuating his neanderthal features, decided to investigate and had his pitchfork held ready to dispatch whatever sort of vermin was exciting the dog. But he had not expected vermin of the human kind.

He looked at the desperate beggar in disbelief before making a half hearted lunge at him with the pitchfork. The beggar hastily gathered up his cloak and his small bundle, stumbled over the hay to the jeers of the men, grateful that they were in a good humour and prepared to let him go without a beating. If it had been earlier in the day and their wits had not been dulled by the contents of the leather bottles they carried with them, he might not have escaped uninjured.

He stumbled away from the barn, running until the men were out of sight and he was sure that nobody followed him. His heart beat so fast he was sure it would burst within him and he sat down against the wall that marked the boundary of the Crosse Hall lands longing for a drink. He still had four pence left so he would make for the town and buy refreshments.

But he had lost his makeshift lodgings and he needed a safe base if he was to continue to watch. And watch he must...until the affair was ended one way or the other.

The beggar had filled his belly with warm stew and good ale, purchased with the charity of a rotund burgess of Liverpool who had been on his way home from the Mermaid in a warm ale-glow of benevolence. Now to find somewhere to lay his head for the night. Anywhere warm and dry would do; anywhere out of the damp night air and biting river winds.

He walked down the quiet evening streets towards the townfield. There were barns there - shelters for the animals - and no inquisitive human eyes: all work on the burgesses' plots would have been abandoned by sunset. Now - in between the curfew and the hour when the taverns spewed forth their night time drinkers - was the best time to look for a bed without interference.

He passed the Old Hall, his cloak pulled around him, keeping against the high stone wall that edged the garden of the big house. The first building he saw as he reached the open expanse of the townfield was the old empty mill.

His heart beat faster. There was a time, a few weeks back, that he had seen the one he feared at the mill's entrance, probably waiting for the girl. But now all was quiet and he moved silently, pushing open the disintegrating wooden door. He looked about and he could just make out a ladder in the dim light. The upper storey would be more comfortable and would make discovery less likely. He climbed the ladder carefully, testing each rung, and to his surprise it was intact. This was better than he'd hoped. And he found that the boards of the first floor were covered with straw: to the beggar with one hand this was luxury fit for the King himself.

He settled himself against a pile of filthy sacks and prepared for sleep. There were noises; but then there were always noises in such places where rats and mice scampered to their hearts content, unbothered by humans or cats. After a while, exhausted, the beggar with one hand drifted into a deep dreamless sleep.

Mires watched the beggar from behind the pile of hay in the corner of the mill's upper chamber. He looked round the small room he had made for himself, with its straw pallet and hay bale walls. It was such a perfect hiding place. It was a pity that it had to be abandoned.

Mires sat in his straw-lined cell, stock still, desperate to empty his bladder. When he heard the gentle snores of the one handed beggar, he pushed out a hay bale as carefully as he could and crept past the sleeping man and out into the night.

It was then the idea came to him. If the beggar's body was burned - unrecognisable - then the matter would be closed, the problem solved. Mires pulled a small tinder box from the pocket inside his cloak and went to work. With all that straw, the mill should burn well. He said a silent goodbye to the beggar who was soon to perish, and hoped that his soul would burn in hell as his body would burn on earth. Mires did not stay to see the result of his work but made for the castle...and safety.

It was the smoke that awakened the beggar. And the crackling of flames from somewhere below. His eyes stinging, he rushed for the ladder but the heat drove him back. Then, like a moth, he made for the silvery moonlit square of the window. He could not see what was below but, with a quick prayer, he jumped.

The old mill, now a tower of flame, began to collapse and crumble. Sailors on the ships moored on the river Mersey watched it, fascinated, as it blazed like a beacon against the velvet sky.

Thadeus Wharton could not sleep. So it was with some relief that he rose from his bed in the early hours of the morning, summoned by the message that he had a visitor.

But his heart sank when he saw who was waiting in his private chamber. Something had convinced him that his caller would be Rosina, having left her brute of a husband and come to him at last. During the walk down the chilly stone passageway, he had dared to contemplate the delights that awaited him; Rosina's final surrender in his bed.

Mires was the last person he wanted to see but he would not have dared say so to his face. The man still filled him with an unhealthy fear. With the help of Satan, Mires was capable of anything. Wharton greeted him with a geniality he did not feel.

"My hiding place is discovered. It is burned."

"The old mill?"

Mires turned away impatiently. Why was the man wasting time? "I need somewhere else. Somewhere over the water. I take a risk each time I walk the streets of Liverpool. I know of a place. You must take me there."

"Now?"

"Get your clothes, man. I want to be there before light. And I'll need supplies. Food...candles."

"But..."

"I'll say to you what I said to those men of yours guarding the gate. I could ruin you and this garrison with what I know" He grinned unpleasantly. "I've been of help to many in this castle."

"I shall deny it," Wharton said, suddenly defiant.

Mires put his face close to Wharton's and spoke in a whisper...almost a hiss. "Do not forget, Captain, that I have certain powers. It would not be well to cross me. Do you understand?"

Wharton nodded nervously. I will get my men to fetch provisions and row you over the river. Where is it you would hide?"

"I know of a place. There is a chamber beneath the old Priory that will serve my purpose...for the moment. When my business here is finished I shall leave this cursed town and head for London. You shall hear of me no more."

"And the business...when is it to be?"

"That is your task to find out, Captain. Keep watch and let me know. I wish to know everything. Mark that? Everything."

Wharton nodded again. "And in return?"

"You have your share. And the fair Rosina to enjoy it with."

Wharton smiled to himself. With any luck it would soon be over and his visitor would be but a distant and unpleasant memory.

CHAPTER 13

Katheryn rose early next morning and resolved to go for a walk. She needed to think. Jane insisting on accompanying her and wanted Will to go too as she was still afraid to venture out unprotected in a town. But Will was cutting wood for the fires so Katheryn was firm.

"There are not cut-throats lurking around every corner in Liverpool, Jane." Katheryn said, gently mocking the country girl's fears. "The town is full of ordinary God-fearing folk going about their daily business. We shall be quite safe alone."

"But what about Agnes, my lady? And there was that priest. That makes two people. The town is not safe."

"They were not walking down the strand in broad daylight. Now come, Jane, don't be such a coward."

Jane began reluctantly to walk towards the shore. Katheryn was right, she conceded. No harm could come to them on the strand. The place bustled with sailors about their business and fishermen unloading their catches. Some liveried retainers of Lord Derby leaned against the formidable red stone walls of the Tower chatting with the fishermen and choosing the best of the catch for the tables of their household. On the strand, at least, life continued as normal.

Bartholomew raised a hand in greeting as they passed his jetty. He was busy helping an elderly farmer to load several hens in wicker cages aboard his ferry.

Katheryn turned and they strolled back slowly along the busy sands. As she passed the chapel of St. Mary del Quay her conscience began to trouble her. Recent events had so much taken up her time and thoughts that she had forgotten to say her offices. A few minutes prayer would make up for some of her omissions.

"Why do we not go to the big church, my lady?" Jane asked, curious, when she saw where they were heading.

"This place is more private, Jane. Come, let us go in."

She pushed the ancient door open and paused at the entrance while her eyes adjusted to the gloom.   As she stepped inside there was a banging sound from near the altar. Katheryn could make out a shape: a man. As he walked towards her she could see he was dressed in the gown of a priest. Then she recognised him.

"Father James. Good day to you."

He did not look straight at her but his eyes darted this way and that, as though planning his escape. "Good day, er..."

"I am staying with Brother Valentine. My name is Lady Katheryn Bulkeley. I was formerly Abbess of Godstow." She thought this information might help to gain the man's confidence since she knew his opinions on the fate of the country's religious communities. "I came to Liverpool to help one of my sisters but alas she was buried by you some days since."

His eyes focused on her face and he visibly relaxed. "Of course, madam. I remember you well. You were at Agnes Moore's requiem mass. You are staying in Liverpool for long?"

Katheryn watched his face carefully. "I have resolved to stay until Agnes's killer is discovered."

"It is a terrible thing when violent death comes to one so young and...."

"Innocent, Father? She had a lover. Did you know that?"

Jane stood behind Katheryn studying her feet, embarrassed by her mistress's bluntness.

"I had heard something of the sort. You must excuse me, my lady, I have urgent business."

Father James hurried from the chapel as though the devil himself was after him.

Katheryn turned to her maidservant. "I think something has disturbed Father James, do you not agree, Jane?"

"Surely Agnes would not... I mean...he's old."

"Some women prefer an older man, Jane. Not you or I perhaps, but some. Was it my question that disturbed him, do you think? Or did we startle him before that?"

"I could not tell. But all was not well with him."

"I did not cast him in the role of Agnes's lover. I thought him too passionate about the King's new laws to concern himself with lower things. Maybe I was wrong."

"I do not know, my lady."

"Let us have a quiet time of prayer now, Jane. We will seek God's guidance on these matters."

The two women knelt on the stone floor in front of the statue of the Virgin surrounded by her firmament of glowing candles. As she knelt Katheryn found herself wondering what Father James had been doing behind the altar. Agnes had claimed to see the devil behind that same altar. What exactly was Father James involved in that made him so fearful of discovery....if not murder?

When Father James left the chapel he hurried towards the Mermaid Inn. He ordered ale and sat down by the man he had arranged to meet there.

"How goes it, Father?" Francis Wells, once cellarer of Birkenhead Priory, whispered conspiratorially.

"All is well...and ready. We wait only for Estgate."

"When will he come again?"

"Monday at sunset."

"Let us drink a toast then, Father. To the Brotherhood of the Five Wounds. May we succeed this time where others failed...God rest their martyred souls."

They raised their tankards solemnly and drank.

Wells leaned forward. "And there is further news. One of our brothers stayed at my inn last night. Today he moves up to Lancashire. Support is growing for our cause. He swears that Lincolnshire and Yorkshire are ready to rise up again."

"You are sure?"

"He seemed most certain. And if we can raise Cheshire and Lancashire... You look fearful, Father. You are still with us, I trust?"

"Have I not been faithful, Brother?"

Francis Wells looked at the priest whose face was drawn with strain and worry. "You have, Father. Let us drink another toast." He lowered his voice. "Let us drink to the demise of our sovereign lord King Henry the Eighth. May his soul rot in hell."

Katheryn had resolved to go straight back to Dale Street but as she passed near the Old Hall she noticed the smell of burning hanging in the air. She walked slowly up Mill Street to investigate and looked beyond the main house to where the old mill had stood, now reduced to a pile of smouldering rubble.

Without a word to Jane she approached the great oak front door of the Old Hall and announced herself to the servant. She was ushered into Mistress Moore's presence in the parlour and the lady of the house greeted her warily.

"I see you have had a misfortune, Mistress," Katheryn began.

Marjory looked at her enquiringly, taut with disapproval.

"Your mill. It is burned down."

"It was but a derelict shell, my lady. No great misfortune to lose it. I am sure you didn't come here to discuss my losses."

Katheryn hadn't expected such open antagonism. She chose her words carefully.

"I came, madam, to pay my respects. And to enquire if you have heard anything of Agnes's young man. If he is a sailor of this port then he may return at any time to hear the tragic news," Katheryn said with as much innocence as she could muster. She leaned forward. "Though I did hear a tale that I could scarce believe."

"What is that, pray, my lady?" said Marjory coolly.

"I did hear say that Agnes's lover was a priest. I am sure it is some nonsense dreamed up by an idle gossip. Do you not think, Mistress?"

Marjory nodded curtly, her expression giving nothing away.

Knowing she would discover no more, Katheryn stood. "I will take my leave, madam. Thank you for giving me your time. May God bless you. And I am sure you will join me in praying that Agnes's killer will be brought swiftly to justice."

Marjory made no comment but bade the lady farewell with as good a grace as she could muster and watched her walk off with Jane towards the town.

When they were gone Marjory left the parlour and made a swift reconnaissance of the hallway. The servants were all about their business. How glad she was that they were too occupied to pry into the business of their betters. She walked silently down the kitchen passage and out into the herb garden. John the gardener, she knew, was tending to the new knot garden at the east end of the house. There was nobody about as she let herself out of the wooden gate that led to the mill path. The mill, or what remained of it, smoked and smouldered in front of her. As she drew closer she could still feel the heat. She took up a half charred piece of wood and poked about in the rubble. How easy, she wondered, would it be to find a body after such a fire. Would it be recognisable? Would anything remain at all? She dug the wood into the blackened masonry. There was no sign of any human remains. But then, that might mean nothing.

Marjory Moore threw down the wood and hurried back to the her house before anyone could see her, none the wiser.

Valentine's visits to the sick of the town had taken longer than he had anticipated so he was late returning to Dale Street. He found that he was running short of mint for his medicines: it was time to harvest some more from the well ordered garden at the back of his shop. The commissioners had not objected when he had dug up his herbs from his garden at the priory. They had thought it a harmless and eccentric request: after all, the King could raise no money from a few plants. Their sole interest had been the confiscation of the priory's treasures and the lead from the roofs. But to Valentine the means of healing were far more precious than gold.

He was surprised to find Katheryn helping Ralph in the shop. She bustled round in her plainest gown, fetching and putting away the jars, hanging up bunches of drying herbs, chattering away to the apprentice and asking questions about the various potions on the shelves. She looked up and smiled when Valentine came in.

"I have been making myself useful, Valentine." He eyes were bright. She was enjoying her task. "The shop has been busy while you were out and I thought Ralph needed some help. I hope I have not got in his way."

Ralph shook his head. He had been glad of an extra pair of hands.

Katheryn continued. "I have found it most interesting. You must teach me more about your trade, Valentine. I was too busy at Godstow to take an interest in the infirmary...and Sister Helena, our infirmarian, guarded her secrets jealously."

"I should be glad to show you anything you wish, Katheryn. I had not realised you had an interest in such matters."

"I do not like to be unoccupied and there seems little more I can do to bring Agnes's killer to justice until Sir Thomas returns to the castle. Though I did see Father James this morning: he seemed much disturbed about something."

"Whatever that something is, I am certain it is nothing to do with Agnes's death," said Valentine decisively.

Katheryn nodded, not yet convinced. "And Mistress Moore's old mill is burned to the ground."

"No great misfortune, surely. The place was derelict."

"That's what Mistress Marjory said."

He smiled. "Then she and I agree about something."

Valentine began to gather medicines together and put them in the bag he carried.

"Are you going out again so soon?"

"Alas, I am needed at the Tower. One of Lord Derby's household is sick with the flux."

"May I come with you?"

"The flux is not a pleasant condition."

"I do not mind."

"Do you think I cannot discover anything of the priests who minister to Lord Derby's household without your help?" He grinned at her.

Katheryn knew when she was defeated. He went alone.

It wasn't far to the Tower, home to over a hundred of the Earl of Derby's retainers. It was a square fortified house of rough red sandstone, squatting on the edge of the strand, almost a rival to the castle itself. The Stanleys, Earls of Derby, and the Molyneux had been rivals for as long as the port of Liverpool could remember, each in their respective fortresses, a mere arrow shot apart, while the rest of the town looked on with interest...and occasionally fear.

It was William Staines who greeted Valentine...better known to the apothecary as Brother William, late of Birkenhead Priory. The Earl of Derby's clerk was a tall, dark haired, good looking man in his mid twenties with a velvet gown and confident manner that told of his growing prosperity.

"Valentine...brother. It is good to see you. We are like a town within a town here in the Tower and we keep ourselves to ourselves. It must be almost a year since our paths last crossed."

Valentine smiled. "I am glad you enjoy such good health. You are doing well, I think. Fine gown," he said teasingly.

William took the remark in good part. "I am indeed. His lordship is most generous to those who work hard. You have heard I am to marry?"

The King's new law worried me for a time, but then I asked myself if it was right for a King so much married himself to forbid the marriage of those who once made vows of chastity but who are forced by his laws and actions to live in the world. Besides, who is to know that I was once a monk?" He laughed and patted the rich material of his gown. "Do I look like a monk, eh? The two years I spent at Birkenhead Priory are but a distant memory...and in hindsight I was never well suited to the cloister. Besides, I have the blessing of his lordship and my future father in law so all will be well."

"My congratulations. Who is the lady?"

"Her name is Elizabeth Crosse, a distant relative of Mayor Crosse of Crosse Hall," he added proudly. "Though not so wealthy, alas. But her father is a ship's captain and owns three fine vessels in the port. Captain Crosse is a well regarded man."

"So you marry well?"

"Well enough. And she is young and lively: much to my taste. The past three years have not increased my taste for chastity. And what of you, brother?"

Valentine smiled and shook his head. "I keep to my medicines. Have you seen Brother Bartholomew since last market day?"

"No. I rarely have need to cross the river. Why do you ask?"

"It was last market day that Bartholomew discovered the body of a young woman in the river: Agnes Moore her name was. Did you know her?"

William shrugged, hardly interested. "One of the Moores, eh? Who would have thought one of that family would meet such an end?"

"Who indeed?" Valentine had learned all he needed. William did not know Agnes Moore. "I must see my patient. We must not prolong his suffering."

"Quite right, Valentine. I will take you to him. It is one of his lordship's servants. A young man...strong."

"How is his lordship's chaplain, Father Michael? I have not seen him lately."

"He is much the same, brother, a martyr to his back."

"He came to me a while ago. I could do little for him but prescribe rest and something to kill the pain. He is no better?"

"He - how shall I put it? - takes refuge in his lordship's wine cellars."

"I see." Valentine was silent for a while, contemplating this professional failure. "Tell him to visit me again, William. There may be something more I can do for him."

"I will indeed. But he is a stubborn man, as you know."

They reached the servant's chamber which he shared with several others, and William rushed back to his duties. There was much work for an ambitious man to do.

Valentine tended to his patient, content that his former brother, William, was not Agnes's killer. And as for Father Michael, a man with a sore back does not ravish a young woman and hold her face beneath the water. The riddle of Agnes's death was not to be solved at the Tower.

Mires sat in the crypt beneath the ruins of Birkenhead Priory and shivered. The journey over the river in that tiny craft the night before had chilled him to the bone. And the place was so silent...so empty.

He sat back and assessed his situation. He was rid of the beggar: he congratulated himself on his ingenuity in finding a neat solution to a potential problem. And he had Wharton where he wanted him, frightened and compliant. Soon Mires would be away to London a rich man. What delights would await him there after the dull entertainments Liverpool had to offer.

Now all he had to do was to wait for the traitors to show their hand. He lay back against the flock mattress Wharton had supplied from the castle stores dreaming of London, wealth and, who knew, even a place at court. The King and his ministers were always ready to employ the talents of the ruthless and amoral.

CHAPTER 14

Matilda had just served the mid-day meal when the soldier came. Valentine looked at the thick stew on his bowl. He was hungry but his services were needed at the castle. Torn between the murmuring of his empty belly and the duties of his calling, he decided on compromise. He took several hasty spoonfuls of the stew and asked Matilda to keep the rest warm until his return. Then, breaking off a large chunk of bread from the freshly baked loaf in the middle of the table, he put on his gown and went into the shop to gather together some medicines and bandages.

He had not asked Katheryn to go with him to the castle. She had only just started her meal. So when he had packed his medicines, he was surprised to find her waiting at the door with her cloak thrown around her shoulders.

"I have asked Matilda to keep my meal warm too, Valentine. If you go to the castle, I should like to come with you."

"It is but two of the garrison involved in a fight. There will be broken heads to mend, I expect, but nothing of much interest to you, Katheryn. Are you sure you wish to abandon Matilda's stew and come with me?"

"Quite sure. There is no need to deprive Jane and Will of their meal. We need no servants to accompany us."

Out in the streets, the pie shops were doing good trade, filling the bellies of hungry townsfolk. Savoury smells wafted from food sellers and inns, reminding Valentine and Katheryn of their hunger. The soldier who had been sent to fetch the apothecary led them past the sentry at the castle gate and up stone spiral steps to a roughly furnished dormitory. Valentine went about his business swiftly, patching up the wounds of the groaning soldiers, the reason for their fight forgotten in its aftermath of pain.

Katheryn recognised one of the soldiers. The large mass of

Manners' body lay on his stained pallet. Blood seeped from a wound in his head.

Valentine spoke with professional matter-of-factness. "What was the fight about, my friend?"

It was the other man who answered. He hauled himself upright and looked across at Manners with surprisingly little animosity. The fight had cleared the air. "I told him how that whore he had lost me two shillings."

Valentine smiled. "Oh yes? Let that be a lesson to you then: sin always leads to trouble in the end," he said good-humouredly as he dressed Manners' wound.

The man, who introduced himself as Tilletson, continued. "Manners here had a whore and Sir Edward found him with her and took her for himself. I got sent to guard the gatehouse. I was playing at dice and winning. I lost two shillings by..."

Katheryn, hearing Sir Edward's name, looked up from the jar of ointment she was holding for Valentine. "When was this?"

Tilletson answered. "Last Friday night it was."

Manners suddenly looked uncomfortable as he remembered Wharton's orders not to discuss the matter of Sir Edward's whore. But it was too late: there was no way he could warn Tilletson not to say anything now.

Katheryn turned to Manners and looked him directly in his bloodshot eyes. "I remember asking you sir if you saw a young lady. Were you speaking the truth when you told me you saw no one?"

Manners began to sweat with panic. Tilletson spoke up again. "Of course he saw a woman. He tried to have her...until Sir Edward took her for himself."

"You're wrong. It was a different night, you addle brained son of a pox ridden whore." Manners' agitation made him forget he spoke in front of a lady.

Katheryn smiled sweetly and decided to appeal to his better nature. "Please, Master Manners. It is most important that I know what became of the young lady. Did you see her?

Edward by sheer chance. He saw her, thought her a lady night and took a fancy to her."

"Then why did she go with him willingly?"

"That I do not know. Maybe she knew him. Maybe he was acquainted with her lover or said he was. It's something v must discover. Let us consider what we know of Agnes's lover?" She looked at Valentine.

"Nothing very much. He was bound by a vow of chastity; that is all."

"And was willing to break that vow, do not forget that."

"Can you think of a circumstance where the breaking of the vow would lead to inconvenience? In spite of the new law, priests and former religious now marry quite openly in far flung parts of the country. Father Nicholas is an example. He lives with his wife and still keeps his post."

"Maybe Agnes's lover is married or betrothed already."

"Agnes was unworldly and gullible. If he had said they must keep their love secret because he had vowed never to have dealings with a woman, she would have believed him. Do you not agree?"

Valentine nodded. "Alas, you are probably right. Agnes was an innocent. We live in a wicked world where innocence is so rewarded."

"But who was her lover? He has to live nearby or they would not have met. And she said that she saw him pass her window. Come, let us consider all the priests and monks of this town."

Valentine thought for a moment. "There is Father James of course. Master Culver the schoolmaster has recently come to his post. He was once a monk, although I do not know if he was acquainted with Agnes. And Father Nicholas...he was a Cistercian from the Abbey of Whalley."

"What of Master Culver?"

"He is new to the town, recently come from Yorkshire."

"And his predecessor?"

Captain Wharton need never know that you told the truth, be assured of that."

Valentine ceased his bandaging for a moment, not wishing to distract Manners from any confession.

"She was pretty. I thought her a whore. There are enough of them hang round the garrison for business. I thought she was playing games..."

"What happened?"

"I was, er...talking to her when Sir Edward appears; gives me a right good kick up the backside he did. Anyway, he sends me away; leaves the gate unguarded and says for me to send Tilletson out. Wharton was mad when he found out. I thought he was going to have me hanged for deserting my post. He sends me back and by that time Sir Edward and the, er...young lady were gone. And that's the truth, as God's my witness, Lady. Captain Wharton said I was to tell nobody. He doesn't want to get on the wrong side of his Lordship, you see."

"Did the young lady tell you her name?"

Manners shook his head.

"You did not think to ask?" Katheryn said pointedly.

"Well, er... you don't." Manners looked deflated.

"Did she say why she was here?"

"Said she would speak with Captain Wharton. Didn't say why and I didn't ask. I thought he most likely owed her money...begging your pardon, my lady."

"And did she get to see Captain Wharton? Did Sir Edward take her to him?"

Tilletson shook his head. "No, ma'am. The Captain was playing cards with some of the sergeants. It was a game likely to go on into the night. The Captain was having good fortune with his winnings. I saw him myself when I reported to him. I do not think the girl got to see him but when I was sent to the postern gate, I did see Sir Edward go into the tunnel... and the girl was with him."

"What tunnel?"

"It leads down to the strand." He looked round uncomfortably. "It is hacked through the rock in case of siege. Supplies could come to the castle by water."

"And where does it come out?"

"Near the brothers' old boathouse, just beneath the castle rock."

She turned to Manners. "Did you think that she knew Sir Edward when they met?"

"He shook his head. "I did not think so, ma'am. I think he fancied having a...begging your pardon...whore, just like the rest of us. The girl was pretty and that would have been enough for Sir Edward."

Valentine dressed the wounds in silence. Katheryn had learned all she wanted to know. It was Sir Edward who interested her now.

When Valentine's work was done he packed up his things, ready to go. Manners looked at Katheryn. "I'm sorry if I spoke roughly, ma'am, but I'll get into bother if Captain Wharton thinks I've been blabbing about..."

"You have no need to fear. As I said before, I shall tell no one of what you said." Katheryn thought for a moment. "You are frightened of Captain Wharton?"

Manners looked uneasy. "There are things about the Captain it's better not to ask, ma'am. I just try and keep my head down: that's all a man can do."

The two men lay back on their pallets, the clean white of their dressings contrasting with the grubby grey of the stained sheets. They were simple soldiers who liked their food, their ale and their whores and Katheryn thought it unlikely that they were involved in what had happened to Agnes.

The young soldier who had fetched Valentine from his shop accompanied them as they walked through the busy courtyard towards the gatehouse.

"While I am here, Valentine, I should like to pay my compliments to Sir Edward Molyneux."

"Take care, Katheryn. If he is our killer..."

Valentine looked alarmed as she ignored him and addressed the soldier who was walking in front of them. "I am acquainted with Sir Thomas Molyneux. I am aware that he is away but I would speak with his brother, Sir Edward."

The soldier bowed. "Sir Edward is not in the castle, ma'am and is not expected back until late tomorrow.

Katheryn smiled. She would have to be patient. Sir Edward would have to wait until another day.

Matilda's stew awaited them back in Dale Street, hot and tasty. The visit to the castle had given Katheryn an appetite but had caused Valentine to lose his. He munched on a piece of brown bread while Katheryn talked.

"Come, Valentine. Tell me your thoughts."

He looked up at her. Her eyes sparkled and he found it hard to imagine that she would have chosen freely a life confined in a nunnery. He was not surprised that she had been elected by her sisters to the position of Abbess. There would have been few, if any, in her cloister to match her.

"So Sir Edward is our killer?" he began.

"It is possible. But we must not forget that Agnes asked for Captain Wharton."

"But, according to the soldiers, she never got to see him. Do we tell the constable and have Sir Edward arrested on his return?"

"There is his position to consider. He is Lord Molyneux son. He is no vagabond or beggar who can be thrown into the town gaol on the slightest suspicion. Justice should not depe on wealth and influence, but alas, Valentine, that is the way the world. Before we accuse the man we must be sure of his guilt and we must have proof. Sir Edward cannot have been Agnes's lover. Whatever else the man may be he is no prie nor ever has been. And he would hardly have taken a vow chastity, from what his brother said of him. We must look elsewhere for her leman. From what Manners said she me

"That was Master Chadwick. He disappeared without explanation about three months ago. I have wondered what became of him."

Katheryn looked up with interest. "Was he a priest?"

"He was in holy orders, I believe. He acted as priest in the chantry of St. Catherine as well as his teaching duties."

"And he disappeared you say?"

"He left the town suddenly that is certain."

"I should like to discover more of Master Chadwick. Pray continue your list of holy men," she said with a smile.

"There is Bartholomew of course. And myself," he added seriously. "And the late Father Clement. There is the chaplain of Lord Derby's household at the Tower, Father Michael, who is a likeable man, though fond of his drink and a martyr to his sore back. And one of my brothers from Birkenhead, William Staines, is clerk to Lord Derby...and about to take a wife. I spoke with him when I visited the Tower yesterday."

"And have you reason to suspect any of them?"

Valentine smiled and shook his head. "I know of none who had particular dealings with Agnes. William Staines almost certainly did not know her. He thought it odd that one of the exalted Moores should meet with such an end."

"He may have behaved thus to mislead you."

Valentine shrugged. "It is possible, of course, but I think not."

"And Father Clement? What of him?"

"He is dead. Agnes's lover still lives, as far as we know."

"But had he enemies? Could he have known of Agnes's indiscretions and been silenced? He had dealings with the castle. And your Manchester merchant saw him with that juggler."

"There are other priests who visit the castle regularly. The Molyneux family have their own chaplain but he travels with his lordship so other priests say mass for the garrison. That is why Father Clement had dealings with Captain Wharton. I believe Father Nicholas visits the castle occasionally; and Master

Culver, the schoolmaster, when his duties permit; and Father James too."

"Can you think of anyone else in the town?"

"If we are listing all the priests in the district there are the vicars of nearby villages and their curates and chantry priests and..."

"Stop, Valentine, it is too much. I had not realised there would be so many. Let us keep to those in the town who were likely to be acquainted with Agnes."

"Where shall we begin?"

"I shall visit the school. I have not yet made the acquaintance of Master Culver."

"You suspect him?"

"How will I know until I have spoken with him, Valentine. Let us consider the facts." She took a deep breath. "Agnes has a lover she keeps secret because he cannot or will not marry her. She finds herself with child and she is attacked in the chapel of St. Mary del Quay. Was it the lover who attacked her, hoping to cover his indiscretions by her death?"

Valentine made no answer. She continued. "The lover makes no effort to find out what has become of her. That indicates his guilt, do you not think? Then she sees him from the window. What was he doing near the Old Hall? Then she goes to the castle and asks for Captain Wharton but goes off with Sir Edward. Why?"

"And who killed Father Clement? And why was his right hand hacked off?"

Katheryn looked up sharply. "His right hand? You didn't mention that."

"Father Clement was found with his right hand roughly hacked off at the wrist."

"If they wanted rings they would just have cut off the fingers, surely."

"That's what I thought. But there are other reasons for obtaining the hand of a dead man."

"What other reasons?"

"The dead man's hand is valuable in certain ceremonies held by those who worship Satan, Katheryn. I fear to think such things go on in Liverpool. This is more than just some old crone making love philtres. I detect the presence of true evil here and it frightens me."

"Agnes said she saw the devil and Griselda spoke of Satan in the old mill that is burned." She shook her head. "I do not understand all this. The devil himself...and all these priests..."

Valentine laughed. "The town is full of them when you start to consider. I sometimes feel it would be better for the King's safety if they were all confined to their monasteries instead of walking free giving the King's subjects ideas of dissent."

"You agree with their ideas?"

"I am no Father James. I keep silent and wait for better times."

"As do we all. I saw Father James in the Mermaid with a man. They had the manner of conspirators and if I noticed it I am sure others did. I fear for his safety."

"Whatever he is involved in, it is better for us not to know." He stood up. "What say you we take Brother Bartholomew's ferry over to Birkenhead and visit our Prior. He will be glad of the company and he may know the whereabouts of more of my brothers."

"Are there any brothers in particular you would suspect of such things? You must know them well. Can you see any in the role of Agnes's lover?"

"There might be one or two; but I would not name them, you understand. And there is Norton Abbey further down the river. Many brothers of that house must have found posts as curates and chantry priests nearby. I thank God that the chantry chapels provide employment for those ejected from the monasteries. There will always be those glad to pay for prayers to be said for the souls of their loved ones."

"Let us hope the King does not turn his greedy eyes towards them. It would not surprise me if he looked to them next when he has spent the treasure from the monasteries."

"Do I detect a hint of treason there, Katheryn?"

"I am saying nothing, Valentine." She smiled. "Let us go and seek out Bartholomew. A trip across the river is just what I need to clear my head. All this thinking is making my senses spin."

Katheryn had heard that many experienced an unpleasant feeling of nausea when travelling by boat: she was glad she was not one of them. She found the sail across the Mersey in the open craft exhilarating and she enjoyed the feel of the chill wind on her face.

When they reached Birkenhead and the other passengers left the boat, she and Valentine hung back to talk to Bartholomew who was tying his ferry to a stout wooden post on the end of the jetty. Katheryn shivered. It seemed colder on shore without the excitement of the wave tossed journey to distract her and she was glad of her warm woollen cloak with its fur lining.

"Have we far to walk?" Katheryn asked.

"No. The Prior has not moved a great distance from his old home."

Valentine and Katheryn walked past the deserted shell of the priory. It stirred memories for Katheryn that she would prefer to forget. How many more memories, she thought, would the weathering stones hold for Valentine and Bartholomew who had spent the best part of their lives there?

They came to a small stone built manor house, comfortable but by no means ostentatious. An elderly man was cutting wood in the courtyard and Valentine recognised him as one of the priory servants. The man's eyes lit up at the sight of one of the brothers returning to see his prior and he greeted him like a long lost friend, taking his hand and shaking it for a full two minutes whilst exclaiming how well the brother looked in his new gown. He introduced Katheryn as the Abbess of Godstow and the servant, pathetically impressed bowed low and said he would announce them to the Prior.

"The changes have been too much for old Meading. Half the time he believes the priory is still in existence, poor man," Valentine whispered as the servant disappeared into the house. "I am glad to see Prior Sharp has taken him into his household."

The old man almost ran back to tell them that Father Prior would be delighted to receive them and that he would fetch refreshments immediately. They were led into the Prior's parlour where he awaited them, warming his backside by a roaring fire. He too greeted Valentine like an old friend.

"Brother, I cannot say how pleased I am to see you. I get so little company here. My brothers are all busy with their own lives in the outside world and..."

"May I introduce Lady Katheryn Bulkeley, formerly Abbess of Godstow, who is my guest over in Liverpool."

The Prior gave Valentine an enquiring look then bowed low to Katheryn. "I am most delighted to meet you, my lady. I assume your house has met the same fate as my own?"

Katheryn nodded. "I held out for as long as I could but I had no wish to anger Master Cromwell more than was necessary as I was afraid my sisters would pay for my defiance."

"I am glad of civilised company, my lady. It was a condition of my receiving this house and my pension that I engage in no form of employment and I do miss my brothers although they visit me from time to time. A few have gone to our order's abbey at Chester - that still has not been closed, though it is only a matter of time I fear."

"I saw Brother William a few days back."

Prior Sharp looked disapproving. "I hear he is about to break his solemn vows and take a wife."

"But he looks well on it, Father Prior - and his intended wife is a maid of virtue."

"You approve, Brother Valentine?"

"Marriage is a sacrament, Father. Surely better that than to indulge in sin."

The Prior nodded sadly. Katheryn studied him. He was a small shrivelled man in his sixties. He wore a long plain black gown, as much like a monk's habit as he could manage without resorting to the genuine article.

"And our Brother Bartholomew of course. He brought us over here today."

"He is a good boy; a true brother. I pray he is not distracted by the desires of the flesh."

"No indeed," Katheryn said solemnly, trying to hide a smile. It was clear Prior Sharp had quite decided views on the desires of the flesh. She changed the subject, explaining her presence in Liverpool and the reason for their visit. The Prior's eyes, sunk as they were in the wrinkled flesh of his face, lit up with interest.

"I will pray that you catch the poor sister's killer. The desires of the flesh are responsible for much of the evil in the world. Our present sad condition was brought about by such desires, you do realise that, my lady. When the King was struck with lust for that Boleyn woman and left his lawful and virtuous wife, the late Queen Katherine, just look what it led to." The Prior sat down, unable to contemplate the desires of the flesh in an upright position for much longer.

"We wondered, Father, if there were any of our brothers living close by, other than the ones I already know of. I should like to contact them very much. I too miss my brothers." He glanced at Katheryn, who smiled to herself at his subterfuge. This request would go down better with Prior Sharp than a suggestion that one of his former monks may be a killer.

"There were but sixteen of us, brother. As I said four went to Chester; Brothers Bartholomew and William you know of. Brother Francis our cellarer runs an inn nearby, and runs it well by all accounts. Brother John, I understand, has a post as schoolmaster in the town of Warrington. Brother Anselm has a post as a clerk in Chester. The others, I fear, are scattered.

They received their forty shillings and their new gowns and went on their way without a word to anyone. It is a sad end to a way of life, is it not, brother?"

"I am sure they will prosper, Father." Valentine said comfortingly to the old man who had had to watch all he had worked for destroyed in a matter of weeks.

"And you, brother? How does your trade fare? You were always skilled at healing...a true gift from God. I hope you use it well."

"I try to Father." He looked across at Katheryn. "We must go and catch the tide. I thank you for receiving us. It has been good to see you again."

Prior Sharp took Valentine's hand as if reluctant to let him go. His now empty life had been temporarily lightened by this visit from one who reminded him of past contentment. He bowed to Katheryn and said that he hoped they would call on him again. As they stepped out into the courtyard, it began to drizzle. Katheryn put her hood up against the damp air.

"Poor man," she said when they were out of earshot of the ancient servant who saw them off the premises. "The ruins of his priory must always remind him of what he had lost."

"He has changed, Katheryn. He used to be an enthusiastic man, always ready to encourage and correct. He has lost all his spirit. I was shocked to see him thus. He deserves better. Come, let us seek out Brother Francis's inn. It is not far away."

The Priory Arms, as its name suggested, was on the fringe of the priory lands, near a small village populated by workers who once made their livings on the priory estates. Valentine hoped that their new landlord would be as benevolent as the brothers had been.

The inn was low and thatched and seemed to be fairly full for the time of day. The floor was clean and well swept and the furniture plain but plentiful and in good repair. Valentine stepped over the threshold first but he felt someone pulling him back. Katheryn had hold of his cloak. She stood on tiptoe behind him and whispered in his ear.

"Come away. I do not wish him to see me." Valentine looked into the inn. He could see the portly Brother Francis Wells pouring ale from a barrel on the great table that stood opposite the door. "That man...I saw him in the Mermaid deep in conspiracy with Father James. I think it best he does not see me here: he may think I spy on him. Is he your Brother Francis?"

Valentine nodded, not quite understanding, but he indulged Katheryn's misgivings for the moment. They turned away from the inn and headed back for the ferry.

As they passed the priory church, they were surprised to see Captain Wharton emerge from behind the wall of the south transept. He had seen them; there was no way they could avoid this meeting...nor did Katheryn want to.

"Good day to you, Captain. I had not expected to see you in such a place. Are you checking that the King's commissioners have done their work thoroughly?"

He missed the humour of her question and looked alarmed. "No indeed, madam." He then stopped, lost for words. It was clear he had no explanation for his presence.

Katheryn looked down at the small sack he carried. "You are taking the air, Captain? I hope the drizzle will not spoil the meal you have brought with you."

Once more the Captain looked uncomfortable and attempted an awkward smile. What, Katheryn wondered, was he doing in such a place? She was intrigued and couldn't resist unnerving him further.

"Captain Wharton, are you certain you are not acquainted with the young lady I mentioned the other day...Agnes Moore from the Old Hall? Maybe you have had time to search your memory?"

For a moment Wharton looked relieved. "No, ma'am, I assure you I've never heard of the young lady."

He nodded curtly, desperate to get away. The sun was trying to set and Mires would be waiting. To his relief Katheryn and Valentine bid him good day and took the path to the ferry.

Those two asked too many questions. But he hesitated to mention them to Mires. He wished them no harm...as yet.

Captain Wharton entered the shell of the church and strode across to what was left of the cloister. In the north wall was a small door, hidden by the encroaching vegetation. The door opened smoothly to reveal a narrow flight of worn stone steps and Wharton took a deep breath, hoping his fear did not show. He went down carefully into the crypt, holding the sack of provisions in his left hand and steadying himself with his right.

Wharton's eyes slowly accustomed themselves to the dark and he could just make out the pillars and the vaulted ceiling. A cloaked figure rose in the shadows and Wharton shuddered involuntarily.

The shape spoke. "So you've come at last, Wharton. I hope you have brought me all I need."

Father Nicholas ignored his wife's advice and went to the strand to seek out the captain of the Santa Isabella in daylight.

The priest stood on the jetty under the bulk of the great wooden merchantman, conscious of the activity going on around him. Dark haired, sun bronzed men, shivering in their inadequately thin clothes made for a warmer climate, loaded barrels and boxes into the ship's hold, supplies for their homeward journey to their native land. Father Nicholas asked one of the men if Captain Sanchez was on board but the man, having no English, gibbered back at him in an incomprehensible foreign tongue.

At last he spied the captain up on the richly carved forecastle. He was a tall, dignified man with a natural air of authority. The sailors worked silently under his supervising gaze as they loaded the ship's cargo.

Nicholas, desperate to complete their transaction, forgot that fact that he had no wish to draw attention to himself and called up. "Captain Sanchez. Good day to you, sir. May I speak with you?"

The captain peered down at him from his lofty position and nodded. He signalled to one of his officers who led Father Nicholas up the unsteady gangplank onto the ship.

The details were soon agreed. Nicholas found Sanchez a most efficient man to do business with: a man who knew what he wanted.

An end was in sight. Soon Nicholas would not have to look over his shoulder. On Monday evening he would complete his business with Captain Sanchez before the Santa Isabella sailed back to Cadiz.

Nicholas strode back up the strand towards the church, his eyes on the fishermen and their nets. He knew that the river claimed many lives when the currents ran fast. If any drowned bodies had been brought ashore, he would offer his services. The more who were claimed by the Mersey's treacherous tides, the more masses he would be paid to say. The river, in many ways, was a friend to Father Nicholas.

"Good day to you, Father Nicholas."

Nicholas jumped at the mention of his name and looked round guiltily to see who addressed him. Katheryn stood there, smiling pleasantly, refreshed after her journey back across the river. Nicholas bowed his head, his eyes darting, looking for escape.

"You are well, I trust? And your wife?"

"Indeed, madam, we are in good health I thank you."

"The day has turned out fair has it not?"

Nicholas was in no mood for small talk. He had duties to perform, masses to say, candles to replenish in his chapel. He shuffled his feet nervously. "If you will forgive me, madam, I have much work to do." He bowed quickly and set off, half running, towards the church.

Katheryn turned to Valentine who was hovering behind her. "That makes two men we have disquieted today. First Captain Wharton on the other side of the river and now Father Nicholas. Are we so fearsome, do you think, or have they some dealings they would rather keep secret?"

Valentine laughed. "I suspect the latter. Did you see Father Nicholas was speaking with that foreign captain? He looked too anxious for one arranging to say a mass or two."

"We shall have to watch our Father Nicholas. He has something to hide certainly."

"Perhaps he fears that we disapprove of his marriage. You cannot suspect that he was Agnes's lover, surely."

"Until we know the truth, Valentine, we must consider all possibilities. What if he killed Agnes and he now tries to obtain passage on a ship to leave the town before he is discovered?"

Valentine sighed. The thought had crossed his mind. They would have to watch and wait.

As they reached the church of Our Lady and St. Nicholas, Katheryn turned towards the gate.

"We cannot go in, Katheryn. Father Nicholas will think we follow him. If we are to discover anything he must be at his ease."

"It is not Father Nicholas I would see," she said. "I have a desire to see the school. It is held in the chapel of St. Catherine I believe."

"The schoolmaster will not thank you for distracting his pupils."

"Then I shall watch unseen. I would speak with Master Culver. He was in holy orders was he not?"

"Yes. He still performs the duties of chantry priest when his commitments allow. But the boys occupy most of his time, you understand."

"You know him well?"

"Not well. He is new to the town and has enjoyed good enough health to need my services but once. He seems to me an amiable man."

They entered the church by the great oak door. Incense lay heavy in the air and the only sound that could be heard in the echoing building was the drone of latin verbs being chanted in the far chapel. There was no sign of Father Nicholas. Katheryn led the way to the far end of the church where the partitioned chapel of St. Catherine was occupied by a huddle of chanting schoolboys, their master standing before them, stick in hand.

Katheryn and Valentine hung back behind the partition and were relieved to hear that their wait would not be long. The schoolmaster was instructing the boys to go outside and run off some of their pent up energy in the churchyard; but to be mindful of the fact that he didn't want to have to treat any broken heads or damaged limbs. The master, Katheryn thought, had a pleasant way with the boys. He called their names: Robert Crosse....John Crosse....Richard Crosse....Were they all called Crosse, Katheryn wondered.

This was the first thing she asked Master Culver when he emerged from the chapel after instructing his charges not to run in the church. "William Crosse," he called out. "Remember you are in the house of God."

"Are all your pupils called Crosse?" asked Katheryn. The schoolmaster swung round. He had not seen her waiting there. He smiled and his pale face lit up. He was a thin man in his late twenties with an amiable twinkle in his dark blue eyes.

"Indeed, madam. It was a stipulation of the will of the late Master John Crosse of Crosse Hall, that a school be founded in his chantry chapel and that boys of the name of Crosse should receive a free education. There are boys with other names, but most are Crosse. I hope our Latin did not disturb your prayers."

"You need have no worries about that, sir. It is good to see the boys so hard at their tasks. You clearly enjoy your work."

"They are good boys; a little boisterous at times like all boys. But, yes...I do enjoy my work."

"Have you always taught, sir?"

"I was a monk of Riveaux in Yorkshire; then I was chantry priest in Chester when my house closed. My family came from that town so I returned there. I heard of this appointment when the last master left and was keen to do more than say masses all day."

Valentine spoke for the first time. "You have a true vocation for teaching, Master Culver, that is clear."

The schoolmaster looked at him with recognition. "It is good to see you again, Master Valentine. You are well, I trust? With God's grace I have enjoyed good health since we last met so I have not had need of your services."

Valentine nodded. Katheryn nudged him, keen to continue her questions. "This lady is Lady Katheryn Bulkeley...formerly Abbess of Godstow."

Master Culver bowed to Katheryn. "This is indeed an honour, my lady."

"I came to Liverpool to the aid of one of my sisters, a young novice named Agnes Moore. Did you know her?"

"Was that the poor girl who was drowned? I did not know her. I am acquainted with the Moore family by reputation of course even though I have been in the town but a short time, but I did not have the honour of knowing Mistress Agnes."

Katheryn nodded. Was the man was telling the truth? His easy manner and the assumption that Agnes was a respected member of the Moore family indicated that he was. If he had been intimately acquainted with the girl he would have known the truth of her situation... But perhaps that was what she was meant to think.

Valentine asked the next question. "What of your predecessor? Father Chadwick was it not?"

"I know little of him except what Father James and the boys have told me. He was over strict, it seems. The boys came to school each day fearing a beating. He left the town three months back but I do not know what became of him."

"Do you say mass at the castle for the garrison there?" asked Katheryn casually.

"I have done so on occasions when I am free of my duties here and there is no one else to render that service." He smiled. "The payment is most welcome. I will never make my fortune as a schoolmaster."

"And did Father Chadwick visit the castle?"

"I believe so, yes."

Katheryn thanked the schoolmaster and made her way out of the church, avoiding the boys in the churchyard who were running, shouting and whooping amongst the grave slabs and wooden crosses.

"I do not think our Master Culver had anything to do with Agnes's death but I may be mistaken." She thought for a moment. "And Father Chadwick. If he did not leave the town..."

"If he had not left the town it would be known. Liverpool is not such a large place. You must not let your imagination run away with you, Katheryn."

"But people come and go - merchants and sailors: the river ensures that. I would speak to one of the boys. They will have no scruples in telling the truth about their old schoolmaster, especially if he was not popular."

Before Valentine could stop her, she had turned back to the churchyard and was speaking to a small freckled red-headed boy; the William Crosse who had been told to walk in church. It was a wise choice, Valentine thought. If any boy was likely to have seen the dark side of Father Chadwick's nature, it would be the one who ran in church. She gave the mischievous lad a sweet smile and returned to Valentine in triumph.

"Young Master Crosse has told me all I wish to know. It seems that Father Chadwick beat a boy to within an inch of his life and that boy's father - a ship's captain - threatened to kill him. It was then Father Chadwick disappeared. Father Chadwick was feared by the boys and there are hints of even darker deeds although my young friend was not specific of course. But he assured me that no boy ever wished to be on his own with Father Chadwick."

Valentine frowned. "The man should never have been appointed as schoolmaster," he said sternly.

"It is possible that he disappeared to avoid the captain's vengeance or a scandal. Tell me about Father Chadwick. What was he like?"

"About my age. A tall man...dark. I did not know him well and I never treated him."

"If we have discovered a priest with evil inclinations and if he had a taste for innocent young people...Agnes or his pupils... The thought makes me shudder but..."

"Father James may know something more of the man's disappearance."

"And where is Father Chadwick now? That's what I wish to know." Katheryn shook her head. So many possibilities. So many priests.

Katheryn and Valentine found Father James in his cottage, eating a simple meal of bread and cheese. He offered them ale, more out of politeness than a true desire for company. The priest looked uncomfortable, preoccupied, and kept glancing anxiously at the window. Katheryn sensed that their visit was not a welcome one.

"Forgive us for disturbing your meal, Father, but we have learned something today that worried us deeply." she began. "A few months ago a Father Chadwick was employed as schoolmaster in the chapel of St. Catherine."

Father James nodded warily.

"I have heard a tale that he beat one of the boys there and incurred the wrath of the lad's father. Is that correct?"

James sighed. "Captain Crosse is a hot tempered man. There was trouble, yes."

"And there was more. Matters that the boys are reluctant to discuss."

"James looked at her. It seemed that this woman knew everything. Or did she? "There was talk but nothing was proved. Father Chadwick left the town and the school is now in good hands. Master Culver is a most excellent schoolmaster and the boys have naught but good to say of him."

"Where did Father Chadwick go when he left Liverpool?"

Father James, uneasy, took a drink of ale. "I don't know. He would not have confided in me. He went. That's all I know."

"Was he close to anyone in the town? Father Nicholas...or Father Clement?"

"He was friend to none that I knew of. He kept himself private."

Valentine, who had been listening silently, stood up. "We must go, James, I have much to do. Come, my lady, we are expected back at Dale Street."

Katheryn, having no choice, bid James farewell, annoyed with Valentine for cutting her questioning short.

"Did you notice," she said quietly as the cottage door was closed behind them, "Father James was most uneasy. Do you think he knows where Father Chadwick is now?"

"I couldn't say. But whatever he knows of the matter, he is not prepared to share it with us." He frowned, trying to capture an elusive thought, then looked up in triumph. "William Staines, Lord Derby's clerk at the Tower who was a brother at Birkenhead, is to marry an Elizabeth Crosse, a captain's daughter. I wonder if she has a young brother at the school. If so, it might be wise to speak with the good captain about this Father Chadwick."

Katheryn nodded. "Do you know Captain Crosse?"

"I know of him. His house is on Bank Street. He is a man much respected in the town and there is talk of his being elected to the town council. If his future son in law could introduce us..."

"If Father Chadwick made such a powerful enemy, maybe he was wise to disappear," Katheryn observed thoughtfully.

Father James stood at the window and watched Katheryn and Valentine walk away, thankful that they had left. He would not have wanted them to meet the visitors he expected. There were some things that were best kept secret. James knew that only too well.

It was night time when Father James's visitors eventually arrived.

Father Nicholas's wife, Mary was taking some broth to an old lady in one of the cottages near the church when she saw them knocking furtively on Father James's door. She recognised one as Brother Francis from Birkenhead and wondered what he was doing so far from his inn at this time. The other she did not know. Mary, with the natural curiosity of one who liked to know what was going on around her, rushed back to her husband with the news.

But Nicholas looked at her fearfully. "Mary....do not interfere in matters that don't concern us."

"But husband, I only meant..."

"Have a care Mary or who knows what might become of us if we involve ourselves in the dangerous deeds of others." He turned to her and put up his hand to touch her face. "We must take care in such perilous times. Who knows, we might have a child to think of."

Mary blushed and touched her belly. "How did you guess, my love."

Nicholas took her in his arms, kissed her and began to undo the laces of her bodice. She pushed him away gently.

"Why are you so afraid, Nicholas? What can Father James's visitors mean to us?"

"We must not be involved. If Father James is meddling in treason we must stand apart. After all, we have our own secrets, do we not, Mary."

He led her to the bed in the corner where they pleasurably put all thought of Father James's visitors out of their minds.

CHAPTER 15

Katheryn rose early and, after Jane had helped her to dress, decided to pay a visit to the castle. There was no need to involve Valentine in her plans - he was already busy in his herb garden. She would take Jane with her and introduce herself to Sir Edward. She had been patient long enough.

Katheryn judged that it would be best to arrive on horseback: speaking to the guards at the castle gate from an elevated position on a fine white horse would give her the psychological advantage. Will was only too happy to saddle her mare. He had polished the leather of her harness and it gleamed in the autumn sunlight. Katheryn was pleased it had stopped raining. It would be hard to make an impressive entrance sopping wet.

Her efforts paid off. The guards let her through with a deferential bow and messengers were sent to seek out Sir Edward, Lord Molyneux and Sir Thomas being absent.

She was shown to a comfortable chamber, part of the constable's private quarters in the keep. No soldier, even an officer, lived with such rich hangings to the walls. She sat down on a well carved chair and fingered the beautifully woven carpet that was draped across the polished oak table. A fire burned cheerfully in the grate and the room smelled sweetly of herbs.

The door opened and a young man stepped in. He was only about two inches taller than she was but his lack of height was compensated for in good looks. Katheryn stood up and he bowed as he kissed her hand. "Lady Katheryn. It is a great pleasure to meet you. "

"Oh, I have visited the castle before, Sir Edward."

He smiled charmingly. "Of course. My brother entertained you did he not. That time I was not told of your visit and I apologise for such a lack of manners: I shall have whoever was responsible for such an oversight punished, I assure you, my lady."

"There is no need for that." The social niceties were over. It was time to come to the point. "I came that time to pay my compliments to your father and your brother was kind enough to receive me. I also took the opportunity to speak with Sir Thomas of a matter that has been concerning me. Please sit down, Sir Edward."

He did as he was told. There was something in his expression that suggested guilt. Something was troubling this young man...his conscience perhaps?"

She smiled to put him at his ease. "I shall tell you what this is about, Sir Edward. It may be that you can help me."

"Of course, my lady. If I can help you in any way..." Sir Edward began to look uneasy.

"Before the closure of the religious houses, I had the honour to be Abbess of Godstow Abbey near Oxford."

Sir Edward looked mildly surprised. She was not how he imagined an Abbess to look...elderly and dried up from a lifetime of self denial.

"And in my charge was a young woman who was soon to take her vows. She was young, unworldly and very pretty." She watched Edward's face carefully. "Her name was Agnes Moore."

Edward was not adept at hiding his feelings: he had never had to be. Katheryn saw the flash of alarm in his eyes and knew she had come to the right place.

She continued. "This girl, Agnes, was alone in the world. Her only living relative was here in Liverpool, Mistress Marjory Moore. Mistress Moore agreed to take her in but Agnes was not afforded the dignity of a member of the family. She was treated as a poor relation, an unpaid servant. The girl was deeply unhappy."

Edward swallowed hard.

"Agnes met a man who, for some reason, could not or would not pay court to her in the usual way; who used her. She became pregnant but lost the child. The man, whoever he was, did not show himself interested in her fate and did not contact her. But she was loyal to him, most likely misguidedly so - she had been brought up in innocence after all - and she never disclosed his identity. Are you all right, Sir Edward?"

He slumped in his chair and took a long drink of wine. "She was a Moore, did you say?" Katheryn nodded. "I did not know. I would never...I did not know. I thought she was just a serving wench after a tumble. If I'd known..."

Katheryn leaned forward and spoke quietly. "You know something of this matter, Sir Edward?"

"I meant her no harm. I thought her willing."

"You realise she is dead, Sir Edward?"

The expression on his face told her that he did no

"She was found dead in the river. Master Valentine says there are signs that she was held beneath the water and drowned."

"I had nothing to do with her death, you must believe me, my lady. I wished her no harm. She fled from me and it was dark so I could not see where she went. I meant her no harm."

He looked down, studying the goblet in his hands. Maybe the shock of this would cure his disregard for the feelings of the young women he thought of as fair game...but Katheryn doubted it. After the initial remorse had worn off, he would be back to his old ways.

"You must tell me what happened, Sir Edward. From the beginning."

He looked at her sheepishly. Normally he had no qualms about boasting of his sexual conquests, but he did not relish doing so before a lady...and a former Abbess at that. But she was not going to give up until she knew the truth. And the truth would exempt him from the suspicion of his having been Agnes's truant lover. She had spoken of a priest, after all.

Edward took a deep breath. "One of the guards was with this girl. I thought her one of the whores of the town. They hang about the garrison like flies around a dung heap because this place is good for business."

Katheryn nodded. "Go on."

"She was pretty and I fancied her for myself. She thought I was Captain Wharton and I did not disillusion her."

"Did she say why she wanted to speak to Captain Wharton?"

Sir Edward's handsome face was a mask of concentration as he tried to remember. "She mentioned a priest of their mutual acquaintance. I think she was looking for him." He smiled unpleasantly. "I wondered what secret dealings such a pretty one could have with a priest. She seemed most anxious to find him and she even came with me willingly to a little place I know on the strand on the promise of a meeting with this, er... man of God." He laughed. "I guess that what they say about priests is true: they are just like the rest of us. But whoever he was, he was a fortunate man. She was a lovely girl."

One look at Katheryn's face made him regret having spoken so frankly. "She was indeed a lovely girl, Sir Edward...and one whose life has been destroyed."

Sir Edward looked suitably chastened. "You must believe me, my lady, I had no part in her death. I have my weaknesses but I am no killer."

"No, Sir Edward, I don't believe you are." She paused to take a sip of wine. Edward looked at her appealingly. She could see his attraction, his charm, but fought against being taken in by it. "Tell me, Sir Edward, where did you take Agnes?"

"A boathouse, not much used now. It used to be owned by the brothers of the Priory and it is a quiet and private place."

"And what did you do in this boathouse?"

Sir Edward had the grace to blush. "She was willing: I assure you that I did not force her."

Katheryn looked sceptical. "And she fled, you say?"

"Like the devil was after her. It's the first time I've had that effect on a woman," he added immodestly.

"And you saw nobody else?"

"I saw nobody in particular. But there were many on the river and the strand that night."

"Somebody killed Agnes, Sir Edward, and I have resolved to find out who it was."

"Then I wish you good fortune in your quest, my lady. But as you see, I cannot help you. The one you seek is elsewhere. It has been a delight to meet you, my lady, and I hope you will dine at the castle soon. But now you must excuse me, my lady. I have duties to perform which can wait no longer."

He stood up and bowed low. His manners, Katheryn noted, were impeccable. If he went to court, this young man would rise quickly in the King's favour...and in the favour of the ladies of the court.

"There is one more matter, Sir Edward. I crave your patience for a few more moments." He sat down again, concealing his anxiety to be away. "You have a chaplain at the castle?" Sir Edward looked relieved. "What manner of a man is he? Could he have been Agnes's lover? I apologise for my forthrightness but I would value your opinion."

A grin was forming on Edward's face. "Our chaplain would not know what to do with a woman if she lay naked before him." He suddenly remembered who he was talking to and checked himself. "No, my lady, I do not think he was the kind to play the lover. Besides, he is in London with my father. Our chaplain was not Agnes's lover, I am certain. She was far too good for him." He smiled to himself, recalling his encounter with the dead girl.

Katheryn, trying hard to conceal her disapproval, stood up. She would leave Sir Edward to his carnal memories and his mysteriously urgent duties.

Valentine was much relieved when Katheryn returned to his shop in Dale Street. When he had noticed her absence he had assumed that she had left early to look round the market. But when he had seen that her horse had gone, he had asked Will where she was.

Will's reply had unnerved him. If the inhabitants of the castle were involved in murder, Katheryn's persistence could put her in danger. Her rank, he knew, would afford her some protection, but if she were to get too close to the truth - if the killer thought himself in peril - then who knew what action he would take to avoid discovery. It took a great deal of effort for Valentine not to scold her and he did his best to listen without comment when she reported her conversation with Sir Edward.

"Then Lord Molyneux' younger son is a violator of young women but no murderer. Is that what you would tell me?"

"That is about the truth of it. But he insists she was a willing party to their dalliance."

"He would say that, wouldn't he." Valentine shook his head. He had seen the bruises.

"Her killer might have..."

"That is always possible." Valentine didn't want to consider such unpleasantness and he changed the subject swiftly. "While you were at the castle William Staines called for medicine for the steward at the Tower. He also invited me to his wedding next month. I questioned him about Captain Crosse and it seems that his future wife does have a young brother at the school...a scallywag by the sound of him."

"Can we speak with the captain?"

"He is in port now and William will tell him that we wish to see him."

"That is good. We must discover more of Father Chadwick."

"I heard another piece of news today from one of my patients - it is the talk of Liverpool until tomorrow when they find something else to gossip about," he smiled. "It seems that the village of Childwall not far from here has been plagued by grave robbers."

"Grave robbers?"

"Their motives, whatever they are, can be naught but evil. It seems they robbed the dead of parts of their earthly bodies. I thought of Father Clement's hand."

"Come, Valentine, have you, as a man of medicine, never been tempted to discover more of the workings of the human body? In Oxford I heard that such things went on."

Valentine looked horrified. "I should not disturb the dead in their place of rest to do it."

"Of course. But there might be some with fewer scruples."

"I think it more likely that the dead are disturbed in the interests of Satan than of knowledge, Katheryn."

"You are probably right." She smiled at him. "You usually are. Where is Childwall?"

"Quite close. Half an hour's ride...less."

Valentine sighed. He wanted to get out, to clear his head, to get away from the stinking town and its market day crowds. "Shall we ride to Childwall and talk with the vicar at All Saints church there? It will not take long."

Katheryn agreed with this suggestion: her desire to get out into the fresh air matched Valentine's own. Will saddled Valentine's ageing brown cob for him and then helped Katheryn back into the gleaming saddle of her white mare.

Childwall was a small village of a few farms and cottages, an inn, a manor house and an impressive church which also served several nearby communities, not unlike Katheryn's own village of Cheadle.

Valentine was acquainted with the vicar: he had treated him for a persistent skin condition which, Valentine was delighted to see, had improved considerably. He was an elderly, unworldly looking man.

"A bad business, Vicar," Valentine began after introducing Katheryn. "It is the talk of Liverpool this day. Have you any idea who would do such a thing?"

The vicar shook his grey head sadly. "I have no idea. I am sure it can be no one in the parish. I know all the people here. There are good, there are bad; honest men and rogues. But nobody, I am certain, would indulge in such practices. I should have had some inkling if any of my flock were followers of Satan, surely. A priest knows these things."

"Then whom do you suspect?"

"There are many beggars and vagabonds ready to kill a man for a few pence or commit evil deeds that honest men would tremble at. There have been such passing through the village...many such. Nowhere is safe, as you know Valentine."

"What has been done in your churchyard?" Valentine asked quietly.

Katheryn felt sorry for the elderly priest who looked as though he carried the worries of the world on his shoulders.

"They dug up three graves: old Randle Carter who died a week since; Jinny Myat...a poor young maid who died of a fever eight days back; and Matthew Potter who passed from this life but ten days ago. All recently buried; the earth freshly piled on their graves and easy to dig, I don't doubt. I came into the church gate on Monday at daybreak and found the graves dug up." He swallowed hard as though the memory disturbed him. "The bodies could be seen and there were...parts missing. Forgive me. I cannot bear to think about it. I fetched the sexton and we covered the graves. Then I said the prayers for the dead afresh. It was a terrible business....a terrible business." He shook his head again as though in disbelief.

"It is indeed terrible, Father." Katheryn spoke for the first time. "Have you any idea why this abomination was committed?"

"I can think of no other reason than the service of Satan, madam. I have heard that such, er...things are needed for the ceremonies performed by those who have the devil as their master."

"And can you remember anyone - any stranger to the village - who has been seen in the district?"

"There was a ragged woman begging with her child and a couple of men who looked like cut-throats passing through frightening the farmers' wives. And the juggler."

Katheryn looked at Valentine. "Juggler? What juggler?"

"I was passing by the inn on Thursday on my way to visit Mistress Walsh who is sick, and he was displaying his skills outside. No doubt he went in there and drank his takings afterwards. I thought no more about it until now."

"What did he look like, this juggler?" asked Katheryn.
"He was a tall, gangling fellow. Yellow hair."

The yellow haired juggler made his way to the old mill.
There were things he had to show: things he would be well paid
for. He had intended to wait until later in the day when he had
earned enough for the next week's food and lodging by
displaying his skills to the market day crowds. But what he had
in his leather bag would not wait. It was best to get it to its
destination without delay.

He reached the Old Hall and stood for a while staring at
the old mill which was now a pile of charred bricks and timbers,
dampened by the persistent drizzle. Where was Mires? This
had been his refuge of late; the place where he had been assured
of secrecy for his practices.

There was one who might know where Mires was; one
who had used that man's skills to his own advantage many
times.

The juggler pulled up his hood to hide his greasy yellow
curls and made his way quickly to the castle to seek Captain
Wharton.

Captain Wharton looked from his window and thought of
the woman he had seen that morning walking across the castle
yard escorted by Sir Edward. Lady Katheryn Bulkeley; what
was she about? Would she never stop asking questions?
Wharton hoped his involvement in the matter would soon be
over: he was a frightened man.

And the visit of the juggler - the creature with the pallid
face and the yellow hair - had only added to his fear. He had
asked Wharton to deliver a message: he was to tell Mires that

the juggler would meet him in the Mermaid that very evening to take delivery of certain items.

What those items were, Wharton did not care to imagine and he shuddered as he contemplated a row across the choppy waters of the river to deliver his message.

Surely this thing would be over soon and Rosina would be

in his bed.

CHAPTER 16

Katheryn and Valentine exchanged few words on the ride back from Childwall, but their thoughts were the same. Somewhere in the town was one who would mutilate the bodies of the dead for the glorification of Satan. It explained Father Clement's missing hand: it explained a lot. Somehow the yellow haired juggler was involved: he had been seen with Father Clement on the night he disappeared and he had been with Melisanda on the night Agnes was killed. Always the yellow haired man. How Katheryn would like to question him.

Valentine had work to do in his shop. It was market day: many would call in for ointments and medicines and he couldn't leave Ralph in charge indefinitely, the boy was overworked as it was. Katheryn, refreshed after her ride, handed her horse to Will to be unsaddled and peeped into the kitchen. Jane was busy helping Matilda, and Katheryn had no wish to disturb their happy chatter.

Her visit to the church the previous day had been spent talking to Master Culver and her offices had been left unsaid. She considered that she would be quite safe walking to Our Lady and St. Nicholas alone so she set out down Dale Street past the Guildhall and the bustling High Cross.

She dodged her way through the market day throng and resisted the temptation to look at the wares on offer, holding firmly onto the purse which hung from her waist: there were many cut-purses about on such a day. She reached the strand but there was no sign of Bartholomew. He would be on the water, she thought: his ferry was much in demand on market days. Several fishermen nodded to her as she passed and she smiled back at them, trying hard not to wrinkle her nose against the stench of yesterday's rotting catch. The heavy grey of the sky was reflected in the river. It might rain soon. She quickened her pace but the fine damp sand caught at her feet and slowed her steps.

She reached the church and went in, glad to exchange the smell of fish and seaweed for that of incense. The building was quiet except for the low murmur of voices coming from one of the chapels. Katheryn knelt and began her own prayers. She was annoyed with herself when, after five minutes or so, the sound of footsteps distracted her from her devotions and made her look up.

Marjory Moore was hurrying from the side chapel of St. John, tears on her cheeks. She saw Katheryn and their eyes met momentarily. As Marjory ran out of the great west door Father James emerged from the chapel, nodded to Katheryn and walked quickly out of the church. Katheryn resumed her prayers, adding an extra request that she might soon be able to bring Agnes's killer to justice.

Marjory hurried back to the Old Hall, trying hard to compose herself before facing the servants. Any hint of weakness and they would take advantage.

Since she had discovered the mill burned to the ground she had known no peace. Had she been wise, she wondered, to confess all to Father James; to admit that she had been foolish and that her foolishness had led her into sin. Even though she had received absolution, she still felt guilty...contaminated. And that interfering Lady Katheryn had been in the church. If she had overheard anything...

Marjory, reaching her front door, scolded a maidservant for her clumsiness and marched angrily through to the parlour. She called imperiously for wine and tried to concentrate on her embroidery.

Her heart began to beat faster when Katheryn was announced. She snapped at the maid to bring her in. If her confession had been overheard she would soon know.

Katheryn greeted her civilly. "Good day to you, Mistress Moore. I saw you in the church. You looked unwell so I called to see if you were better."

"I am indeed well, my lady. You need not have concerned yourself," Marjory replied stiffly.

"I also wish to speak with Griselda. She told my maidservant, Jane, that she had seen someone in the old mill. Has she said anything to you or any of your household?"

Marjory hoped that Katheryn could not hear the beating of her heart. "No, she has said nothing...and she is about her duties." Her voice was tense.

Katheryn, realising that she would be offered no refreshment or any other encouragement to stay, took her leave. She would discover nothing from Marjory that day.

Katheryn made her way slowly across the bustle of the cobbled courtyard. Servants bobbed curtseys as she passed but she resisted the temptation to ask where Griselda's was as such enquiries might be reported back to Mistress Marjory. But she kept her eyes open and hoped that any meeting would seem accidental to the casual observer.

Her swift prayer that she would find Griselda was soon answered. The maidservant appeared round the corner of the house carrying a basket of herbs on her arm. Katheryn smiled, feigning surprise that they should meet by chance.

"It's good to see you, Griselda. You have not visited us for a few days. I hope you will do so soon as Jane misses you."

"Mistress Moore keeps me busy, my lady. And..." She bowed her head as though embarrassed. "She said I was not to speak with Jane. She says I waste time gossiping."

"I'm certain that's not true. Can you walk with me awhile? I shall take the blame if we are discovered."

Griselda looked up at the diamond paned windows of the house. No one was watching. She grinned at Katheryn and nodded eagerly. The two women walked out onto Mill Street and headed in the direction of the White Cross and the town.

"Does Mistress Moore know of what you saw in the old mill?"

Griselda nodded. "The housekeeper told her and the mistress sent for me and said I was never to repeat such nonsense. But it is no matter now: the mill is burned...and a good thing too."

"Does anybody in the household know what caused the fire?"

"The men think it was young lovers lighting a fire to keep themselves warm. But that's nonsense...who would be foolish enough to do such a thing?"

"And what do you think caused it?"

Griselda looked Katheryn straight in the eye as though the answer was obvious. "Why, who would bring fire with him from hell but Satan himself? There has been much happening in this town of late and I don't just mean cutpurses and whores and the usual wrongdoings: there is something evil. I heard that in the village of Childwall nearby the dead have been torn from their graves." Her eyes were alight with superstitious relish. Griselda was treading the fine border between fear and the enjoyment of fear.

"I know what happened in Childwall," Katheryn said, matter of fact. "I want to ask you a question, Griselda. Please think hard and answer honestly."

"I will if I can, my lady." She tilted her head to one side to show willing.

"Did you ever see Agnes in the company of a priest?"

Griselda looked crestfallen. The question was disappointingly mundane. She had expected to be asked if she had witnessed any member of the household consorting naked with the devil at least. She shrugged. "She saw Father James when she went to mass."

"But apart from at her confession, did she speak with any priest alone?"

"Griselda shook her head. Then her hand went to her mouth in sudden realisation. "There was that time I saw her by the old mill, when she first came here it was. She was talking with a man in a priest's gown but he had his back to me. I didn't see who it was because I was too far away." The corners of her mouth turned upwards in a mischievous grin. "You think her sweetheart was a priest? Did he kill her do you think? Some man of God to cover his sins with murder."

"I cannot say as yet who killed her, and I should be grateful if you would say nothing of the matter."

Griselda tried her best to look solemn. "Indeed I will not, my lady. You can trust me."

"Did you see this priest again?"

Griselda thought carefully. "I'm sure I saw him talking with Mistress Moore on the same spot a few weeks after, although I did not see clearly. I was gathering herbs at twilight and I wasn't going to loiter and get a thrashing for spying on my betters. I thought no more of it till now. You must ask Mistress Moore and see what she says." Griselda glanced anxiously over her shoulder. "I must get back, my lady, or I'll be missed. I'm sorry I could tell you nothing of importance."

"On the contrary, Griselda, I owe you my thanks. You have told me a great deal."

When Griselda had hurried back to her work, Katheryn returned to Dale Street in the fast fading light. The market stalls were being dismantled and the population of the town was on the move through the littered streets, homeward or tavernward bound. When she reached Valentine's shop she found Ralph putting the shutters up at the windows. She had not realised it was so late.

It was Saturday night and Master Jacob Multhorpe had stayed on in Liverpool longer than he had intended. His business with Captain Flynn successfully concluded, he was now negotiating with a Captain O'Rourke whose price was even more competitive. And there were carters to arrange and loading to supervise. It would be a few days yet before he would set off back to Manchester and the unwelcoming bed of Mistress Multhorpe. He would stay there in the Mermaid for as long as he had business in the town. The inn had its attractions in the shape of a young redhead named Nan and he was in no hurry to get back home.

He ate Master Turner's meat pie carefully, chewing every mouthful. He had learned his lesson and he had no desire to call upon Master Valentine's services again to relieve the agonies of over-indulgence. He looked about him as solitary eaters do. The inn was packed with a mixture of townsfolk and sailors and the tapsters and serving wenches were kept busy under the landlord's all-seeing supervision.

The door opened and Multhorpe looked round. Standing there was a tall man, strangely dressed in brightly patched clothes with curly yellow hair and a shabby cloak of motley hanging loosely from his shoulders. He approached Master Turner and exchanged a few words with him. The landlord shook his head and the yellow haired man sat down in a private corner and ordered ale, placing the heavy leather sack he carried carefully on the ground.

Multhorpe knew him. This was the man who had been talking to Father Clement the night he disappeared. Jacob Multhorpe remembered his duty as an upright citizen and his promise to Valentine. The merchant beckoned to a boy who was weaving between the tables collecting the pots. He held out a shiny coin and the boy's eyes lit up with sudden interest.

"You know Master Valentine, the apothecary?" The boy nodded. "This coin is yours if you fetch him this instant and tell him the juggler's here. He'll understand." He returned the coin to his purse and watched the boy bob out of the door. At the speed he was travelling, the message would not take long to reach its destination.

Katheryn and Valentine, sharing the day's news by the fireside, were surprised to receive Multhorpe's message. But they threw on their cloaks and followed the lad to the Mermaid. When they arrived Valentine raised a hand in greeting to

Master Multhorpe and proceeded to stare at the juggler who was seated in his private alcove eyeing the serving girls. Valentine had worked out his approach and congratulated himself that his idea was quite a clever one.

He approached the juggler, a look of grave concern on his face. "My friend, you must feel most unwell. I suggest you ask the landlord for a room where you can rest. May I introduce myself, sir. I am Master Valentine and I am an apothecary of this town." Valentine looked the man up and down, keeping his distance. "Those spots...how long have you had them?"

The juggler felt his face, he was starting to grow restless with panic. "Spots? What is it, I pray you, Master, what is it?"

Valentine nodded knowledgeably. "I have the very thing for such a condition in my shop but first I would ask you some questions."

"Please hurry...will I live?"

"Have you been in contact with any priests, say a few weeks ago. There is one that I know of who had such a condition...a Father Clement. If you had been near to this man..."

Katheryn stood behind Valentine, her expression serious. She could not help but admire his acting ability.

"I meet many on business. I might have met your priest."

"And the village of Childwall. Have you been there in the past few days?"

This time the juggler looked alarmed. He stood up, pushed Valentine aside and ran from the inn."

"There is your answer." Katheryn looked down. In his panic, the juggler had left his bag behind. She opened it carefully, dreading what she might find. Underneath the coloured balls and the other tools of the juggler's trade were some small packs of oilcloth, well sealed but ominously stained with dark red. Katheryn hardly liked to touch them. She stepped back and let Valentine investigate.

He took the packs from the bag. "I will have these taken back to Childwall for decent burial. Let the man come to reclaim his bag. He will find his gruesome trophies gone. The man is a trader in such things for those who indulge in the black arts. They are usually too cowardly to mutilate the bodies themselves but they will pay handsomely for others to do so."

Master Multhorpe came over and slapped Valentine heartily on the back. "Well done, my friend. You gave that rogue quite a shock. And what was in his bag?" He peered over to see but Valentine hastily concealed the items. He did not want to start a panic in the inn.

"It is best that you do not know, Master Multhorpe."

"Fair enough. I had a word with the landlord while you were at your work. It seems that our yellow haired friend was asking for a certain gentleman. The landlord had never heard of him of course but he remembered the name. The rogue was asking for a Master Mires."

Mires had been watching the inn from the shadows of a doorway opposite, making sure that all was well before he ventured inside. The juggler had expected him to be waiting inside but Mires was no fool. He was not going to hang about the taverns of Liverpool, where somebody might recognise him, any longer than he had to.

When he saw the juggler shoot from the inn as though the hounds of hell were after him, he knew his caution was justified.

Let the juggler take the consequences. Mires still had enough objects of evil to impress Wharton with...and keep him compliant.

Mires would lie low; he would take care. And patience would bring its rewards. He would soon be a very wealthy man.

CHAPTER 17

After high mass Father Nicholas returned home, took the thing out of its soft leather pouch and looked at it. Captain Sanchez was almost ready to do the deal. It had taken persuasion of course. The Captain had had to be convinced of the power of the object...and that it was what Nicholas claimed it to be. And when Nicholas had told his story, the Captain's eyes had gleamed greedily. He wanted the object...wanted to possess it.

Mary strolled over to see what was preoccupying her husband. She gasped in horror when she saw the object. "Put that away. It makes me feel sick."

"You don't appreciate how important this will be to us, Mary. It will make all the difference. And with our child on the way..."

"I don't care. I don't want to see it."

He placed the thing carefully into its pouch, taking care not to disturb the rotting skin that hung round the joints. He would hide it until he handed it over. Women in his wife's condition often had sick fancies. He went to her and put his arm about her shoulder, reassuring her that it would soon be out of her house.

It was early afternoon when the messenger came from the castle to say that Sir Thomas had returned and would be honoured if Lady Katheryn would dine with him that evening. Katheryn accepted graciously, regretting that the invitation hadn't extended to Valentine. But she was confident of her abilities to discover information by herself: putting people at their ease and encouraging them to talk was one of the talents God had given her.

She asked Jane to lay out her best gown and spent the afternoon in preparation. She had already decided to go on horseback to protect her gown from the filth of the streets, so the castle servant who had been sent to accompany her - a fat good natured fellow called Pouch - walked ahead of her, leading her mare's reins, while she chatted easily to him about the garrison and the castle. She listened patiently to the saga of the cook's toothache and Captain Wharton's fancy for the wife of one of the town's more prosperous merchants, throwing in the odd question to keep the flow of information coming. Although she sympathised with the cook, it was Wharton who interested her.

"So what will be the outcome, Master Pouch? Will the merchant discover Captain Wharton's intentions towards Mistress Rosina?" she asked conspiratorially, hoping Pouch would think she possessed an interest in general gossip rather than a particular concern for the affairs of Captain Wharton.

"I couldn't tell you, my lady. But if I know anything of the Captain, whatever he wants he gets. It's strange indeed. When he first came here from Chester castle he was under a Captain March and they didn't get on. Then three weeks later March's dead...fallen from the castle rock...broken neck. Not that I'm blaming Wharton, mind; he was elsewhere at the time. But what a piece of luck for him, eh. I've heard tell that something like that happened in Chester too. Nothing stands in our Captain's way for long. He's a good commander, mind. The men respect him. But I'll warrant Mistress Rosina's husband won't stop him getting what he wants. I hear say the man's sick already."

Katheryn was disappointed to see the castle gate looming in front of her. The man Pouch was a natural gossip and she had discovered more than she had dared to hope during her brief journey. She gave the servant a beaming smile as he helped her from her horse. "I hope you'll do me the honour of accompanying me home, Master Pouch. I have enjoyed our conversation. Who would have thought Liverpool castle to be such an interesting place. You must tell me more on our return journey."

Pouch bowed low, blushing with pleasure. Here was a lady who enjoyed gossip just as much as he did; not like Mistress Pouch who swore he would hang one day for not guarding his tongue.

Katheryn was received with due ceremony by Sir Thomas while Sir Edward hung in the background sheepishly. When he spoke to her it was with a cautious formality. This woman knew too many of his secrets and he could feel her eyes on him, watching him. For the first time in his easy, over-indulged life, Edward Molyneux felt the pangs of an uneasy conscience.

Katheryn was pleased to see that Captain Wharton had been invited to join them. He greeted her courteously, giving no hint that they had met before, and sat as far away from her as possible at dinner.

Sir Thomas, the perfect host, kept the conversation going, enquiring after the well being of the Bulkeley lands and steering carefully away from any subject that might be considered controversial; a difficult task but somehow he managed it well. The meal was as good as any Katheryn had presided over at Godstow: suckling pig and a huge freshly caught salmon, followed by rich pastries and sweetmeats. The cook at the castle, she was told, had been in Lord Molyneux' service for many years and had excelled himself in spite of his toothache. His Lordship was a fortunate man to have harnessed such talent in a small town like Liverpool.

An excellent wine helped to relax the atmosphere and loosen tongues and a pair of household musicians provided the discreet strains of lute and viol as they ate. Both Sir Edward and Captain Wharton were looking more relaxed and Katheryn thought that, in view of her previous occupation, a few questions about the religious life of the castle might not be considered out of place.

"I have nothing but praise for the sustenance you have provided for the body, Sir Thomas." Sir Thomas, gratified, bowed his head to acknowledge this praise for his hospitality. "But I hope you provide equal sustenance for the soul. Do the men of the garrison hear mass often?"

"The men's spiritual well-being is taken care of I can assure you, my lady."

Katheryn turned to Wharton who was toying with his goblet. He reached out for the silver flagon and helped himself to more wine.

"I expect the priests of Liverpool are glad of the extra fees they can earn for saying mass for the garrison, Captain. Their salary is hardly sufficient to live on, I understand."

Wharton nodded stiffly. "That is indeed the case, ma'am. There is no problem persuading them to do that service for the souls of my men. And the poor creatures look half starved when they arrive so they usually enjoy a good meal into the bargain. As you see, we have an adequate cook."

There were well fed chuckles of agreement from Lord Molyneux' sons whose consumption of wine had made them more relaxed. Sir Edward, his inhibitions lowered, was staring at Katheryn's figure appreciatively which was his natural reaction to any attractive woman.

Katheryn continued. "I believe the late Father Clement visited the castle often."

Sir Thomas nodded. "Ah yes. His murder was a dreadful business. There is much danger to the innocent in these times. The lower orders no longer have respect for their betters but to kill a priest..."

"Indeed, Sir Thomas. A dreadful business, as you say. And the schoolmaster, Father Chadwick, did he visit the castle?

Thomas nodded. "Yes, but it was Father Clement who came most often."

"You knew Father Clement well?"

"Not well. He was of more service to the garrison than the family."

"Then Captain Wharton must have been well acquainted with him." She turned to Wharton who quickly drained his goblet and poured himself more wine. Katheryn repeated her question. "You knew Father Clement well, Captain? Were you not both in Chester? Did you know him then?" She put her head to one side ingenuously, awaiting an answer.

Wharton's unease seemed to turn almost to panic. He finished his wine and stood up. "I hardly knew the man. We never talked. If you'll excuse me, my lady...gentlemen. I have matters to attend to."

He bowed stiffly and marched out of the room with determination. Katheryn sat back and sipped her wine. Her suspicions had been confirmed. Captain Wharton was deeply involved in whatever was going on in Liverpool Castle and, if she was not mistaken, was somehow involved in Father Clement's murder.

Sir Thomas swiftly covered up the Captain's abruptness by changing the subject to the latest court rumours concerning the King's marital future. The death of Queen Jane in childbirth had left the King a widower with a weakly son and the necessity to secure the future of the Tudor dynasty with more male heirs. It wasn't long before he had begun to cast his eyes about for a new wife...but who would be the fortunate (or, Katheryn thought treasonably, the unfortunate) lady? The court was rife with speculation about Jane Seymour's successor: a German princess had been suggested. But whoever the lady might be, Katheryn did not envy her...though she kept all such thoughts to herself.

The evening drew amicably to a close and, as Katheryn made her farewells, Sir Edward took her hand and kissed it lingeringly. She shot him a warning look. The man clearly had no conscience about what had happened to Agnes: he probably considered it his right to satisfy his desires with any woman who was available at the time. Katheryn made a mental note to pray for his immortal soul and for his repentance. But he was no killer - she was sure of that.

A yawning Pouch brought her horse round to the courtyard and helped her mount. The man was well versed in castle gossip so the question was worth asking. When they were out of earshot of the Molyneux brothers she spoke.

"Tell me, Master Pouch, did you know of the priest who was lately murdered...Father Clement?"

For the first time Pouch looked away and did not answer. They walked on for a while in silence, the only sounds being the rhythmic clip clop of the horse's hooves on the hard packed ground and the noise of revelling and argument from the numerous taverns which lined their route. When Pouch spoke he did so quietly. "He was very thick with Captain Wharton, he was. More than that I cannot say."

"He visited the castle often then?"

"Oh aye. From what I heard he was closeted with the Captain for hours on end...and mass left unsaid. That's only what I've heard, mind: I could not vouch for the truth of it."

"And Father Chadwick, the schoolmaster? Did he know Captain Wharton?"

"Oh aye, he used to say mass for the garrison. Not seen him for a while; I think he's left the town."

She decided to try another question: a longshot. "Have you heard the name Mires mentioned?"

Pouch shook his head. "Can't say I have, my lady. But then I don't hear everything," he added regretfully.

They had reached Valentine's shop. A candle burned in the window and Katheryn knew that the apothecary would be waiting up for her. She pressed a coin into Pouch's hand and was thanked with an eager grin and a low bow. "It's been a pleasure to make your acquaintance, my lady."

"And yours, Master Pouch. Thank you for escorting me and keeping me entertained."

Katheryn was just wondering whether Pouch would have anything more to tell her when Will appeared to take her horse. The moment was missed. Pouch bowed low again and disappeared, running, into the darkness of Dale Street.

Valentine had a warming infusion of camomile waiting for Katheryn on her return. He was in the habit of taking such a drink himself before bed, knowing that it helped him to sleep. They sat before the embers of the fire, sipping their drinks.

Katheryn looked across at him. Was this, she wondered, what marriage was like; the silent companionship; to be in the company of another without the necessity to make conversation. Valentine looked at her and smiled.

"Did you dine well at the castle? And did you discover anything of interest?"

"I dined very well. Their cook was most skilled, in spite of his toothache." She grinned. "And I learned enough to suspect Captain Wharton of being involved in Father Clement's death." She went on to recount the events of the evening.

"But what of Agnes? You suspect Sir Edward?"

She shook her head. "No. The man is a seducer and a rogue and a danger to the whole female sex...or he would like to be. But I do not think him a killer. I feel we must look for our priest, whoever he may be. It seems we are still no nearer discovering his identity. Though I would know more of Father Chadwick's whereabouts: we must enquire of your friend William Staines when Captain Crosse can see us. But now we must sleep on the problem."

Katheryn rose from her seat. Valentine stood up at the same time and they paused there before the fire, so close that the desire for contact was almost irresistible. Valentine put out his hand to take hers and drew her towards him. At first she did not resist but after a split second she stepped away. "Brother, we have both made certain vows."

Valentine closed his eyes and took a deep breath. "Katheryn, forgive me."

She stepped forward again and touched his face gently, her hand brushing against the evening stubble of his chin. "I forgive you readily but we must remember that vows made to our creator are of more importance than our own inclinations."

Their eyes met in understanding. They were still friends. No harm had been done.

She left him alone. He listened to the swish of her skirts as she went up the stairs to her chamber. She had spoken of "our" inclinations: did hers match his own? Valentine knelt there on the rushes before the dying fire and prayed for strength to resist the desires of the flesh.

CHAPTER 18

Valentine slept badly that night and left his bed early to attend to some overdue tasks in his shop. Ralph, sleepy eyed, found his master up and about and restless. The apprentice was surprised when the apothecary went out without telling him his destination as he usually did.

Valentine walked through the bustling early morning streets, hardly hearing the shopkeepers call their greetings to him as they let down their wooden shutters to form their shop counters and set out their wares to attract the people of Liverpool to part with their money. A pair of beggars, recently wakened up in a doorway and chased off with a broom by the mistress of the house, squatted on the ground and whined for alms.

Valentine wondered what had become of the beggar with one hand. No doubt the man had moved on to find fresh sympathy. He tossed the beggars a halfpenny, all he could spare, and let them fight over it: if they were wise and didn't let self interest get the better of them, they could buy bread with the coin and share an adequate breakfast.

When he reached Father James's house, Valentine hammered on the door. It was early still; early enough for the priest to be at home rather than about his duties in the church. Father James opened the door, surprised to see his visitor; and even more surprised when Valentine told him the reason for his visit.

"I will gladly hear your confession, brother," he said, concerned. "If you have anything on your conscience that troubles you, it is only right that you should confess it."

Valentine followed James into his small thatched house, knelt and confessed the innermost thoughts of his heart. Father James nodded with understanding. He had seen the Abbess: she was indeed an attractive woman...and living beneath the same roof. He murmured the absolution and Valentine felt a renewed strength. Katheryn was his sister in Christ and he must regard her as such.

Valentine changed the subject. "I hope the questions Katheryn asked on market day about Father Chadwick the schoolmaster did not disturb you."

James shook his head. "Sometimes, as a priest, there are things that one would rather not know. Chadwick is gone. Let us leave it at that. No good can come of pursuing the matter."

"I rather think that Katheryn suspects him of some connection with Agnes Moore's death."

James shook his head again. "You must take my word for it. The man sinned and now he is gone." James pressed his lips tightly together. The subject was closed.

Valentine's departure from Father James' house was watched by Captain Wharton and his companion who stood hidden against the churchyard wall, their cloaks pulled about them, shielding them from the sharp river wind and hiding their faces from prying eyes.

"Is the apothecary one of their number? Mires spoke softly to the other man even though there wasn't another soul about.

"I have not seen him in their company. And there are many reasons for an apothecary to visit a priest, none of which are of any interest to us."

"We must not be deflected from our purpose. If the apothecary is not involved then we must forget him. We must interest ourselves only in those who can lead us to our goal."

Wharton looked at Mires and saw the fire of lust burning in his eyes: lust for the riches of this world and the power they could bring.

Katheryn also rose early, but by the time she had come downstairs, Valentine was gone and Ralph could not tell her where. Jane had gone down to the kitchen after helping her lady dress, and was now busy gossiping with Matilda and bantering with Will, who was sitting like a lord by the roaring fire sipping his breakfast ale.

Katheryn peeped round the door but did not announce her presence. She would go out by herself: there were times when she preferred to be alone.

She walked through the streets, that were already filling with goodwives and servants shopping for the day's provisions, and headed for the strand.

At first Katheryn took little notice of the young woman who walked a few yards ahead of her. But as she followed her down Chapel Street it came to her that the plump figure belonged to Father Nicholas's wife, Mary. Katheryn, not wishing to waste the opportunity, quickened her pace until she caught up with her. Mary turned round, wary at first in case the hurrying footsteps belonged to a cutpurse or foist. But when she saw Katheryn a welcoming smile lit her pretty face.

"My lady, it is a pleasure to see you. You are alone?" She looked round for a servant: it was uncommon for a lady of position to walk the streets unaccompanied.

"I prefer to walk alone at times. Solitude, I find, is necessary for thought. At my abbey I had the cloisters but here the streets must suffice. How is your husband?"

"He is well, thank you my lady." Something in Mary's expression told Katheryn that she was not telling the whole truth. She looked down at the basket the priest's young wife was carrying: a small loaf, yesterday's by the look of it; a couple of small eggs; a small bag of flour: hardly the raw materials for a feast. Mary saw her looking at her purchases. "One of the fishermen knows my father and he is most generous. We get by with what he gives us."

"It is not easy living on the salary of a chantry priest," Katheryn stated simply, without judgement.

"You are right, my lady. And when he left the abbey at Whalley, the brothers received no pension as they had incurred the anger of the King." She paused, a smile playing on her lips. "But we expect our fortunes to improve shortly." Katheryn could see Mary weighing up how much information it was safe to give out. "My husband has made the acquaintance of the captain of a Spanish ship moored here in the river, the Santa Isabella," she said proudly, almost preening herself at her husband's influential connections. "This evening he is to do some trade with him and the captain is willing to pay well." She stopped herself before she gave too much away.

"I am pleased to hear it," said Katheryn in the hope of encouraging more confidences. But none came. In view of the secretive nature of her husband's dealings, Mary had said too much already. Katheryn, sensing that the subject of Father Nicholas's business was now closed, tried steering the conversation in another direction.

"I was a guest of Sir Thomas Molyneux at the castle last night." She watched Mary's reaction. It was not Katheryn's habit to try to impress with her rank and good connections, but this time it was unavoidable. "He mentioned to me that chantry priests often say mass at the castle. Perhaps your husband might render the garrison that good service more often. I could speak to Sir Thomas..."

"That would be most kind, my lady," said Mary gratefully. "He has said mass there on a few occasions but if it were to become a regular..."

"I understand that the late Father Clement often said mass at the castle. Did you know him well." Katheryn inclined her head expectantly, pleased with herself for introducing the subject of Father Clement so casually. She was unprepared for the reaction she received.

Mary pressed her lips together disapprovingly. "I knew the man more than I should have liked."

"You mean he was unsuited to his calling?"

Mary nodded, her eyes filled with righteous indignation. "When my husband began to court me, he did so in honour. He was a priest but one who sought Christian marriage: not every man is suited to abstinence."

"And Father Clement?"

Mary took a deep breath. "There was no honour about that man. He fancied himself handsome and some might have thought him so. But he was a disgrace to his calling."

"Did he...make advances to you?"

"When I was a bride of but three weeks, he called when my husband was about his duties. He asked me if...if I liked priests. The way he said it, I felt most uneasy. Then, when I was about to pour him some ale - I had thought to show him the hospitality due to a colleague of my husband's - he grabbed my wrist and..."

"Go on." Katheryn nodded in encouragement.

"He tried to kiss me...and touch me. I freed myself and shouted at him to get out of my house. He laughed and said I should have been flattered that he found me attractive. Then he left."

"Did you tell your husband?"

Mary shook her head. "I said nothing. I thought it best. Please, my lady, say nothing of this. I should not like it known...or my husband to hear."

Katheryn agreed to keep Mary's confidences and took the opportunity to bring up the subject of another priest. "Were you acquainted with Father Chadwick, the schoolmaster?"

Mary looked relieved at the change of subject. "I heard dark tales of him and some say it was a relief to his pupils when he left the town. But it is but gossip. I did not know the man myself so I can tell you no more."

Katheryn thanked her and took her leave, assuring her that she would recommend her husband's services to Sir Thomas.

But as she walked slowly back to Dale Street she wondered if Father Nicholas had found out about Clement's advances, in spite of Mary's efforts to keep the knowledge from him.

Was Father Clement's murder an act of vengeance by a wronged husband? And here was a priest who liked dalliance with the opposite sex: could he have been Agnes's lover? But then again, her lover had been alive after Clement's death - unless she did not know of his death and her sighting of him was all the feverish imagination of an impressionable girl. And what mysterious trade was Father Nicholas to transact with the captain of the Santa Isabella tonight?

Katheryn walked back to Valentine's shop, oblivious to the sights and smells of the streets and the raucous shouting of the traders. Soon she would face Valentine again and she felt slightly nervous at the thought. Perhaps she should turn back and seek out Father James to hear her confession.

After a midday meal of freshly baked bread and cheese, Valentine rose from the table ready to resume his work in the shop. But Katheryn begged a moment of his time while Matilda and Jane cleared away. He smiled at her shyly and she suspected that he was as confused about the events of the previous evening as she was. As they sat before the roaring fire, Katheryn spoke first.

"I talked with Father Nicholas's wife, Mary, this morning. She told me something that might be of interest to us and I would value your opinion. Father Clement, it seems, was not a man who lived up to the standards of his calling and his behaviour was dishonourable in any man, let alone a priest. He made advances to Mistress Mary shortly after her wedding."

Valentine raised his eyebrows. "Father James had his reservations about the man, I know.

"Could he have been Agnes's lover? It is possible she did not hear of his death and thought that he had abandoned her. The news might not have reached her at the Old Hall as Mistress Moore kept her close confined."

"Then who killed her?"

Someone who thought her privy to Clement's secrets; someone who was afraid she would discover the truth about his death. If she had only confided in me..."

"The world is full of ifs, Katheryn," he sighed. "I have had no word from Captain Crosse yet: I hope William Staines has reminded his future father in law that we wish to see him. I spoke with Father James this morning about Father Chadwick but he was reluctant to discuss the man. I fear he was hiding something."

Katheryn sat forward. "Then we must discover what it is. Is William Staines a reliable man?"

"I always thought so when we were brothers together at Birkenhead - and my Lord Derby clearly thinks so. His promotion in his lordship's household has been swift."

"Then we shall hear from Captain Crosse by and by. We must be patient." She smoothed her skirts and looked up. "And there is Father Nicholas to consider. What is he about? He is to do some mysterious business tonight with a Spanish captain: his wife spoke of it as a way of overcoming their poverty. What is it that could earn a humble chantry priest such a fortune? I am certain that it was something secret; something she should not have told me."

"There is but one way to find out."

As their eyes met they both knew how they would be spending that evening.

Katheryn's trust in the word of William Staines was justified. He sent word by one of the Tower's kitchen lads, that Captain Crosse would receive them that afternoon if their business would not take up too much of his time.

Katheryn did not hesitate. She threw her cloak around her shoulders and looked at Valentine expectantly.

"I'm sorry, Katheryn," he said, "I have much to do. The constable's wife is with child and needs my services. And then there is a child on Moore Street who has a fever and..."

"Very well. I shall go alone. Where is the captain's house?"

Valentine knew better now than to argue with Katheryn once her mind was made up. "He lives on Bank Street near the strand. Be careful. Be mindful of the captain's temper."

"If I cannot charm the captain, Valentine, then there is no hope for me. Have no fear." She grinned at him and swept out.

"Should you not take Jane?" he called after her. But it was no use. She would go her own way. It was hard to care for the safety of one who had no such cares herself. He went about his business and tried not to let worry distract him.

Katheryn found Captain Crosse's tall stone house easily enough and a servant announced her to the captain who stood formidably in the spacious parlour with his back to the fireplace.

"My lady, this is an honour." He bowed awkwardly. He was a large, bear-like man with a gruff voice, more at home bawling at recalcitrant sailors than playing host to a lady. "I had expected the apothecary."

"I apologise, captain. He was called to a patient and I have come in his stead. I wish to clear up a matter that concerns one of the novices lately in my charge. I was, until a few months ago, Abbess of the nunnery of Godstow near Oxford." Captain Crosse raised his eyebrows in surprise. "One of my novices came to Liverpool to stay with relations when our house was closed. You are acquainted with the Moores?"

"All Liverpool is. A family fond of money and power. So your novice was one of them?"

"A poor relation only. She was murdered and I seek her killer."

The captain looked at her. This woman was worth listening to. He called a servant and ordered ale.

"And what is my part in this, my lady. I did not know the girl and I arrived back in port only two days since."

"The girl was enamoured of a priest."

The captain leered knowingly. "Really? Anyone I know?"

"He took great care to avoid discovery. There was a priest who disappeared, I believe. If he should still be in the town..."

The captain took a long drink, avoiding her eyes.

"His name was Father Chadwick. He was master of the chantry school at Our Lady and St. Nicholas. I believe your son received a beating at his hands."

The captain looked up sharply.

"If this priest was a man of violence, then he could be the murderer we seek. My novice, Sister Agnes, was an innocent young girl, unused to the ways of the world. How old is your daughter, captain?"

Captain Crosse's expression softened. "Eighteen years. She is to marry soon, as you no doubt know. Why do you ask?"

"Agnes was the same age, sir. As her Abbess, I felt the responsibility of a mother towards her. Please, sir, if you know anything of this priest you must tell me."

Katheryn's words struck home. For all his rough sailor's ways, Captain Crosse was a sentimental man. He would be a tough captain to his men but an indulgent father to his children.

"I only know that Chadwick is not the one you seek. You must look elsewhere for your sister's murderer."

"But he is a most likely culprit. Do you know if he still dwells in Liverpool?"

The captain shook his head sadly. "He is not the one you seek."

"But how can you be so sure? He did your son a great wrong and that proves he is capable of..."

"He is dead. That's how I know." He blurted out the words and took another drink of ale before replenishing his tankard from the jug on the table.

"Dead? How?"

"I would not have this spread abroad because I take no blame, but I would not welcome questions. Father James knows the truth but he is bound by the seal of the confessional." He looked at Katheryn awkwardly. "Are, er...abbesses bound by such a seal?"

"If you wish it, captain, our conversation will go no further."

"If I had known the apothecary's business, I should never have consented to this meeting, you understand? I wish to forget the sorry incident. But I will tell you if I can trust your silence."

Katheryn nodded. "You have my word."

The captain walked over to the window which overlooked the street and stood there in silence for a while before beginning his narrative.

"Chadwick was vermin. He called himself a priest but he had...certain inclinations. I should never have sent my lad to his school if I had known. One day my Matthew came home in great pain, bruised black and blue. Chadwick had beaten him and tried to...touch him. I was mad with rage and sought the creature out. I was not in control of my temper, I admit. He ran from me out of the churchyard to the part of the strand past the Old Hall. Beyond the sand dunes there are quicksands which can suck a man down in minutes. He made for them then..." He took another drink of ale. "I stopped but he kept running. Then he disappeared...sucked into the sand. There was nothing I could do and - like I said to Father James - nothing I would have done. I was glad the world was rid of such a man. But I was not to blame - Father James said that. It was an accident. Though I had no wish to save him even if I had been able to."

He finished his ale and put the tankard down on the rough oak table in the centre of the room.

"So he is certainly dead?"

"Certainly. He is beneath the sand somewhere...all the easier for his soul to travel to hell."

Katheryn stood. "Father James was right, captain. You have nothing to blame yourself for. I will take my leave and wish your daughter happiness in her marriage."

"I thank you, my lady." He bowed clumsily, his expression still troubled. Captain Crosse would not readily forget the death of Father Chadwick but, Katheryn hoped, with a few lively grandchildren to distract him, the memory and the guilt would fade in time.

The sick of Liverpool kept Valentine busy that afternoon. But the news he had gleaned during his visit to the constable's wife, who was with child for the ninth time, lifted any tiredness he felt and made him hurry back to tell Katheryn what he had learned.

On his return, he found her helping Ralph in the shop. He took her arm and gently drew her into the parlour.

Katheryn told her own news first. She had no wish to betray Captain Crosse's confidences, but she told Valentine with certainty that Father Chadwick could no longer be suspected of any connection with Agnes's death.

"And I heard some talk while I was about my work," Valentine said when she had finished. "The constables have arrested two men for the murder of Father Clement."

"And are they guilty?"

"That I cannot say, of course. But they are held in the jail beneath the Guildhall."

"Is there evidence against them?"

"They had cut the purse of a baker near the Townsend Bridge. The baker raised the hue and cry and the villains were caught. They had the baker's money all right and they were on their way to town to spend it in an ale house."

"But what evidence is there that they killed Father Clement?"

"They possessed a crucifix. As far as I know that is all."

"That means nothing. They could have got that from anywhere. What do the villains say?"

"They deny everything. But then they face the gallows so they would deny it."

"Has the crucifix been identified as Father Clement's?"

"I do not know, truly. I know only what I have told you. Surely this has nothing to do with Agnes's death."

Katheryn put down the pot of ointment she was holding and turned to face Valentine. "I should like to question these villains. If you wish to come with me..."

"This is foolishness, Katheryn. You cannot go questioning the King's prisoners."

"My duties of an Abbess included visiting those less fortunate. Did not Our Lord...?"

"The town jail is not a pleasant place. There is disease and..."

"If we are to find out the truth, we must ask questions. I wish to know if these men killed Father Clement. That is all."

Valentine saw that he would lose the fight. But he couldn't let her go alone to such a place. They knew him at the jail and he would be let through without question. Katheryn needed him.

"Very well, but remember that I advised against it. I will come with you, of course."

"Your presence will make the task so much lighter."

A few minutes later Valentine walked with Katheryn to the Guildhall, just fifty yards down the street. The town gaol occupied the ground floor and up a flight of steps was the well appointed meeting place of the mayor and his council. A stark contrast under the same roof.

The gaoler, a big sweaty man in a stained leather jerkin that strained at the seams against its wearer's bulk, greeted Valentine like an old friend and launched into a recital of the symptoms of his chronic stomach ache. Valentine listened patiently while Katheryn hung back just within the doorway. After giving some advice and promising to drop off some medicine later which was bound to give relief, Valentine made his request. The gaoler looked slightly uncomfortable but could hardly refuse.

He unlocked one of the fetid cells and Valentine entered, Katheryn following, her hand to her nose. On the filthy, flea ridden straw pallets sat two sorry looking creatures, probably in their twenties but with the wizened, weary look of old men; their lank straggly hair was a uniform grey with filth. They looked up with defeated eyes. They were used to visitors, all of whom were hostile.

Valentine greeted them courteously and Katheryn could see the surprise on their faces. These men were used to being treated little better than dogs. All human dignity had left them a fair while ago. She took her hand from her nose: these men stank but she did not wish to remind them of the fact.

"My friends," Valentine began. Katheryn noticed Valentine's gentle greeting kindle a spark of humanity in the villains' eyes. "I hope it will be in order to ask you a few questions."

The men made no reply but stared dumbly. Valentine continued.

"I understand that you are accused of robbing a man, a baker?" The men again stayed silent. This crime was not in dispute. "And the magistrates would like to convict you of another, more serious crime - murder."

One of the men hauled himself upright. "That's a lie. We never murdered nobody. I swear on my dead baby's grave...we never. We robbed that fat bastard to eat. He was on the bridge, his purse bulging and our bellies empty. Believe us, sir. We took only money. We meant no harm to no one."

Valentine looked the man in the eye. "I believe you, my friend. But I have heard tell that a certain item was found in your possession: a crucifix. The murdered man was a priest so you understand the reason for the constable's suspicion, do you not?"

"I told them. It was given me by one of the fathers when I left the abbey lands. When they closed the abbey we were all thrown off and Father Gregory gave me his crucifix and his blessing. I swear on the Holy Book. Believe me sir."

"Which abbey was this?"

"Norton. I worked on the land. I had no skill but the Fathers were good to us."

The second man, thin and sick looking, nodded weakly in agreement. He looked too ill to speak but Valentine turned to him. "And you, my friend...have you anything to say?"

The voice was weak, barely audible. "Hodge speaks the truth, sir. We stole from the baker and others like him, but we have never harmed any of God's creatures. And we would never do harm to a priest: believe us, sir, we never would." He sank back against the verminous pallet, exhausted by the effort of speech.

Valentine turned to Katheryn who stood silently listening by the door. She nodded. She had heard enough. He turned back to the sick man.

"I will visit again, my friend and bring some physic. Until then, I bid you good day."

When they were out of earshot of the prisoners Valentine gently upbraided the gaoler for not calling him to treat the sick man. "Did you not see that he was in need of my services?"

"I did not think it worth it, Master, seeing the rogue will hang soon."

"I shall be back soon with some medicines for him. And as for hanging, you may be mistaken about that."

Valentine swept from the gaol and out into Dale Street with Katheryn following behind. She drew alongside him and she could tell he was angry.

"You did well in there, Valentine. The men are innocent of Father Clement's death."

"But can we prove it?"

"If we find Father Gregory, he will vouch for the truth of their story. They are poor lost souls - there are many such since the religious houses were closed. We got pensions and rewards, but our workers - those who tended our land and our farms and those who worked in our kitchens and households - what became of them?"

"Father Gregory might not be easy to find. He could be anywhere."

"We gain nothing by talk. If we visit the Norton lands, someone might know the whereabouts of some of the Fathers. Is it far?"

"Not far. A few hours' ride on a good horse. But first I must see the Constable. He is a fair man and will listen to me. I tended his wife today and I saved the life of his last baby so he owes me a favour."

"See him now, Valentine. We must ensure that those men do not hang for a murder they did not commit."

"They may hang anyway for the theft."

"They are poor men, Valentine...and desperate. If you spoke to the Magistrate..."

"To Master Crosse? Katheryn I could not..."

"Another Crosse? What manner of man is he, this Master Crosse?"

"Owner of Crosse Hall, Mayor of Liverpool, Justice of the Peace and a reasonable man."

"Then he will listen. Mercy and charity cost a man nothing but they ensure a reward in heaven. Tell that to Master Crosse."

"I will try. Meanwhile I must talk with the constable."

"I shall be praying for you." Katheryn touched his arm gently.

Valentine turned back towards the Guildhall and Katheryn walked the short way back to the shop, narrowly avoiding being drenched by the contents of a chamber pot flung into the street from an overhanging upstairs window.

As she walked, she made plans. A trip to Norton might prove fruitful in other ways. Maybe there were other priests from that house in the town: maybe Agnes's lover had been a canon of Norton. And if they found Father Gregory, he might know where his brothers had headed when Norton Abbey had been so cruelly despoiled... if not what fortunes had awaited them.

But Norton would have to wait for tomorrow. That evening they had another matter to attend to.

CHAPTER 19

There was nothing more that Katheryn and Valentine could do for Hodge and his friend that night. The constable had promised to inform the Magistrate of their misgivings: they could only trust in his fairness.

But now they stood on the strand in the gloom of dusk, well wrapped against the cold. The Santa Isabella lay at anchor some way out in the River Mersey and rowing boats and small sailing craft scuttled around the larger merchantmen like insects skimming on the oily water.

The strand was filled with the songs and chatter of sailors and fishermen about to set out for a night on the water. Katheryn and Valentine stood by the sheltering walls of the Tower and waited, hoping they wouldn't miss Father Nicholas in the dimming light.

Katheryn stamped her feet on the sand to ward off the cold: how Jane would scold her for spoiling the fine Spanish leather of her boots on the damp sand, saying that the marks left by salt water were the devil's own job to clean.

The sound of oars on the water nearby alerted them to the approach of a small rowing boat. In the half-light Katheryn could make out two figures in the craft. One, a roughly clad sailor, jumped from the boat and dragged it up onto the shore. The other man sat, straight backed, until the boat was far enough out of the water for him to disembark without wetting his feet. The seated man, dressed in a fine soft leather coat and velvet cap, barked an order in Spanish to the sailor who then helped him out of the boat. The well dressed man looked around impatiently, and muttered something to his companion that Katheryn, being a short distance away, could not make out.

She touched Valentine's arm. "Let us walk along the Strand towards the church. If Father Nicholas has a meeting with these men, he will come that way and I do not wish to encounter him when he is in their company. If he should be up to anything amiss..."

Valentine took her arm and they strolled past the two Spaniards who were looking about restlessly as if they were expecting someone to join them. They looked nervous, uneasy.

Katheryn and Valentine didn't meet Father Nicholas until they reached the churchyard gate. He had the anxious look of somebody in a hurry.

"Good evening to you, Father Nicholas."

He nodded to Katheryn curtly, as though he dreaded any delay. Valentine caught his arm and Nicholas looked at him in alarm. "Please, brother, I am late for an appointment."

"With a Spanish captain perhaps?"

Nicholas looked at Valentine, quite crestfallen. "How did you know? Have I been watched?"

"Not by us, Father. We discovered your meeting by chance."

"So what will you do? My wife is with child. We need money to live. If there was another way I should have taken it, but when Captain Sanchez came to confession and told me he had a particular devotion to the saint, I told him my secret. He offered me so much...a fortune and I could not refuse. Say you will not betray me to the authorities."

Katheryn spoke gently. "I have no wish to betray you, Father. I think you an honest man...and so does your wife. But if you wish us to harbour no suspicions, I suggest that you tell us the truth. What is it you would trade with the Captain of the Santa Isabella?"

Nicholas looked surprised: this woman seemed to know so much and telling the truth would do no harm: she was no sympathiser with the despoiler of the monasteries. Reverently, he pulled a soft leather bag from the inside of his threadbare cloak. "It has brought me much good fortune," he said. "I am loath to part with it but I know the captain to be a devout man."

Father Nicholas opened the bag and gently pushed its folds aside so the contents were visible. Katheryn's hand went to her mouth to suppress a gasp of horror. Against the leather of the bag lay a hand, the skeletal fingers blackened with the remnants of leathery skin.

"It is the hand of Saint James, torn from its casket when the commissioners visited our abbey at Whalley and flung to the ground. The casket was gold and inlaid with jewels so you can guess what happened to that: the rogues stole everything of earthly value. But the hand itself I rescued and kept safe." He stroked the thing lovingly. "Captain Sanchez has offered me a great deal of money for it, more than I could earn in three years."

Nicholas looked down the strand to where the Spaniards were waiting. "He waits for me and I must keep my part of the bargain." He packed the relic carefully back in its bag. "I wish I did not have to part with this holy thing but I am a man of my word. The captain agreed that I should keep it with me until it was time for him to leave Liverpool. He sails tonight on the tide."

Katheryn nodded. She understood the priest's feelings. The relic had been a comfort in adversity. Whether it was actually the hand of Saint James, Katheryn doubted: spurious relics were only too common. But Nicholas believed it was real and drew comfort from it.

"You must go to the captain and complete your transaction," she said gently.

They watched as Nicholas strode purposefully along the sand to meet Sanchez. Their business took but a moment then Sanchez bowed and, holding the leather bag like a delicate and precious thing, climbed into his boat and was rowed off towards the shadowy bulk of the Santa Isabella, now displaying lanterns that reflected ribbons of light onto the darkening water.

It wasn't long before Nicholas returned, a purse of gold clutched tightly to his chest. Katheryn and Valentine turned to walk with him towards his cottage. Valentine did not like to think that the money gained by the priest's personal sacrifice might be gone in a moment if he encountered thieves on his journey home.

It was nearly dark when they passed St. Mary del Quay. The windows of the chapel glowed golden from the candlelight within. A tall limping figure was approaching the chapel door. Nicholas stopped.

"What is it?" asked Valentine.

"That man. I know him. Even in this poor light...I know him."

"Who is it?"

"His name is John Estgate. He was a brother of my abbey at Whalley. He used to travel with me to tend to the abbey's lands at Stanlow over the river and the grange at Aigburth nearby. We both spent much time near Liverpool so I came to know him well. But I have not seen him since we were forced to leave the abbey. He stood trial for treason with others. They were executed - even our Lord Abbot - but John was acquitted. It shows there is some little justice for I know that he was innocent - as were the others, God rest their souls."

John Estgate looked about him, opened the door of the chapel and slipped inside. His manner suggested that he had no wish to be seen.

"Will you go into the chapel to greet your brother, Father Nicholas?" asked Katheryn, watching the priest's face carefully.

Nicholas shook his head. "I think not. I would guess that he does not wish to have his business disturbed."

"And what is his business, I wonder?"

Nicholas looked Katheryn in the eye. "There are many, my lady - I am not one of them for I lack the courage - who would defy the King's laws if those laws contradict the laws of God. I ask no questions and I do not want to know."

"And John Estgate?"

"He has every reason to join their number. His own brother, Richard Estgate, met his death at the hands of the King - as did our Abbott and another of our brothers in Christ. If John is now engaged in any plot that might restore God's rule to this land, I keep silent about it. Come, let us go."

He turned away and began to walk towards Chapel Street and his home. Katheryn and Valentine followed. Whatever was going on in the chapel of St. Mary del Quay was none of their concern.

The three soldiers seemed to appear from nowhere. Nicholas stopped and pressed himself against the wall that separated the churchyard from the strand: Katheryn and Valentine did likewise. The soldiers, silent and well disciplined, approached the chapel. Katheryn recognised Captain Wharton as one of the men who was kicking at the wooden door.

"I'll fetch Bartholomew," Valentine hissed. "Stay out of sight...both of you." He ran down the strand past fishermen who were studiously minding their own business: they had no wish to become involved and risk the wrath of the King's garrison.

Katheryn stayed, pressed against the wall, her heart pounding. Wharton and his men were trained and armed fighters; there would be no deflecting them from their purpose. For the second time in her life she felt helpless - the first time being when she and her sisters were ejected from the peace of their abbey. Helplessness was not a condition Katheryn felt comfortable with.

"We must do something," she whispered to Nicholas who stood, fearful, beside her.

"It would be of no use. They would cut us both down and make their excuses afterwards. I beg you, my Lady, do nothing foolish."

But Katheryn had no intention of abandoning caution. She waited.

It was not long before the soldiers reappeared. Under Wharton's watchful eye they carried a large wooden chest, staggering under its weight and they made their way across the strand to a small single sailed barque at the end of a wooden jetty. Katheryn and Nicholas watched as they lowered the chest carefully into the boat and then rowed away into the gathering darkness.

Katheryn had supposed that Wharton had come to arrest conspirators, but they had left not with prisoners, but with a heavily laden chest. She thought it unlikely that they would find the men in the chapel alive.

Wharton's boat was disappearing out of sight when Valentine returned with Bartholomew, who looked tired after his days work.

"The men in the chapel may be in need of our help, brothers," said Katheryn quietly before climbing the steps to the churchyard gate.

The men followed, apprehensive, each one praying that they would not find a scene of bloodshed in St. Mary del Quay.

Nervously, Bartholomew pushed the battered chapel door open. The damage inflicted by Wharton's kicks was clearly visible. The others hung back as he entered but then he turned and signalled them to follow.

They found the chapel littered not with bleeding corpses, but with the fragments of the statue of the Virgin that had stood by the altar. Two men sat amongst the debris, their faces showing the marks of their defeat. Luckily, it seemed that the men had received no injuries more serious than a black eye or a superficial sword slash. Many would have thought Father James and John Estgate fortunate in the circumstances.

Father James spoke first. "They smashed her with their swords. They smashed Our Lady." He mumbled, close to tears. "They said they came to finish the commissioners' work. We hid her safe when they came last...hid her inside the altar. We did not think they would return."

"What else did they do, Father?" Katheryn asked firmly. "They took something. What was it?"

Estgate sat silent. James spoke again. "It can do no harm to tell these good people, John. They have all suffered at the King's hands."

Estgate looked up and nodded: then he spotted Nicholas hovering anxiously in the background. "It is good to see you, Brother Nicholas," he called across the chapel. "I should have asked you to join our cause but Father James here says you are now a married man with much to lose...unlike myself."

Nicholas stepped forward and clasped Estgate's hand. "I have prayed for you often, Brother. I am glad you are safe. It is a miracle."

"It is indeed. Our fellowship of the five wounds has much support. I and others hope to raise another Pilgrimage of Grace to plead with the King to dismiss his ungodly ministers and restore the church to her former power."

Katheryn saw the fire of idealistic fervour burning in Estgate's eyes. The man was naive, she thought, if he considered the King to be a puppet of wicked ministers: King Henry the eighth was well capable of indulging in wickedness without any help from others.

But there were many like Estgate, trusting and unworldly: many who had paid for their defiance after the last uprising in the north with their earthly remains dismembered and hanging from trees and town walls as a warning to others. John Estgate and Father James had not heeded that warning. The five wounds of Christ had been the badge of the northern rebels three years before. And if Estgate and his fellows hoped to revive the spirit of the first northern rising, they were playing a dangerous game.

She looked Estgate in the eye. "What was in the chest that the captain of the castle garrison and his men carried away from here and took across the river?" Directness was usually the best way to obtain answers.

It was James who answered. "Brother John here has been travelling the north gaining support for his holy cause. But his work needs money."

He turned to Valentine and Bartholomew. "The treasure of Birkenhead Priory, brothers...the commissioners did not steal it. They took two small chalices, a jewelled cross and three patens but they got no more. Prior Sharp managed to hide the bulk of it when they came calling. I was saying mass when they came and I helped him....so did Brother Francis the cellarer. At first we hid the treasure in the passageway that leads from the priory crypt to the shore. Then we thought Brother Francis's corn bins a less obvious place. When the priory was left to ruin we moved it over the water to our hiding place here in the chapel."

He walked over to the altar and Katheryn followed him. Behind the altar was a sliding panel which James drew aside to reveal a spacious hiding place, big enough to contain the chest she had seen Wharton take across the river.

"When I heard the commissioners were due to visit here, I fixed the panel so that it would move aside. I hid the statue of Our Lady there: I knew that they intended to harm her." He looked at the fragments on the floor and tears brimmed in his eyes. "She has been good to the people of this town."

"I 'm sure God and His Mother hear your prayers, Father James, statue or no statue." Katheryn touched his arm comfortingly.

James nodded and continued. "When the commissioners left we put Our Lady back in her place where she has stood for hundreds of years, and we brought the priory treasure over here and hid it inside the altar. We thought it would be safe there until we could use it for our work. There was but one moment of danger. It was on St. Matthew's Eve. Brother Francis was taking a small chalice from the chest to give to Brother John to sell - he needed money from time to time, you understand - when that unfortunate girl, Agnes Moore, came in to pray. I had just entered the chapel and I noticed that Francis, thinking himself alone, had risen up from behind the altar. I did not wish Agnes to see him. If our secret should be known..."

Katheryn smiled. "She did see him. The candles must have cast his shadow on the wall for she thought she had seen the devil: she thought it a judgement for her sins."

James looked troubled. "The poor child," he said simply.

"Did Brother Francis see who attacked her?"

James looked down at the floor. "I did not wish to hurt her, just to stun her while we made our escape. I could not risk our secret being discovered." Katheryn looked at him in disbelief. "I did not know she was with child. I did not wish her to come to any harm. Do you think I have not repented of my sin a thousand times. Yet in a holy cause, maybe it was permissible." James looked unsure of his ground.

Katheryn stared at James, her heart pounding with fury. "I am sure it is not the Lord's will that you cudgel my novices to prosper your deeds," she hissed.

James bowed his head sheepishly as Katheryn turned away from him, trying to contain her wrath. With effort she managed to compose herself. "There is nothing more we can do here, brothers. I fear we shall see no more of Birkenhead Priory's treasure as I suspect it is gone to line Captain Wharton's pockets."

"Wharton threatened us with hanging if we spoke out," said John Estgate bitterly.

Bartholomew shook his dark tousled head. "I hate to think of the holy treasure of our priory in his filthy hands."

There was nothing more to be done. Katheryn swept from the chapel, still furious with Father James. She had never thought him to be Agnes's killer, but now that she knew him to be capable of violence against a young woman she began to reconsider her opinion.

Valentine and Bartholomew followed her, as did Nicholas who was torn between the company of his old friend John Estgate and a desire for a safe escort home with his purse of Spanish gold. The latter won. He bid a hasty farewell to John, inviting him to take a meal with him and Mary when times were better.

When they reached Valentine's shop, Katheryn went straight to her chamber and prayed that her anger would soon subside.

CHAPTER 20

Valentine was working in the shop when Katheryn came down the next morning. Jane had found her mistress uncharacteristically quiet as she brushed her hair and helped her dress. Something was wrong.

Before Valentine could bid her good morning, the shop door opened and Bartholomew entered, breathless. "I need to talk to you, brother. I know where they have taken the priory treasure."

Valentine looked sceptical. "It could be anywhere. Wharton's no fool. He'll have a safe hiding place."

Bartholomew shook his head. "I have seen him cross the river often. When he lands on the Birkenhead side, he goes off in the direction of the priory. I think he's taken our treasure back home, brother. Who would think to look for it there?"

"Even if you are right, who would dare to recover it and risk hanging? I beg you, Bartholomew, don't let the lure of gold cloud your judgement. Attend to your ferry. It is safer."

"But..."

"But nothing, brother. Keep out of the matter, I beg you."

"So you would let that rogue steal it for himself? He will not hand it over to the King, of that I'm sure."

Katheryn had stayed silent, but seeing Bartholomew's obstinacy, she felt compelled to speak. "Valentine is right, brother. Unless we have good reason for alerting the constable to Wharton's treachery, we must let the matter lie. He could betray Father James and John Estgate and they could hang or worse for their treason. Unless we have proof that Wharton is a thief we cannot move against him. He could say he was storing the treasure in a private place for safe keeping until it could be handed to the King's officers."

The conversation ceased abruptly as the door opened and a large gentleman of middling height and years stepped into the sweet-smelling shop. The man had a round shiny face and his steel grey hair fell in a fringe round a large bald dome in the centre giving the effect of an exaggerated monk's tonsure. He wore a rich brown velvet coat over a crisp linen shirt. His demeanour and apparel proclaimed him to be a man of substance.

Valentine greeted him. "Master Crosse, this is an honour indeed. May I introduce Lady Katheryn Bulkeley who is my guest."

Katheryn smiled and inclined her head. Master Crosse did likewise. Bartholomew stepped into the background, trying to make himself inconspicuous in this auspicious gathering.

Valentine continued. "Please step through to the parlour, Master Crosse. How may I be of service to you?"

After niceties were exchanged, Master Crosse of Crosse Hall, Justice of the Peace and Mayor of Liverpool, seated himself comfortably by the fire and sipped a cup of the best wine Valentine could offer. He quickly came to the purpose of his visit.

"Although I have much pleasure in our meetings, Master Valentine, I am afraid that this time I come on the King's business. As Magistrate I am to deal with two villains now incarcerated in the town jail."

Katheryn, seated on the other side of the fireplace, noted that his voice was deep and pleasant. Here was a man who was used to authority, but used it wisely.

Crosse continued. "I am told by the constable that you have visited these men?"

"I did indeed...and Lady Katheryn with me. They are sorry rogues and no mistake."

"I understand you have some doubt as to their guilt," said Crosse, concern in his voice.

The men were most fortunate, Katheryn thought, that such a man would decide their case. There were many who would hang them without bothering to question their guilt: the mere fact that they were destitute would be enough to condemn them.

"If I may speak, Master Crosse," said Katheryn. "I formed some opinion of the unfortunate men."

Crosse studied her. Valentine clearly valued this woman's opinions...and the apothecary's judgement was usually to be trusted. "Pray tell, my lady, what is your opinion?"

"I think the men's poverty has forced them into wrongdoing," Katheryn replied with determination. "They admit taking the baker's purse but they utterly deny the murder of Father Clement and I am inclined to believe them. The Father's hand was severed from his body, if you recall. Master Valentine and I have discovered one who robs graves to obtain such objects for use in the worship of Satan. He is a juggler with yellow hair. We encountered him once but he escaped us. I suggest you order the constable and his men to keep a lookout for him next market day...if he dares to show his face in Liverpool now that his evil has been uncovered."

"So you are convinced of our rogues' innocence?"

"Of the murder, certainly."

"And the crucifix they had in their possession?"

"They said it was given to them by a Father Gregory, a canon of Norton, when they left the service of the abbey there." She looked across at Valentine. "If you would allow us, Master Crosse, Master Valentine and I would be happy to verify this...if we can find the good Father in question. Would this satisfy you as to their innocence?"

"It would go a long way to convincing me, madam." He smiled at her, business like. Here was a woman who spoke straight and knew her own mind. If only Mistress Crosse and his giddy daughters had been gifted with such sound common sense.

Norton Abbey was a few hours ride away on the far banks of the Mersey near the village of Runcorn and the King's castle at Halton. Katheryn said a prayer of thanks that the weather had held fair. It was not a journey to be undertaken in the wet. The land around the abbey was prone to flooding; a fact which had caused the Augustinian canons who lived there much concern throughout its history.

The tower of the great abbey church grew closer as they approached. From a distance the buildings seemed intact. The two visitors could almost imagine that they were back in the days of peace before the King's commissioners had shattered their ordered world, and that they would be greeted as guests by the hospitaller at the end of their journey and taken into the presence of the Abbot in his well appointed lodgings.

But such idle musings receded as they drew nearer. The lead had been stripped from the roofs of church and monastery buildings alike, leaving only the strongest stone walls standing and the wood of the beams and floors rotting and splintering away. The local people had helped themselves to the stone, causing the walls to tumble here and there.

Surprisingly, in the outer courtyard, stood a statue, some eleven feet high. A bearded giant of a man carried a child on his shoulder, his feet immersed in a great block of stone covered in carved fishes. St. Christopher, the patron saint of travellers, looked down on Katheryn and Valentine benignly, blessing their journey. How this great figure had escaped the commissioners' axes, Katheryn did not know. But she was glad the saint was still intact to guard the abbey as he had done in happier times.

Slowly, on horseback, Katheryn and Valentine rode about the buildings, alighting to enter the doorless, roofless church, its size, tiles and remaining carvings giving an indication of its former glories. The tombs of the abbots and of the Dutton family - once the abbey's benefactors but more recently the means of its destruction - lay open to the elements; their carvings and recumbent figures wearing away in the river damp and the rain.

The place was silent apart from the song of the birds and the restless stamping of their horses' hooves.

"We cannot hope to find any of the brothers here," said Katheryn without emotion.

"Some might serve in churches nearby...or work in other ways. There was an inn we passed on the road. We can ask there and beg a night's lodging from the landlord: we can't return to Liverpool before dark." He suddenly frowned. "If that suits you, Katheryn."

"If we must stay, so be it. There are many in the land who cannot afford a bed for the night. We must count ourselves fortunate."

The landlord of the inn, a tall lanky man with a long solemn face which belied his good humour, greeted them effusively. Travellers, he said cheerfully, did not often come this way and he and his good lady would be honoured if her ladyship and her companion would be their guests for the night. They were shown to their rooms by the landlord's wife who was a short round woman with a retiring disposition; the opposite of her husband.

The rooms were simple but spotless and joined by a communicating door. Katheryn, in a moment of irresolution, wished she had brought Jane or Will with her: in the presence of another there would be no question of temptation. Then she said a quick prayer of contrition for even thinking such thoughts. Her relationship with Valentine had been decided: they were friends...nothing more.

After an ample meal of freshly baked bread, cheese and meat pie washed down with a good strong ale, Katheryn asked the landlord to join them and tell them something of the district. It wasn't hard to bring the subject round to the Abbey.

"I hear that Abbot Birkett's out of prison," said the landlord confidentially. "Though they say he's much changed."

"Indeed? How changed?" Katheryn leaned forward encouragingly.

"They say that prison has broken him. I had a man from Chester here a week past. He'd met the poor Abbot and spoken with him. Poor man, he was ever a good landlord to us: and the fathers were much loved in the district."

""Do you know what became of any of them?"

"Father Gregory has a post as chantry priest in the church at Runcorn. Father Edmund, Father Theobald and Father John were taken by Sir Piers Dutton and imprisoned in Chester castle with Abbot Birkett. I hear they have now been given their freedom, thanks be to God. I feared they would face the rope."

"And Father Clement? Did you know him?"

The landlord smiled. "A true Christian man if ever I met one was Father Clement. He was good to us when our daughter died; said her requiem for no fee. Though I don't know what became of him."

"I'm sorry to bear bad tidings to you, landlord," said Valentine softly. "But Father Clement was cruelly done to death by robbers in Liverpool not long since. He served as chantry priest in the church of Our Lady and St. Nicholas there."

The landlord made the sign of the cross and looked genuinely upset by the news. Here was one who held a high opinion of Father Clement, whatever others might say. The man shook his head. "We live in terrible times."

Do any other former monks of Norton live hereabouts?" Katheryn asked, changing the subject. As well as speaking to Father Gregory about the crucifix, she was now full of curiosity about the true nature of Father Clement. The landlord here painted him as a saintly man: in Liverpool she had heard a different story. She wanted to hear the truth.

"There is Father Robert Janyns who farms the Abbey lands. You'll find his house half a mile east of the Abbey church. He stayed on here and married a local girl...Margaret, the miller's daughter." The landlord looked slightly disapproving of this last fact.

There would be no time to find Robert Janyns and ride over to Runcorn before darkness set in. After a brief discussion, Katheryn and Valentine agreed to see the monk turned farmer that afternoon and seek out Father Gregory in the morning on their way home.

Robert Janyn's farmhouse was easy to find and they were received by a plain, fair haired woman in her thirties whose face was transformed to prettiness when she smiled to greet them.

She rocked a wooden cradle with her foot as she wrapped her cheeses in muslin. Her husband Robert, she explained was out in the fields tending the cattle. The little farmhouse was well kept and humbly prosperous. Robert Janyns had not suffered much by the closure of Norton Abbey.

They found him, as his wife had said, in the fields leading down to the River Mersey in the company of half a dozen healthy looking cows. He had the contented look of a born farmer whose land was prospering well.

He greeted his visitors courteously and listened to their questions. As they spoke the expression on his placid, almost bovine, face became troubled. "You ask about Father Clement? I don't understand."

"He was a priest near my home in Liverpool," Valentine explained again patiently. "He was done to death by footpads."

Robert shook his head. "That's not possible."

"Please explain," said Valentine, growing impatient.

Robert Janyns leaned on his stout staff and regarded the cows, calmly chewing the cud around him: it seemed that Janyn's thought processes were starting to match the pace of his animals. It was no use hurrying him.

"Father Clement was a good man," he began. "An example to all of us weaker vessels." He smiled to himself and continued. "There was a worker on our lands who sought his help. He feared his wife was being unfaithful. His name was Walter de Daresbury and his wife was much younger than him...a pretty little thing she was. It seemed that when Walter was away working, the son of our steward would keep her company. Walter was older than his wife as I said and they'd not been blessed with children...but soon Lucy, his wife, was with child."

"Tongues wagged and fingers pointed and it was said that the steward's son was the child's father. He was a wicked lot. He'd gone to Liverpool to work for a wealthy family there for a while but then he came back and we cursed the day he did." Robert shook his head in disgust. "No maid was safe and he used all folk alike for his own ends. He was bad before he went to Liverpool but he came back worse. There were some said he had powers beyond that of a common man; that he consorted with Satan...but I never knew of it." He fell silent for a while, ruminating on the nature of evil.

"So what happened?" prompted Katheryn.

"Things began to happen...bad things. Walter de Daresbury was arrested for stealing a gold plate from the Abbey. The steward's son bore witness against him and the plate was found beneath Walter's mattress. He was thrown in jail and his right hand was cut off as punishment. By the Abbot's charity, Lucy was allowed to stay in their cottage but she died in childbed and the babe with her. They were healthy enough till the steward's son visited to see his bastard. There were some spoke of poison. A few days after she died the commissioners came to the Abbey."

He paused for a few moments before continuing.

"It was in the October three years back. They were late finishing their thieving and destruction so they decided to stay the night at our Abbey. The people round about were angry. The Abbey and the fathers were well regarded. Our Abbot, John Birkett, led the tenants and the commissioners took fright and hid themselves in the tower. Walter de Daresbury and his wife were forgotten in all the excitement." He smiled at this memory: getting the better of the King's commissioners, even for a few hours, must have been a satisfying experience. "Such a feast we had. We roasted an ox and great fires burned. And we thought to give those robbing King's men a message they would not forget." His eyes gleamed at the recollection of that night when spirits and hopes had been high.

"What happened then?" asked Valentine, guessing that the outcome of the story would not be a happy one.

"I don't know how they did it, but those men in the tower managed to get a message to the High Sheriff, Sir Piers Dutton. He and his men came upon us suddenly and there was a great flight. We escaped by swimming across the Abbey pools: it was the only way. The Abbot and three brethren were taken to Halton as the King's prisoners and it was all over...finished.

The Duttons had always been benefactors of our Abbey: if it wasn't for that, I reckon Sir Piers would have hanged them there and then."

"And what of Father Clement? What happened to him?"

"In truth I don't know what took place that night. I saw them in the distance...that rogue and Clement. I only saw in the light of the fires but they were talking...arguing, I think: after that all was confusion."

"And Walter de Daresbury? What became of him?"

"I never heard of him again. Some say he died in prison but truly I do not know."

"And the steward's son?"

"That I cannot say. He could be in hell for all I know. He is unlikely to be in the other place."

"And did you see Father Clement again?"

"Oh yes, I saw him."

"Do you know where he went?" Katheryn asked anxiously.

"Oh yes. Come. I'll show you."

Katheryn and Valentine allowed themselves to be led back to the derelict shell of the Abbey. Robert Janyns walked slowly: he was not a man to hurry. They stopped in the nave of the ruined church, near where the high altar had been. Janyn's pointed to a patch of bare earth dug in the once magnificently tiled floor of the abbey church. Valentine had noticed it before but had assumed it was the result of villagers plundering the finely decorated tiles.

Janyns stood staring at the spot, his head bowed reverently. "I found him the next morning when all the excitement had died down. He'd been stabbed.

Valentine was puzzled. "Who had?"

"Father Clement. I buried him here; gave him a Christian burial before the high altar where he deserved to be. He was a good man."

Katheryn and Valentine looked at each other. "You're sure it was him?" she asked. "You're certain?"

"I lived with the man for ten years. He was my brother."
Katheryn saw tears well up in the eyes of this simple man who
asked for nothing but a peaceful existence. "He had been
murdered and I did what I could for him. It might have been
Dutton's men but I think not: they harmed nobody else. Their
orders were to detain, not kill."

"So?"

"I think he challenged that creature over his treatment of
Walter and Lucy de Daresbury. Injustice and wickedness
angered Father Clement: he would not tolerate such things."

"And the steward's son...you have no idea what became of
him?"

"He disappeared that night."

Katheryn shook her head. Just when she thought the
picture was becoming clearer all her assumptions had been
shaken by Robert Janyn's revelations. There was one last
question she wanted to ask. "The steward's son...what was his
name?"

"He was a disgrace to the name of his poor father. His
name was Mires...Martin Mires."

CHAPTER 21

The candle guttered as the three men sat round the table. Francis Wells' normally jovial face was drawn with worry. Father James sat brooding and silent, taking frequent sips from his mug of ale. Only Bartholomew seemed restless and wanting action.

"We cannot let the matter rest here, brothers. If Wharton is to keep the treasure for himself, he will not dare to complain of its disappearance. If he did, he would have to admit his wrongdoing. Don't you see, we could get it back."

James shook his head. "Don't be foolish, brother. Wharton would concoct some story; he wouldn't let us get away with it. Besides, John Estgate has fled. We would have to hide it until his return...if that day ever comes. It is useless, brother, and we must do nothing to put ourselves in further danger."

"Even for such a cause as ours?"

Francis and James looked at each other. "Why do you think we did not ask you to join us in the first place, Bartholomew?" said Francis softly. "You were always headstrong. You would have put us in peril by your actions."

Bartholomew stood, spilling his ale as he did so. He marched from the room, angry that these friends of his, these brothers bound to their holy cause, showed such little courage.

He slammed the door of Father James's house and made his way down the moonlit strand towards his boat.

Father Gregory had been easy to find and he had confirmed the story of the imprisoned men. He had indeed given Hodge, the labourer, a crucifix as a remembrance. An expression of deep sadness had appeared on his grey tired face when he heard about the fate of his protégés. He also confirmed Robert Janyns' account of the evil doing of Martin Mires.

They rode home in companionable silence. Katheryn had spent a wakeful night at the inn, looking at the simple wooden door that connected her own room with Valentine's and wondering if she had made the right decision. She did not know that Valentine had spent a similar night thinking similar thoughts. If he had met a woman like Katheryn in his youth, he argued to himself, he would never have committed himself to the vow of chastity.

But neither spoke of it: neither broke their earlier agreement that the subject was dead. They concentrated instead on their new discoveries.

"Mires!" said Katheryn thoughtfully. "The man the juggler was to meet was named Mires. And Master Janyns said that many thought Mires to be in league with Satan. It fits well."

"If Mires is in Liverpool, why is he not known? It is but a small town."

"But not a town like others. It is a port; sailors and merchants come and go without question. A new face causes no comment."

"And the Father Clement who was priest at Our Lady and St. Nicholas? Who was he if the real one was dead?"

"Father James may have been mistaken: he may have been a brother from another Augustinian house. He may have assumed it to be Norton as it was the nearest."

"Father James wasn't mistaken. Clement was recommended by Abbot Birkett himself. It ensured his appointment."

"And how was the abbot to recommend anyone if he was locked up in Chester castle?"

Valentine nodded. What Katheryn said was so obvious. Why had it not been thought of before?

"So the letter he showed to Father James was false?"

"I have no doubt of it. I think Mires took the dead Clement's identity. He went to Chester and become acquainted with Captain Wharton and gained a hold over the captain by means of witchcraft. Then he followed Wharton to Liverpool and obtained his post as chantry priest. He had been raised on Norton Abbey's estates so he'd be familiar with the ways of priests: so familiar he could doubtless pass for one."

Valentine stared at her in disbelief. "So the Father Clement in Liverpool was really Martin Mires? He had killed the real Clement and taken his name?"

"It fits, does it not?"

Valentine shook his head. "Not entirely. The man Mires has traded in the trappings of witchcraft long after the death of Father Clement."

"Mires has killed to change his identity once so why not again? The body of Father James's chantry priest had been in the river for a few days had it not? Was it recognisable?"

"Father James thought so. I did not know the man well as I had only seen him at a distance. There was a ring on his left hand and James said it was the one Clement always wore."

"Then we must speak to Father James." She gave her white mare a gentle kick to hurry her along and she took off at a gallop. Valentine's old cob tried its best to keep up but was trailing far behind when they reached the townsend bridge.

Father James was alone and preoccupied when they came upon him praying in the chantry chapel of St. John. He had unburdened his worries to God but he was still glad to see Valentine. He looked at Katheryn nervously, hoping her anger against him for his attack on Agnes had faded and that she had taken heed of the Lord's commands concerning forgiveness.

He was relieved when she greeted him civilly and he began to voice his worries about Bartholomew.

"Last night I thought he would do something foolish. He thinks he knows where they have taken the treasure and I fear that he might try to recover it on his own. The lad could get himself killed." He looked downcast. "And I should not like another death on my conscience."

Valentine touched his shoulder. "You did not kill Agnes. It was another. Don't blame yourself."

"All Liverpool will blame me."

"Then don't tell all Liverpool. Let the matter rest. The important thing is to catch Agnes's true killer."

"And as to that matter," said Katheryn, "there is some confusion. When you identified the body of Father Clement, are you certain it was him?"

"Yes... but it was difficult. The face was... The creatures of the river had destroyed it. It is often thus with drowned corpses."

"But you are sure it was Father Clement?"

"It was his build and his colouring...and his manner of dress. And I recognised the ring he wore...gold with a black stone. I have never seen another like it: it was his for sure."

"But the body itself may have been another?" she persisted.

"I was certain it was him. I made an honest judgement." Father James was becoming agitated.

"Calm yourself, James," said Valentine gently. "Any mistake you made was made in good faith. What can you tell me of Father Clement?"

James looked mildly surprised at this new line of questioning, then his expression became guarded. He was hiding something. "What do you mean?"

Valentine told him of his visit to Norton and of his conversation with Robert Janyns. Father James shut his eyes. "I knew there was something. But he had been so highly recommended by Abbot Birkett himself. He showed me the letter the abbot had written. It was glowing with praise."

"We searched his quarters," said Katheryn. James looked at her, surprised. "If the letter was genuine, he would have kept it in a place of safety and we found no such letter. I fear it was a forgery. The abbot was in prison when Clement came to take up his post."

James looked away, annoyed with himself, wondering why he hadn't thought of this when Clement first came to him. James made a decision: it would do no harm now to tell the truth about Clement as he had seen it.

"It started soon after he arrived," he began. "I caught him alone with the Mayor's daughter, but fifteen years old. He had his hand on her breast and his expression was one of..." James shook his head in disapproval.

"When he saw me he moved his hand and smiled...as if he was mocking me. Then he spent so much time at the castle. I tried to tell myself that he was attending to the spiritual needs of the men but I suspected there were other reasons for his visits there. His cottage was next to mine and he received visits at night...sometimes from Captain Wharton but more often from women. I heard...noises through the walls. I heard tales about him in the taverns and when I tried to speak with him about it, I was told to mind my own business. I know some priests lead such lives... and I merely thought him one of that kind."

"And was Agnes one of his visitors?" asked Katheryn quietly.

"In truth I don't know, my lady. You should ask Mistress Moore. She knew him. Ask Marjory Moore: she knew him well."

Father James's words jogged Katheryn's memory. Griselda had hinted that Marjory might know something. But Katheryn had been distracted by other events and perhaps reluctant to risk another of Marjory's rejections,. But now that she had new reason to go to the Old Hall, she would not let the woman's hostility discourage her.

Katheryn thought it best to visit Marjory alone so she sent Valentine back to Dale Street to attend to his shop and his patients. Mistress Moore might be unwilling to discuss delicate matters in the presence of a man...and Katheryn suspected that Marjory's revelations might be very delicate indeed. If her suspicions were correct and the wealthy Liverpool family Martin Mires had worked for was the Moores, then Katheryn could only guess what hold Mires might have over Marjory.

She was received coolly at the Old Hall, as she expected. Marjory offered no refreshment but asked her guest sit while she continued with her embroidery. Katheryn came straight to the point.

"What do you know of Martin Mires...lately known in this town as Father Clement?"

Marjory Moore, the authoritative and self possessed mistress of the household, looked as helpless and vulnerable as the youngest maidservant. Her face turned ashen. She opened her mouth to speak but no sound came. Katheryn repeated her question.

"Surely Father James has not broken the seal of the confessional," Marjory whispered, eyes closed.

"He has said nothing, I assure you. The facts were bound to be discovered eventually," Katheryn said confidently. She was making guesses but did not intend to let Marjory know that. "It would be best if you told me everything. It is God's will that wrongdoers be brought to justice."

Marjory nodded. She was a widow with no husband to consider now: and although she had no liking for Katheryn, she presumed her to be a woman who could keep a confidence.

"I was lonely," she began quietly. "My husband was mayor at that time; an important man in the town and much occupied with business. My son had grown and married and had no more use for me."

She looked at Katheryn for sympathy. Katheryn smiled gently and nodded.

"A young man came to Bank Hall as help for our steward there," she continued. "I found myself more and more in his company. In spite of the difference in our ages, he made it clear that he considered me attractive."

She blushed, remembering how her lost youth had been recaptured on a bed of straw above the stables. "Then he began to ask for money and he hinted that my husband and son would find out about... I had some money of my own. I paid him...and I kept meeting him. I know that I was foolish and I hadn't even the excuse of youthful innocence."

"What happened? How did you rid yourself of him?" For the first time Katheryn felt sorry for this woman who must have lived for so many years with the fear that her folly would be exposed to public scrutiny.

"He left," she said simply. "He said he was returning to help his father at Norton. I said a thousand prayers of thanks. I had begun to fear him...especially when he spoke of evil things."

"What evil things?"

"He showed me a doll of wax. He said it was me: he said that he had obtained some of my hairs from my comb and stuck them on the thing's head. It was horrible." She shuddered. "He said he could use it to make me do his will." She looked up at Katheryn, pleading. "But he was most... When we were... He was quite unlike my husband and I wanted him. You have led a life sheltered by the cloister. You could not understand."

Katheryn smiled to herself. She knew the power of sexual attraction as well as any woman. "What happened when he left?"

"I did not hear from him for three years. My husband died, God rest his soul, and I moved here to the Old Hall. I thought I would never see Martin Mires again. I began to lead a life free from lust and sin and I tried to forget the whole episode."

"Then, a few months ago, he called here dressed as a priest. He introduced himself to my servants as Father Clement, Father James's new chantry priest, and had himself shown into this parlour. I came down to receive him unsuspecting and when I saw him there, smiling at me, I almost swooned but I composed myself in the presence of my servants. Then, when we were alone, I asked him his business. He said he'd taken holy orders - which I could not believe, knowing the man's nature - and hinted that he would make my indiscretions of the past known if I did not do his bidding."

She swallowed hard. The memories were painful and embarrassing. "He bid me take him to the old mill. He looked round the place and said it would be ideal for his purposes: I could only guess what those purposes were. He said he needed somewhere private and told me to instruct my servants not to go near the place. Then he...he had his will of me there on the floor of the mill. I did not want to but... He did it to remind me...to let me know I was in his power. I could see no escape from my shame."

Marjory shuddered. Katheryn waited for her to continue.

"When I heard the news that he was dead, I rejoiced. I would be free of him at last. But then I saw him at the mill and I thought he had come back from hell to haunt me. But he was no ghost. He said he had certain business to transact and it suited his purposes for the town to believe him dead. He wished to hide for a while until he could leave Liverpool and he claimed to have important dealings in the town that would make him a rich man. He talked of going to London...of finding a place at the King's court. I don't know who was buried in his place or how he died: it was better not to ask questions."

"And Agnes?" Katheryn asked, almost in a whisper. "Did you know he was her lover?"

Marjory shook her head. "I had no idea. I told him of her condition, never thinking that he had had aught to do with her. Then, after she had been found dead, he told me all. He had met her when they travelled together from Chester and he had found her innocence amusing. She was unsuspecting; she had thought he wanted to court her and gave him her body and her heart...poor silly fool. Of course, I suspected nothing: I thought she had taken up with some sailor or lad from the town." She looked up at Katheryn defiantly. "Do you know what I felt when he told me he had lain with her? I was jealous."

Unable to hold the tears back any longer, Marjory began to sob. Katheryn put a comforting hand on her shoulder and waited patiently for her to compose herself. "He said he had wanted rid of the silly girl; that she had tired him. He told how she would go to him at his cottage and... He was confiding in me and I wanted him still. And I was grateful whenever he tumbled me," she added pathetically. "I was too deep in my sin to see the truth."

"And do you see the truth now?"

Marjory nodded weakly. "I can deceive myself no longer. I was a silly, middle aged woman, enamoured of a rogue. But he is dead: this time I am certain. The mill burned to the ground and I think he was inside. He would not leave without a word. He perished in the fire."

"I think not."

Marjory's eyes lit up with hope. She still wasn't free of Martin Mires. "Where? Where is he?"

"Did he speak of Captain Wharton?"

"Yes, often. He boasted that he had great power over the man; that Captain Wharton would make him rich. That is why he stayed in Liverpool and hid in the mill. When the business with Wharton was over, he said he would go to London."

"In that case, Mistress, I know he is still alive...until the devil claims his own."

Marjory did not reply but sat, staring into space.

CHAPTER 22

When Katheryn returned to Valentine's shop, she found him with Father James who seemed to have grown older and more careworn overnight. When Katheryn said where she had been, the priest gave her a look of sad understanding. Marjory had needed to unburden herself and he hoped Katheryn had been of some help.

Briefly, Katheryn told all she know of Martin Mires, leaving out direct references to Marjory to preserve the lady's confidences.

"So we have discovered Agnes's lover?" said Valentine, sitting back.

"And her killer. The girl was becoming a nuisance and she was too trusting and naive to know when he had grown weary of her. It was an act of great wickedness, to take a young life to preserve his secret."

"But where is he?" asked Father James. "And who is buried in his grave?"

"I think he killed another, dressed the unfortunate man in his clothes and put his ring on the corpse's finger. We were meant to assume that he was dead so that he could take on a new identity...or return to his real identity."

"And the hand?"

Valentine shrugged. "We can only assume it was used for the purposes of witchcraft, as were the desecrated bodies of Childwall."

Father James, who had seemed deep in thought, looked up as if he had received a shattering revelation. "A priest visited me a while back; a Father Theobald from Norton. He had been imprisoned with Abbot Birkett and had just been released from Chester castle. One of his fellow prisoners was another monk of Norton, Father Edmund, who was to have come to Liverpool to board ship for Ireland. He could not be found and had not been heard of. I wonder..."

"If he was killed by Mires to take his place?" suggested Katheryn.

"The description Father Theobald gave of his missing friend could have fitted that of Mires; same colouring, same build. I did not think of it at the time but... Of course, I could be mistaken."

"I think not, James," said Valentine quietly. "The murder of a priest would be of no consequence to Mires."

"Mires boasted of riches and, as Father Clement, he could easily have discovered the secret of Birkenhead Priory's treasure," said Katheryn. "What better way to rob than to use the captain of the king's garrison to do your work for you: who would argue with his authority? Mires plays upon the weaknesses of others to get his will: Agnes's naiveté; Wharton's desire for worldly rewards. Mires used Wharton to plan the theft of the priory's gold and I fear that this man has no conscience and would use any means to get his way."

"Then what do we do?" asked Father James despairingly.

Katheryn stood up. "Captain Wharton is not the only man with authority in this town. He is answerable to Lord Molyneux. And the constables and magistrates would also interest themselves in matters of murder and theft."

She turned to Jane who had been hovering shyly by the doorway. "Jane, tell Will to go to the castle and ask for Sir Thomas Molyneux. Send my compliments and ask Sir Thomas to meet me on the strand by Bartholomew's ferry. And ask him to bring some trustworthy soldiers of the garrison...those not too much in the company of Captain Wharton. Have you got that?"

Jane nodded eagerly and ran off to find Will. She knew he would be in the stables. She sometimes thought he preferred the horses' company to her own...and she had noticed he spent a lot of time in the company of the baker's pretty daughter from next door. Her small shining hopes of love were rapidly tarnishing with Will's neglect. She was glad of any excuse to be in his company.

"I shall go for the constable and send Ralph for Master Crosse," said Valentine. "As Magistrate he should be involved."

Katheryn watched as he left the room and prayed for their safety as she warmed herself by the roaring fire.

"Your servant told me the matter was most urgent," said Sir Thomas Molyneux stiffly as they stood on the sand in the fast fading light.

"It is, Sir Thomas. We are to apprehend the killer of two priests and a young woman...and maybe more besides."

Sir Thomas looked at her in polite disbelief. "And what proof have you, madam? Have you witnesses? Has the man confessed?"

"I have spoken with several who will bear witness to this man's wickedness...and the proof I shall obtain when we confront him," Katheryn said with a confidence she did not feel.

Bartholomew was growing impatient. "We must be away before the tide turns," he called out to them from his ferry. "Please hurry. Wharton went over an hour since."

Sir Thomas still looked sceptical. "And you say Captain Wharton is involved? The man has always been considered most trustworthy by my father. He came highly recommended from Chester. There is nothing known against him."

"He stole the treasure of Birkenhead Priory, Sir Thomas. That is a fact beyond dispute and there are many witnesses to the act. He took it over the river to a hiding place: Bartholomew, the ferryman was a monk of Birkenhead and he knows where it is most likely hidden. Please, Sir Thomas, if we do not act now the treasure will be sold and Wharton and our murderer will be away."

Sir Thomas gave a curt nod. If this lady's suppositions proved true, it would bring him into great favour with his father and the authorities; and who knew where that could lead?"

Valentine appeared from the mouth of Bank Street alone. The constable and his assistant were out arresting a crowd of sailors who had taken too much drink in one of the town's ale houses, he explained, and Master Crosse was away from home on some unspecified business. He looked relieved to see Sir Thomas and the two hatchet faced soldiers who accompanied him. At least they would not have to face Mires and Wharton alone.

Bartholomew's ferry boat was built strongly and on market days even a cow or horse could be accommodated with care. He raised the single sail and the craft skimmed over the dark waters, in and out of merchantmen at anchor, and towards the Birkenhead bank.

Such was the concentration of his passengers that they did not hear the gentle swish of a single oar as a small rowing boat carrying a dark, hooded figure laboured to follow them.

Trapped in the confines of the ferry, Sir Thomas had the chance to question Katheryn further. She explained what she knew as clearly and honestly as she could and Sir Thomas seemed to understand most of the story, although he confessed himself confused when it came to Father Clement's true identity. "You are saying that the priest who said mass for the garrison was no priest but a steward's son who took the identity of a priest he had murdered?"

"You have it, Sir Thomas. In the upheaval caused by the closure of the religious houses there have, I fear, been some who used the confusion as an opportunity for theft and worse."

"Wharton admitted that he and Father Clement - sorry, Mires - were friends in Chester. I didn't see much of Mires but what I saw I did not like."

Katheryn smiled to herself. It was easy to admit to wisdom with hindsight.

The boat jolted gently against the jetty as Bartholomew brought it skilfully back to Birkenhead. The ferryman's mouth was set with grim determination and Katheryn remembered his budding feelings of affection for Agnes; possibly the first time in his life that he had experienced such feelings for a woman. Poor, silly Agnes...Bartholomew might have been her salvation.

But the young man would have to be watched. If he was bent on avenging Agnes's untimely death, she must ensure that he did not take the law into his own hands. Things must be done properly.

Bartholomew left the boat and secured it with habitual thoroughness. He helped Katheryn from the vessel first and the others were left to clamber out as best they could. Katheryn noticed that another smaller boat was moored at the jetty. Wharton had got there before them.

The party made their way up to the Priory in silence. It was dark now and they kept carefully to the trodden path, Bartholomew leading the way. The walls of the Priory stood out black against the night sky and there was no sign of life; no lamp to indicate the presence of others. Katheryn began to wonder if Bartholomew had been mistaken.

The ferryman whispered in the darkness. "You stay back. I'll see if they're there."

Valentine was walking close to Katheryn; she touched his hand. "Do not let him go alone," she whispered. "He will get himself killed." She turned to Sir Thomas and the soldiers. "Sir Thomas, if you stay outside the Priory, I shall go in with Bartholomew and Valentine. They know the buildings well."

Sir Thomas looked alarmed. "My lady, I cannot allow you to walk into danger. If, as you say, the man we seek is a murderer, you must stay here with us."

Katheryn turned round, her eyes blazing with determination. "This man killed one of the sisters whom God entrusted to my care. I have faced danger before, sir." She saw his look of amazement at her boldness and took pity on him. "And besides, Sir Thomas, what harm can come to us when you are so near to leap to our defence?" She smiled at him sweetly and, pulling her cloak closely around her, followed Bartholomew and Valentine into the crumbling Priory buildings.

Bartholomew led the way across the silent cloister. "The crypt would be the best place for a man to hide," he whispered to Valentine. "And we must not forget the tunnels."

Valentine nodded and took hold of Katheryn's hand protectively. She did not pull it away but instead gave Valentine's fingers an encouraging squeeze.

The small door set in the north wall of the cloister opened silently. It had been in use recently, that much was clear. It crossed Katheryn's mind that they should have brought a lantern but, on reflection, she realised that Bartholomew's decision had been a wise one: a lantern would announce their presence as well as any fanfare of trumpets. They tiptoed carefully and quietly down a narrow stone staircase then stood, completely still, staring at the scene before them.

In the far corner of the vaulted crypt, almost hidden by the massive octagonal stone pillars that supported the range of buildings above them, they could see the golden flickering light of a pair of lanterns. There was a low murmur of men's voices. Bartholomew stood frozen, straining to hear, with Katheryn and Valentine behind him. They couldn't make out what was being said but the conversation was punctuated with self congratulatory laughter. The men were celebrating something. In the silences they could hear wine being poured. They were relaxed...vulnerable. Now was the time. Before Valentine could stop her, Katheryn stepped forward.

"I bid you good evening, gentlemen." Her voice echoed confidently through the great vaulted chamber. "Do nothing foolish, I beg you. Sir Thomas Molyneux is outside with soldiers of the garrison."

The two men had swung round to face her, disbelief on their faces. For the first time she took a good look at Mires who was now beginning to relax. He was dark, rugged, well built: a handsome man. Katheryn could see why he had wielded such power over the weaker members of her sex: he would use charm as a weapon when it suited his purposes.

He was already standing, looking at her, a calculating coldness in his eyes and a contemptuous smile on his lips. He bowed low and was about to step forward and take Katheryn's hand when Bartholomew and Valentine stepped forward protectively out of the shadows. Mires put his hand up to indicate that he meant no harm and smiled. The charming, Katheryn thought could be the most dangerous of creatures: had not the serpent charmed Eve in Eden?

It delights me to meet you at last, my lady. I have heard so much of you from my friend, the Captain." He turned to Wharton, who stood nervously playing with the edge of his shirt, and shrugged nonchalantly as though they had been discovered playing cards when they should have been at mass.

"And I have heard much of you, Master Mires."

"It was Father Clement last time I saw him," Bartholomew said, jumpy, anxious to get the affair over with and bring Agnes's killer to justice.

"Yes. It's amazing the opportunities a priest has for sin: it is a great wonder that they are not all corrupted by the power they wield over silly souls." Mires grinned unpleasantly.

"You killed Father Edmund of Norton when he came to Liverpool to seek passage to Ireland. You hoped that he would be mistaken for you and enable you to disappear in safety?" she said with as much confidence as she could muster.

Mires smiled smugly and shook his head. "That's one matter I had nothing to do with. One night I came across a body wearing priest's clothing in an alleyway near the castle. The right hand was cut off and lying by the body." He smiled unpleasantly. "I took it. I need such items from time to time. Then the idea came to me: this dead priest was of my height and colouring and it would suit my purposes to be thought dead. So I put my ring upon his left hand, heaved him to the top of the castle rock and threw him over: it was high tide and I knew the water would do its work. I returned to my cottage to gather some possessions then I sought refuge in Mistress Marjory's mill."

He laughed to himself as if enjoying some private joke. "I take no blame for Father Edmund's murder; he was well dead when I found him. I merely arranged for the disposal of the body. My time spent as a priest was of great use to me for a while but I have larger ambitions...as the Captain here will testify."

Katheryn, surprised by this denial, persisted trying hard not to show her dislike. She knew that if she angered him he would not talk. "And Agnes...she was pretty, was she not?" She heard Bartholomew gasp behind her.

"She would pursue me: the silly creature couldn't accept that it was all a moment's pleasure. I made her acquaintance on the way here from Chester. She was so innocent, so compliant...and a virgin - that was amusing. Then when I had to disappear, I feared she would be a nuisance. She clung to me and I knew she would start asking questions."

"One night I did some business with a juggler, the nature of which I shall not reveal. He went off with a whore and I thought to visit Captain Wharton by way of the castle tunnel and the postern gate. Then I saw Agnes near the boathouse on the strand with Sir Edward. I knew he was no danger to me as his mind rarely rises above his loins...but talk spreads in a town like this. I followed them and when Agnes ran out of that boathouse as if the hounds of hell were after her and flung herself into the river, it was easy to dispose of her: she almost did the job herself. All I had to do was help her on her way to hell."

"You took her across the river?"

"When she was dead. I didn't want her found too near the castle: there might have been questions asked."

Katheryn swallowed hard. She felt sick with disgust at the cool way in which this creature spoke of the young woman's death.

Wharton had remained silent in the background; but now he stared at Mires uncomprehendingly as though he had not known the full extent of the man's evil.

But it was more than Bartholomew could stand. He lunged towards Mires but Agnes's murderer was too quick for him. Valentine rushed forward and hardly saw the flash of the dagger before it was thrust into Bartholomew's body.

The ferryman lay on the floor, gasping, and Valentine jumped to his aid. Katheryn knelt to help Valentine but a sound, a grating of stone against stone, made her turn. In the far wall of the undercroft a black hole, a passage in the rock, had appeared in the solid stone wall, clearly visible in the gentle gold lantern light. Mires disappeared into its depths. Wharton hesitated. He could hear Mires' footsteps receding down the tunnel.

Mires must have stopped in his flight because he called urgently to Wharton "Bring the chest. Move man. Now." He barked out the order and Wharton, dazed, followed the instruction with the automatic obedience of the professional soldier.

Mires must have been well down the passage by the time Wharton picked up the wooden chest he had been sitting on and staggered under its weight, making for the passage entrance.

Bartholomew was losing blood fast. He hissed to Valentine "Forget me. Follow Wharton...get the treasure."

Valentine did not hesitate in his decision. He stayed with Bartholomew, trying to stem the flow of blood. "Sir Thomas's men will see to that. Your life is of more importance than gold." He looked up at Katheryn. "Go and warn Sir Thomas and tell him the tunnel comes out on the sand near the jetty. But first let me have your petticoat. It is only a shoulder wound but I need to tie a bandage tight around his arm to stop the flow of blood." She obeyed at once, lifting her skirts and tearing desperately at the red flannel petticoat beneath. Then she took off her thick woollen cloak, folded it and placed it under Bartholomew's head before running from the crypt to seek out Sir Thomas.

Wharton, now used to the weight of the box and moving faster, vanished into the open tunnel entrance.

After a few seconds there was a shuddering crash which set the floor of the crypt vibrating with noise. The tunnel's entrance had been concealed by a huge flat stone which had balanced as a door. It had fallen on where the Captain and his precious load would have been. There were further rumblings in the tunnel. If Wharton had not been crushed, he would be trapped in the passage to face a slow and unpleasant death. Katheryn listened as the rumblings ceased and were followed by silence. The treasure had been the death of Captain Wharton.

Valentine said nothing but continued his work bandaging Bartholomew's shoulder with the red flannel strips. The ferryman was now unconscious and oblivious to all that was happening around him, but the flow of blood was ceasing and with care his life could be saved.

Katheryn had run, dishevelled, up the dark steps and out into the cloister. She was without her cloak and the night air was cooled by the river breezes but she did not feel its chill. Sir Thomas stepped forward out of the cloister shadows, his hand on the hilt of his sword. "My lady, you are hurt?"

"No," she said breathlessly. "Bartholomew is hurt but Valentine attends him. We must go to the shore. Mires has made his escape by way of a tunnel leading from the crypt. We must be quick if we are to catch him. And you need not concern yourself for Wharton: he is dead."

She lifted her skirts and ran, Sir Thomas and his men following. As she scrambled down the steep path to the beach, she almost fell and Sir Thomas put out his hand to steady her but she shook it off. This was no time for courtly manners.

There were two figures on the sand: as she drew closer Katheryn could see them clearly in the light of the full moon. Surely Wharton could not have escaped from the tunnel alive. The two men were fighting and, from the concentration of the two protagonists, she sensed that this was no drunken brawl, nor even a fight between two rivals over treasure: this was a fight to the death. Even Sir Thomas's men looked dubious about breaking up such a vicious bout.

The two fighters lumbered about the sand. The moonlight caught a flash of metal as the smaller man lunged at Mires. Mires, stumbling, retreated towards the shoreline where a rowing boat lay on the sand.

Sir Thomas, calm and aloof, nodded to the two soldiers under his command. They started towards Mires, who stumbled and fell allowing the other man to catch up with him. Another flash of metal and Mires sank down into the damp sand.

By the time they reached Mires' prone body, the other man had disappeared into the darkness by the cliffs. Mires lay on the sand, apparently unconscious. Blood seeped from his wounds and glistened, dark and oily, in the light of the moon.

"Fetch Master Valentine," Sir Thomas barked to one of his men. "I would not lose this man. I would have him face the King's justice and pay the price for his crimes at the end of a rope."

Sir Thomas ran off down the sand in pursuit of the other combatant, leaving Katheryn alone, bent over the unconscious man.

But she gasped in terror as his eyes flashed open and she felt an iron grip on her wrist. Mires looked up at her, opening his eyes wider, and smiled. Although wounded, he seemed to be gaining in strength. "Where is he?"

"Who?" She tried to sound calm, not to agitate him.

"The one who did this to me. The beggar." He almost spat the word. "He thinks that some time ago I did him a disservice. And he has followed me since he discovered my whereabouts. I thought I had rid myself of him when I burned the old mill as I was certain he was inside. But it seems he shares my power over death." He smiled unpleasantly.

"Why did you burn the mill?"

"I told you. I thought my enemy asleep inside. And it had served my purposes: I had tired of Mistress Moore's sagging body. Do I shock you? I could tell you a thing or two about prim Mistress Moore."

"If you think to shock me, Master Mires, save your breath. I have heard the whole sorry tale. Have you no thought for those whose lives you have blighted and destroyed."

"It is those who take what they want and have no heed for others who prosper in this world, my dear. I think even our sovereign lord the King would not argue with that. I suppose the treasure is gone. I heard the tunnel collapse behind me."

"No thought for Captain Wharton?"

"Another fool. The world is full of fools, my dear. Remember that."

He fixed his eyes on hers and raised his arm. Katheryn was unprepared for his strength as he pulled her towards him and the violent pressure of his moist lips on her mouth. His free hand, iron hard, was on her breast, his fingers thrusting their way inside her bodice. She struggled but he held her tighter. She tried to kick out at him but her skirts had wrapped themselves about her legs, impeding movement.

She felt herself being pushed back until she lay, helpless on the damp sand. Mires was pinning her down, his shape looming above her against the night sky. As she opened her mouth to scream, he stopped it again with his. She could feel the warm stickiness of his blood as it seeped into her bodice and his hand determinedly exploring her skirts. She felt a shiver of revulsion as Mires pressed his tongue into her tightly closed mouth. She bit it hard.

As Mires jumped back with the unexpected pain, he released his hold on her. She seized the chance to make her escape, lifted her skirts, now heavy with damp sand, and took off down the shore. Mires followed her, beginning to stagger now as he lost more blood.

He was closing on her. As she ran she felt something catch her skirt, making her stumble back. She turned to see Mires, fallen to the ground, holding firmly onto the back of her skirt. She tried to pull the material away but he held fast, pulling at her, trying to bring her down. She struggled and tugged, frantic to be free of him.

Then suddenly he loosed his grip and she fell forward and she lay for a second on the cold wet sand, afraid to turn, bracing herself for a second attack The sound of the waves a few feet away was deafening.

It was a few seconds before she dared to look round but it had seemed like an age. She raised herself to her knees. Mires lay behind her looking up at her with glazed, staring eyes, a sardonic smile of triumph on his lips. The life blood had flowed from him. He was dead.

A cloaked figure stood over the body. The moonlight caught the glint of a knife. Katheryn closed her eyes in prayer, only to open them when she felt a reassuring hand on her shoulder. She fell against her rescuer, oblivious to the smell of unwashed clothing and flesh, and sank her face into the coarse cloth of his threadbare cloak.

Walter de Daresbury had dropped the knife and supported Katheryn gently. She took deep breaths while her thumping heart stilled to a comfortable beat. All the time de Daresbury watched Mires to satisfy himself that the man was truly dead; that the deed was finally done.

"Is he dead?" Katheryn whispered.

"Yes."

She made an attempt to compose herself. "I must thank you, sir. You have done me a great service in saving me from the attentions of that rogue."

The man said nothing. He was gaunt, haggard. It was hard to tell his age but he wasn't a young man. Katheryn had seen him before, begging in Liverpool. She looked down at his hands. She knew one would be missing.

"There is no need for explanation, sir. I have been to Norton. I know your story: Robert Janyns told me all. You sought your revenge?"

"The fathers said I should leave all vengeance to God...but they did not see my Lucy in her agony: they were not falsely accused on the testimony of their enemy: they did not have the very means of livelihood cut from their bodies." He held up the stump of his right hand. Katheryn said nothing but let him continue. "For three years I have begged round Cheshire and Lancashire. Then by chance I saw him. I had come to Liverpool. I had been told that the sailors here could be generous when they had spent a day in the tavern. I saw that...devil in the clothing of a priest. I would sooner have seen Satan himself in such attire."

Walter de Daresbury looked at her, puzzled. "I killed him," he said softly. "I lay in wait for him near the castle one evening after dark. He often went there and when I saw him..."

"You stabbed him?"

He looked down as if ashamed. "And I cut off his right hand...as he had caused mine to be cut off. I thought of all he had done to me and I did it in fury. I tried to pray for forgiveness - after all I had killed a man - but when I thought of him I could only reason that the world was better rid of such a creature. I had discovered his dealings with the young girl who lived at the Old Hall and I had watched his cottage and seen them together: I'd looked in the window and witnessed their coupling. I feared for her and I told myself that when he was dead all would be well, that the evil he spread to all he met would cease. But then..."

Katheryn reached out and touched his handless arm. "Then what?"

"Then he returned from the dead. Satan had guarded his own. I was begging near the White Cross and I saw him but I could not be sure. So I followed his leman...the girl from the Old Hall; Agnes I think her name was. She went to the castle one night and I thought she might be meeting him there. I had to know if I'd been mistaken but I did not see him: she had dealings with some soldiers and went into the castle. Then I heard she had been murdered and I knew that I had not been mistaken and that he was still on this earth. I went to the mill by the Old Hall, thinking it a good shelter as the nights grow colder, but he discovered me there and tried to kill me by

burning it down. But I jumped from the window and escaped.
God preserved me to finish my work."

Katheryn shook her head. What she was about to tell him
would cause de Daresbury further pain...but he had to know the
truth. "The man you killed was not Mires. I fear it was Father
Edmund from Norton. He had had been released from prison in
Chester and had come to Liverpool to sail for Ireland. He has
been missing since that night. You killed the wrong priest.
Mires did not return from the dead."

De Daresbury fell to his knees and let out a cry like a
wounded beast. "Why did I not recognise Father Edmund. That
I should mistake him for that devil... May God forgive me."
His face twisted with the agony of his distress.

Katheryn spoke to him gently. "It was dark and you could
not have known. You saw a man in priest's garb and assumed it
was Mires. He was the same height and build."

"Walter de Daresbury broke into sobs. There was nothing
Katheryn could say by way of comfort. The man had judged
himself.

She looked up and saw a figure approaching across the
sand in the dim light of the moon. Valentine: she would know
him in any light. All of a sudden she felt a desire to run to him,
to fling herself into his arms and be held there in safety, taking
refuge against this world of evil and misery. She touched de
Daresbury's arm reassuringly and took off over the sand
towards Valentine, leaving the beggar near Mires' body.
Neither could come to harm and if de Daresbury escaped so be
it. She had no wish to see the unfortunate man dangling from
the gallows. The torment in his soul was punishment enough.

Valentine called her name and as she drew nearer he was
shocked at her appearance. He held out his arms to her and she
ran into them. He held her for a while and she drew strength
and comfort from his embrace. Then her mind began to clear.

"Where is Sir Thomas?"

"Searching the headland. Is Mires dead? Who were you
speaking with?"

She put a finger to his lips. "Mires is dead now but when Sir Thomas left him he was feigning death. He..." She buried her face in Valentine's coat and shuddered.

He said nothing for a while then "You are all right?"

She nodded and looked round at the shoreline where she had left de Daresbury. She could see the waves lapping at Mires' body...but the beggar was gone.

Valentine took her hand and they ran down to the glistening river. When they reached the water's edge, Valentine gave Mires' body a kick as if to make sure that he had not cheated death a second time. Katheryn tried not to look at the corpse but found her eyes drawn to the staring eyes and the still triumphant smile. She shuddered. Poor foolish Agnes, she thought, to have given herself to such a creature.

There was no sign of de Daresbury on the shore but in the distance they could see Sir Thomas and his men returning from their search. Then a movement on the water caught Katheryn's eye. About fifty yards out into the river a boat was being rowed slowly towards the Liverpool side. The water swelled and billowed. The rower, swapping the single oar over from one side to the other, laboured against the force of the tide.

"He is in danger. The currents are treacherous." Valentine kicked off his boots and started to take off his coat. Katheryn, realising what he intended, grabbed his arm.

"If he is taken by Sir Thomas, he will hang. Leave him to God and the river. Please Valentine...it is best."

Valentine did not fully understand but he nodded, knowing that she would tell him her reasons in time. He was bending to put his boots back on when the current dragged de Daresbury's small boat beneath the oily dark waters of the River Mersey. Katheryn stared out across the river. De Daresbury's ordeal was over.

She looked down once more at Mires' body and her eyes were drawn to the outstretched right arm. The hand had been hacked off, leaving only a bloody stump. Walter de Daresbury's justice had been done.

CHAPTER 23

Sir Thomas's soldiers had rowed the ferry boat strongly back across the river to the Liverpool strand. Bartholomew lay quiet but conscious, his head in Katheryn's lap.

Valentine answered Sir Thomas's questions as honestly as he could, explaining that Lady Katheryn was too shocked after her ordeal to speak of the evening's events. Katheryn was grateful. She had no wish to speak of it yet. When she was ready, she would answer Sir Thomas plainly, giving him the bare facts to clear up all doubts about the deaths of Agnes and Father Edmund. But for the moment she needed rest and prayer to gather her thoughts.

Jane ran to her mistress anxiously as soon as the shop door opened, offering warm refreshment; relieved at her safe return.

"Your cloak, my lady? Where's your cloak? Come by the fire. You must be frozen."

Katheryn, who had quite forgotten that she had left her cloak for Bartholomew's comfort, said nothing.

"And your gown....it is covered in....take it off, my lady. I will soak it."

"Jane...calm yourself. I will undress when I have had some of Matilda's excellent broth." She thought it best not to mention to origin of the dark stains on her dress. The mention of blood would only agitate Jane further. "You will be please to know that we can return to Cheadle tomorrow. My work here is done. You may tell Will to prepare the horses."

Jane blushed and shuffled her feet. "Will is not here, my lady."

"Where is he?"

Jane closed her eyes, near to tears. "I cannot say, my lady."

239

Katheryn, aware of Jane's distress, realised that things had been going on in her own household that she had missed, being too preoccupied with other matters. "Come, Jane, you are upset. What has Will been doing? Where is he?" she asked gently.

Jane looked down at her feet. "He is with the baker's daughter next door. They have been..."

"Oh Jane," Katheryn touched the girl's shoulder comfortingly. "I am so sorry. I know your hopes were so high. But if he returns with us tomorrow.... Liverpool and Cheadle are a long way apart."

Katheryn smiled and Jane, looking up, managed a weak smile of hope. But Katheryn knew she would soon have to endure her own parting. What would bring relief to Jane would bring her mistress much regret. Cheadle and Liverpool were indeed far apart...two days' ride. She turned as Valentine entered the room and nodded to Jane who scurried off, leaving them alone.

"I leave tomorrow, Valentine. I have done all I can here."

"I disagree, Katheryn."

"What do you mean?"

"You have not done all you can. There is something more you can do."

She was watching him, sensing that he was uneasy about what he had to say. He took her hand in his.

"Until the commissioners came, I was content to live a life of obedience to the rule of St. Benedict...as you were, no doubt, my dear Katheryn."

She nodded, fearing what was coming, the choice she would have to make.

"I did not live a life of chastity before I entered the cloister. I must confess that to you. I was no libertine, you understand, but a young man encounters temptation in this world. It all finished, of course, when I dedicated my life to the service of God. But since..." He hesitated, trying to find the words. "Since I met you, since I came to know you, Katheryn, I have questioned the vows I made and whether they still bind me...and you."

"Please, Valentine, say what is in your mind." She looked at him with affection. He was clearly nervous, expecting rejection.

"Katheryn, I know the King's new act of the Six Articles says that we are not allowed to marry, but there are many who do...and in such a place as Liverpool nobody would trouble to enforce it. I know the difference in our rank is great. You are a Bulkeley and I...I am a poor man of medicine. But all the knights in Cheshire could not hold you more dear than I do."

He drew her towards him and held her. She closed her eyes, warm in the heat from the dying embers of the fire and in his comforting arms. She was exhausted by the events of the evening and in no state to make a decision of any importance.

"I am most honoured," she looked into his anxious brown eyes. "That you should hold me in such esteem, but I am exhausted. Forgive me." She entwined her fingers in his. For the first time she realised how much pain their separation would bring to her.

"Please, my dear, sleep now. I was thoughtless."

"You were honest. I shall consider the matter in the morning."

They kissed, deep and long before she retired to her chamber and stripped off her bloodstained clothes. The white shift beneath her gown was stained brown and Jane, recognising the colour of the stain, gasped in horror. Katheryn told her to calm herself. All was well and she was not hurt. Jane took the clothes away to soak, holding them at arm's length.

Katheryn washed and fell gratefully into her bed. She slept the deep sleep of one who has completed a task with success. She had fulfilled her obligations to Agnes. As for the other matter, she would make her decision in the morning.

Will looked bleary eyed as he saddled the horses. Jane regarded him sheepishly. There was no sign of the giddy hope she had displayed when they had set out for Liverpool: the baker's daughter had put paid to that.

Katheryn had farewells to make. She took Jane with her, thinking the distraction would be good for the girl, and walked through the morning streets to the church of Our Lady and St. Nicholas to give Father James and Father Nicholas a brief account of the events of the previous night. She then called at Bartholomew's lodgings and found the ferryman in his bed being cared for by his motherly landlady. He assured her that he was recovering well, hauling himself into a sitting position with a gusto that Katheryn thought was probably unwise. When she told him she was leaving the town, he looked disappointed.

"I know of one who will miss you sorely, my lady."

She turned away. She did not need another to remind her of her dilemma. She squeezed Bartholomew's hand in farewell and promised to pray for his speedy recovery.

She set off down the strand with Jane trailing dreamily behind. The waterfront was busy. Cargoes were loaded and unloaded as impudent seagulls helped themselves to the remnants of last night's catch of fish. Katheryn wondered how long it would be before a fisherman found Walter de Daresbury's emaciated body. Perhaps he still lived: perhaps he had escaped the river. Part of her hoped he had...although she would not have admitted that to another living soul.

Jane was far behind when they reached the road up to the Old Hall. Katheryn waited patiently for her. There was one more call to make.

Marjory Moore showed Katheryn into the parlour and there was a new humility in her manner. Katheryn wondered how this change would affect her household.

When Katheryn spoke of what had happened, Marjory closed her eyes in relief. "Thank God," she said. "It is certain this time? He is dead?"

Katheryn nodded and to her surprise the older woman fell to her knees and made the sign of the cross. Her prayer, when it came, was not for the dead man's soul but one of thanksgiving. Katheryn waited, still, until she had finished. "You are relieved, mistress?"

She turned to Katheryn anxiously. "Is it wicked to rejoice at another's death?"

Katheryn considered the question. "Mires blighted the lives of everyone he came into contact with, Marjory. If God has chosen to relieve the world of his wickedness, we can only rejoice at His mercy and wisdom."

Marjory smiled, the first time Katheryn had seen her smile. They parted as friends.

Katheryn and Jane made their way back slowly and turned left at the High Cross into Dale Street.

Valentine rode with them to the Townsend bridge, saying little.

He halted his horse. This was where they had agreed to part. He paused awkwardly before speaking what was in his mind: the only thought he had kept there since the previous evening. "Katheryn...have you an answer for me? Have you considered...?"

"I have thought of little else."

"Please, Katheryn. We are well together...will be well together..."

"I know but... When I was nineteen I made vows before God; the same vows as you made. A vow, once made, binds us for life."

"As will our marriage vows. Will you not stay?"

"I must return. I have promised my brother and he will be concerned for me."

"Send him a message. Will can take it."

"And there is another vow I made...to my brother and to God. Master Cromwell granted me a handsome pension and I vowed to use some of it to build a new chancel for my brother's church in Cheadle. That is a vow I cannot break...do you not agree, Valentine?"

He nodded, acknowledging defeat in this matter if not in the first. "Will you return?"

She turned away from him so that he would not see the tears in her eyes.

"I will pray each day that you will." He grabbed her hand, kissed it and held it. "Take this." He put a ring on her finger: a gold ring set with two stones, a blue and a red. She looked down at it and her heart lurched with indecision. "It was my mother's," he said. "Please take it and think of me whenever you look at it. Take it."

It was time. She took the reins and turned her white mare towards the Warrington road. Then she looked back at Valentine. "We will meet again, Valentine. I know it."

In response to a gentle kick, her mare moved off, leaving Valentine to watch her disappear down the rough pitted track: back to Cheadle...to keep her vow.

AUTHOR'S NOTE

The real Lady Katheryn Bulkeley was Abbess of Godstow Abbey near Oxford in the last two years of its existence before it was dissolved in 1539. In 1538 she refused to surrender her abbey to the King's commissioner, the ruthless Dr. London: her spirited and courageous defence of her abbey and her sisters can be seen in her correspondence with Henry Vlll's Chancellor, Thomas Cromwell. She did not suffer too much for her defiance, however, as she was granted a generous pension of fifty pounds a year (in the days when a labourer's annual wages were a tenth of that sum).

She returned to her home in the village of Cheadle in Cheshire where her brother, John, was rector (her eldest brother, Richard was constable of Beaumaris castle in Anglesey). A local ballad described her then as "A jem of joye, a lamp of godley light". Her burial place lies in the chancel she had built for her brother's church. I am sure she would forgive me for using her in this book to right some imaginary wrongs.

I have used the names of families prominent in Liverpool in the sixteenth century, though individual members of those families mentioned in the story are fictitious. The Moores were indeed a family of wealthy burgesses, reputed for their parsimony and business acumen, who provided Liverpool with many a mayor and magistrate at this time in history. The Crosses likewise played a major role in Liverpool's municipal life. The Stanleys (Earls of Derby) and the Molyneux (later Earls of Sefton) had many interests in Liverpool (the Molyneux were hereditary constables of the castle) and kept large households of retainers there. But, in the manner of sixteenth century nobility, they had estates elsewhere and probably visited the town infrequently.

The famous "ferry across the Mersey" was operated by the monks of Birkenhead until their priory's closure in 1536. It is feasible that one or more of the monks continued to run it after this date. The remains of Birkenhead Priory can still be visited although part of the site has been destroyed by the building of a dry dock. There is a legend which tells of a tunnel from the priory crypt to the nearby river which collapsed, burying several men alive as they attempted to flee with the priory treasure. The start of a passageway can be seen in the wall of the crypt: it comes to an abrupt end.

Norton Abbey near Liverpool was dissolved in 1536. As described in this book, the King's commissioners were imprisoned in the tower while the abbot led a large band of locals in an impromptu celebration, which included the roasting of an ox in the abbey grounds. The commissioners somehow sent a message to the High Sheriff, Sir Piers Dutton, who arrived in the small hours of the morning with a group of his tenants. Monks and locals alike made their escape in the darkness by swimming the abbey pools. The abbot, John Birkett and several of his monks were imprisoned in Chester castle but it is likely that they were later released.

In March 1537 the Abbot of Whalley Abbey in Lancashire, was executed with two other monks for his part in the Northern Rising against King Henry V111. John Estgate, a monk of Whalley, was acquitted: I have used him in this story as a representative of all the religious who must have longed to take action to restore their former way of life.

Many dispossessed monks became priests in chantry chapels at this time, taking payment for saying prayers for the souls of the dead. The salary was small but, with the pension given to most former monks, they could eke out a living. The chantries, however, were to meet the same fate as the monasteries: they were dissolved in 1546.

As for Liverpool's fate...of all the landmarks mentioned in this book, only the church of Our Lady and St. Nicholas (known as the sailors' church) still stands behind the well-known Liver Building; though it has been much altered and suffered extensive bomb damage during world war two. The ancient pilgrimage chapel of St. Mary del Quay became a school after the dissolution of the chantries and was demolished in 1814.

Liverpool castle fell to ruin in the seventeenth century and was finally demolished in 1726. Castle Street, Chapel Street and Dale Street are still there today and other places mentioned in this book are commemorated in street names - Crosshall Street, Oldhall Street, Tower Buildings and the Strand. The present day city would be completely unrecognisable to the Liverpudlians of 1539.